Roger Zelazny's

# The Dawn of Amber

iBooks
Habent Sua Fata Libelli

**iBooks**
1230 Park Avenue
New York, New York 10128
Tel: 212-427-7139
bricktower@aol.com • www.BrickTowerPress.com

Special thanks to the Zelazny family and to Kirby and Kay McCauley.

**Library of Congress Cataloging-in-Publication Data**

Betancourt, John Gregory.
Roger Zelazny's The Dawn Of Amber / John Gregory Betancourt.

p. cm.
1. Science Fiction—Fiction. 2. Adventure—
Fiction, I. Title.

ISBN 0-7434-4552-X
First iBooks printing September 2002

Edited by Howard Zimmerman
Jacket art by Scott Grimando
Jacket Design by Eric Goodman

March 2012

Roger Zelazny's

# The Dawn of Amber

Book One of the New Amber Trilogy

John Gregory Betancourt

ALSO BY JOHN GREGORY BETANCOURT

*Roger Zelazny's The Dawn of Amber*
*Amber and Chaos*

Selected Fiction
*The Blind Archer*

*Born of Elven Blood* (With Kevin J. Anderson)
*Cutthroat Island*
*Horizon*
*Johnny Zed*
*Master of Dragons*
*Rememory*
*Rogue Pirate*
*Starskimmer*
*Star Trek Deep Space Nine: Devil in the Sky*
*Star Trek Deep Space Nine: Heart of the Warrior*
*Star Trek The Next Generation: Double Helix, Book 1: Infection*
*Star Trek Voyager: Incident at Arbuk*

This one is for Roger Zelazny–
the one true Lord of Amber.
For Warren Lapine–
visionary and friend.

And for the millions who have journeyed
to Amber and the Courts of Chaos–
you have made all this possible.

Roger Zelazny's

# THE DAWN OF AMBER

# PROLOG

## ONE YEAR AGO

I felt the world around me bend and sway like the branches of a willow in a storm. Strange colors turned, misshapen geometries that couldn't possibly exist but somehow did, drifting like snowflakes, patterns within patterns within patterns. My vision brightened then dimmed, repeatedly, and in no perceptible rhythm.

Come...

A voice...where? I turned, the world kaleidoscoping.

Come to me...

The voice pulled me on. Come to me, *sons of Chaos...*

I followed the sound across a land of ever-changing design and color to a tower made of skulls, some human and some clearly not. I stretched out my hand to touch its walls, but my fingers passed through the bones as though through fog.

*Not real.*

A vision? A dream?

A *nightmare, more like it.* The thought came from deep inside.

*Come...*the voice called to me.

I gave in to the sound and drifted forward, through the wall of skulls and into the heart of the tower.

Shadows flickered within. As my eyes began to adjust to the gloom, I could make out a stairway of arm and leg bones that circled the inside wall, climbing into a deeper darkness, descending into murky, pulsating redness.

I drifted down, and the redness resolved into a circle of torches and five men. Four of them wore finely wrought silvered chain mail of a design I had never seen before. They held down the limbs of the fifth man, who lay spread-eagled on a huge sacrificial altar, a single immense slab of gray marble threaded with intricate patterns of gold. His chest and stomach had been opened and his entrails spread across the altar as though some augur had been reading the future from them. When the victim shuddered suddenly, I realized the men were holding him down because he was still alive.

I reached instinctively for my sword. In any other time or place I would have rushed them, decency and honor commanding me to try to rescue this poor victim. *Only he isn't real,* I told myself. This was some sort of vision, some kind of fever dream or premonition.

I forced myself closer, staring at the dying man, trying to see his face. Was it mine? Did this vision predict *my* fate?

No, I saw with some relief, it wasn't me on the altar. His eyes were a muddy brown; mine are blue as the sea. His hair was lighter than mine, his skin smoother. He was little more than a boy, I thought, maybe fourteen or fifteen years old;

"Who are you?" I whispered, half to myself.

The suffering victim turned his head in my direction.

"Help me," he mouthed. He seemed to be staring straight at me, as though he could see me.

I reached out for him, but my hand passed through his body and into the stone of the altar. Had I become some sort of ghost? A powerless creature forced to watch atrocities unfold around me, with no power to act?

I pulled my hand free. A mild tingling, like the return of blood after circulation had been cut off, shot through my fingers, but nothing else. I couldn't help him.

The young man turned his head away. He shuddered again, but though tears rolled down his cheeks, he did not cry out. Brave and strong, I gave him that.

"Have courage," I whispered.

He did not reply, but his body began to shake and his eyes rolled back in his head.

Again that wild, uncontrollable rage surged inside me. Why was I here? Why was I having this vision? What could it possibly mean?

I looked at the soldiers, searching their faces for an explanation and suddenly I realized they were not human. Their slitted eyes glowed a faint red behind their helms. Nasals and cheek guards concealed most of their features, but could not hide the faintly iridescent pattern of scales around their mouths and chins. I had never seen their like before. They must have the blood of serpents in their veins, I thought, to kill one so young in such a horrible manner.

The victim on the slab gave one last convulsive shudder, then lay still. They released him.

"Lord Zon," one of the soldiers croaked.

Something stirred in the darker shadows by the far wall. Slitted eyes, much larger than the soldiers' and set a foot apart, opened, then blinked twice. As the creature shifted, torchlight glinted off its metallic-gray scales and the sharp talons of its four spindly limbs.

I felt a sudden chill, a blind panic that made me want to run screaming from this tower. Yet I steeled myself and held firm in my place, facing it, knowing this to be a true enemy–the enemy of all men.

*Yes,* it said. The creature did not speak, but I heard the rumble of its words clearly in my head.

"He is dead."

*Bring* me *the other son of Dworkin.*

A shock of recognition went through me. *Dworkin!* I knew that name. But it had been such a very long time since I had seen him....

Calmly, two of the serpent-soldiers turned and left the tower through a doorway set deep in the shadows. The remaining pair pulled the young man off the slab and dragged him to a small hole in the floor. They rolled him into it, and he plunged into darkness. I did not hear him hit the bottom.

A moment later the other two returned, half carrying, half dragging another man between then, this one older than the one who had just died. He wore the tattered remains of a military uniform, but I did not recognize the design, and his face and hands were bruised and dirty. Still he bucked and fought, kicking and biting, struggling frantically to free himself. He almost threw off the serpent-soldiers several times; he was strong and determined not to be taken easily.

Instinctively, my hand sought my sword again. I wished I had the power to help him. But I remembered how my hand had passed through the body of the last victim and knew I could do nothing but watch.

The two soldiers who had disposed of the young man's body rushed forward, and together the four of them managed to heave the newcomer up onto the altar's slab. All four leaned on his limbs heavily, holding him down despite his valiant efforts to free himself.

The serpent-beast in the shadows stirred, immense scales sliding across the floor's stones. I heard a laugh that chilled my heart.

*Son of Dworkin. You will help me now.*

"Never!" the young man yelled. "You'll pay for this!" And he followed with a string of obscenities.

Then he raised his head defiantly, staring at the giant serpent, and the flickering torches revealed his features for the first time.

*My* features. For he had my face.

I could only gape. How was it possible? Was this nightmare some premonition of things to come? Would this Lord Zon capture me, drag me here, too, and read the future from my guts?

Drifting closer, like a phantom, I peered down at the man. I had to get a better look, had to know more about who he was and how he had gotten into this situation. If this really *was* some future vision of myself–

Fortunately neither the soldiers nor their serpent-master seemed aware of me. I might have been some spectral figure wandering through their nightmare world, unseen and unheard, forced to witness atrocities beyond all human suffering but unable to stop them.

And yet, I reminded myself, before his death, the first victim had seen me. How? What did it all mean?

As I continued to study the man with my face, I began to notice small differences between us. Like the boy before him, he had brown eyes to my blue. But despite our eye colors, there were many uncanny similarities between us. The high rise of our cheekbones, the shape of our noses and our ears...we could have been brothers.

Or father and son.

*My father is already dead,* I told myself. *This cannot* possibly *be him.* Could it?

No, my father would have been much, much older.

This man looked about my own age.

*Tell* me *of Dworkin,* the voice in my head commanded. *Where* is *he hiding? Where else has he spread his tainted blood?* I felt my heart leap. *Dworkin again.* What did my former teacher have to do with all of this?

The man on the slab spat at the creature, then declared, "I have never heard of Dworkin. Kill me and be done with it!"

Let *him go,* I thought desperately, dreading what might come next. *Whatever you are, you're looking for* me, not *him.* I'm *the one who knows Dworkin!*

The serpent-creature didn't hear me. Talons lashed out from the darkness, seized the man, and ripped his chest and stomach open like cheesecloth. I gasped, stunned. The prisoner screamed and kept screaming. With a quick motion, the creature pulled his entrails across the altar's slab like an offering to the dark gods.

Blood sprayed in the air and hung there, forming a cloud, a shifting pattern like the snowflakes of color outside the tower. But this pattern was different, somehow—I could see holes where it was incomplete, jagged, and somehow wrong.

Come to me...

The serpent-creature writhed, body undulating before the pattern in the air, working its foul sorcery. Rings of light burst from the floating droplets of blood, spreading out through the walls of the tower, disappearing into the greater void outside.

Come to me, *sons of Dworkin...*

The air over the altar filled with a spinning lacework design, with strange turns and angles. The hanging drops of blood flattened, rippled like waves of the sea, then grew clear. Each one offered a tiny window into what must have been hundreds of different worlds. I stared at them, the breath catching in my throat. Some had red skies; some had the familiar blue one. Oceans raged in one; mountains moved like sheep in a pasture in another; fires rained down from the sky in a third. In still others I saw towns of strangely dressed people, or what might have been people. Still more showed virgin forests, others empty expanses of desert, or grassland, or thundering rivers.

*Come* to *me, princes of Chaos...*

Like bubbles bursting, the windows began to disappear. The pattern that held them together was breaking apart. I realized the man on the altar slab was nearing death.

Suddenly the last of the tiny windows vanished and beads of red spattered onto the floor, an unholy rain. Coughing, spitting blood, the young man on the altar began to jerk and spasm uncontrollably. Finally, he lay still. It hadn't taken him more than a minute or two to die.

The serpent-creature hissed in anger and disappointment.

*Continue searching.*

"Yes, Lord Zon," said the soldier who had spoken before.

I moved closer, peering into the shadows, trying to see this Lord Zon more clearly. Somehow, I knew the creature was my enemy. It wanted me spread on its slab, *my* blood sprayed into the air and held up in that strange, flawed pattern that offered glimpses of other worlds.

"Who are you?" I whispered.

Like the first victim, Zan seemed to hear me—or sensed my presence. Eyes glinting like ruby chips, it turned, peering this way and that.

*Who is there?* it demanded. *Speak!*

I remained silent, drifting backward, willing myself invisible. Zan's slitted eyes suddenly focused on me. It gave a hiss, and a forked tongue flickering from its lipless, scaled mouth.

*You. You are the one.*

"Who are you?" I demanded. "What do you want of me?"

*Death!*

Its talons reached for me—

—and suddenly I sat up in my bed, drenched in sweat, heart pounding like a hammer in my chest, shaking all over but unable to recall what had terrified me so. A dream–a nightmare–some sort of horror...

I sucked in a deep breath, held it, listening beyond the canvas walls of my tent to the nighttime sounds of a military camp. Boots on gravel, soft whinnies of horses, the *scritch-scritch-scritch* of whetstones sharpening steel knives and swords, a distant "All's well!" call from sentries on patrol.

Home.

*Safe.*

Everything seemed normal.

And yet...and yet, everything had changed, though I did not know how or why.

Reaching out in the darkness, I wrapped my fingers around the cool, smooth hilt of my sword. Tonight, for no reason I could name, I wanted it close at hand.

# ONE

## THE PRESENT

A heavy pounding on the door downstairs roused me from sleep.

"Obere!" came a distant shout.

Damnable timing. I squinted into near darkness, frowned. The hour lay somewhere between midnight and dawn, and blades of moonlight slid between the window shutters, cutting an intricate pattern of light and darkness across the checkered quilt. Off in the night I heard plodding hooves and creaks from some passing merchant's wagon, and from farther off still the distant baying of packs of wild dogs as they scavenged the battlefields a mile to the north of Kingstown.

The pounding on the door resumed. Feigning sleep wouldn't work; somehow, King Elnar's agents—probably that all too efficient Captain Iago–had tracked me down.

I tried to sit up and found a soft arm pinning my chest. Helda hadn't yet heard a thing; her breathing remained deep and regular. I half chuckled to myself. Too much wine, too much love. She would sleep through the sacking of Kingstown, given half a chance.

As gently as I could, I slid out from under her, leaving the warm sweet smells of perfume and sweat and incense that filled her bed. I made a reassuring murmur at her puzzled sound and quickly gathered up pants, shirt, boots, and sword.

Damnable timing indeed. My first night alone with Helda in nearly two months, and King Elnar couldn't wait till dawn to summon me back. Price of being one of his right-hand men, I supposed. Still, Captain Iago—or whoever the king had sent to find me—might have had the sense to let me stay lost at least a few hours more. It was seldom enough we had time to rest, but since the hell, creatures had been quiet now for nearly a week, King Elnar had granted me a night's leave. I had tried to make the best of it, drinking my way through Kingstown's half dozen taverns before joining Helda at her house to continue a more private celebration into the late hours.

Carrying my belongings, I padded quickly down the steps. First things first. I had to halt that racket before the whole town was up in arms. The hell-creatures had driven us back steadily over the last six months, and with the front lines of the war close to Kingstown, King Elnar's troops now policed the streets–not that they needed much attention, since three-quarters of the inhabitants had fled. No need to rouse the night watch for a mere summons back to camp. I sighed, half in apprehension. What calamity had befallen us this time? Something bad must have happened to drag me back in the middle of the night. Had our scouts spotted new enemy movements? Or perhaps the hell-creatures had mounted another sneak-attack on our supply lines?

The pounding ceased as I rattled back the bar and flung open the heavy wooden door.

"By the six hells—" I began.

My curse died away unfinished. It wasn't Captain Iago—or any of the other officers under King Elnar's command. It was a stranger, a thin little man of perhaps forty with long black hair tied behind his head and a sharp gleam in his eye. He raised his lantern and peered up at me.

"Obere?" he demanded.

I towered a good head and a half over him, but that didn't matter. He had a powerful presence, much like King Elnar–the sort of man you instinctively looked at whenever he entered a room, or listened to whenever he spoke. He was clean-shaven, dressed in red-and-gold silks with a strange rampant-lion crest stitched in gold and silver thread on the blouse, and I caught the scents of dressing-powder and lavender.

"Maybe," I said cautiously, feeling for my sword's hilt, wondering who he was and what he wanted. "You are... ?"

"It *is* you!" he said, grasping my arm. "The years have changed you–but it *is* good to see you alive!"

"Who *are* you," I demanded, shrugging off his hand, "and what in all the hells do you think you're doing here at this hour?" No matter who he was, I did not appreciate being awakened from my much-needed and much-deserved rest. It was one thing to receive the king's summons and quite another to be roused by a stranger.

His voice was quiet. "Has it been so long you no longer know me?"

"I have no idea who–" I began. Then I paused and looked at him. *Really* looked at him.

"Uncle Dworkin?" I whispered. It had been ten years since I'd last set eyes on him. He had worn his hair cropped short in those days, and he had seemed much, much taller.

Dworkin smiled and bowed his head. "The very same."

"What—how—"

He waved me to silence. "Later. You must come with me, and quickly. I have sent for a carriage. I assure you, this cannot wait. You will come with me. *Now.*"

It was a command, not a suggestion.

I gave a bark of a laugh. "Go with you? Just like that?"

"Yes."

"I can't. I'm due back at camp in the morning. I'm no longer a child, Dworkin—I have duties and responsibilities you cannot imagine."

"It is a matter of life and death."

"Whose?"

"Yours—and King Elnar's. I cannot say more than that."

That made me pause. "What about King Elnar?" I asked slowly. My duty was clear: to protect and serve first the king and second all of Ilerium. If Dworkin knew something of such great importance that it endangered King Elnar's life, I had to report it at once.

He shook his head, though. "Later. When we are safely away from here."

I took a deep breath. Dworkin wasn't really my uncle—he had been a close friend of my parents. When my father died at the hands of pirates from Saliir shortly after my birth, Dworkin had practically adopted my mother and me. Perhaps it was because he had had no children or family of his own, but I had come to view him as almost a father. It had been Dworkin who played soldier with me, brought me treats on high holidays, and took me hunting in the fields beyond our house at Piermont as if I were his own true son. It had been Dworkin who presented me with my first real sword, and Dworkin who began the training in arms that had ultimately become my livelihood. That is, until he disappeared following my mother's death from the Scarlet Plague. That had been just after my fourteenth birthday. Those had been crazy times, mad times, with death in the air and fear in every heart. After the deathcart  took my mother's body away, she and Dworkin were both simply *gone*. I had always assumed he'd died in the plague, too.

And now he stood before me, smug as you please, expecting me to drop everything and go off with him for reasons he wouldn't share beyond claiming it was a matter of life or death to both the king and me. It was impossible.

Instead of filial love and devotion, I felt a sudden towering rage at having been abandoned.

"I'm not going anywhere," I growled at him, "unless you explain exactly what you mean. See my orderly in the morning, if you like, and I'll breakfast with you in my tent. We can catch up with each other then. And you'd better have a damned good explanation—for everything!"

I started to shut the door. "You will not be alive in the morning if you remain here," he said softly.

I hesitated, looked into his face, searching—for what, I didn't know. Truth, perhaps. Or maybe some sign that he still cared for me. After all, my mother was gone now. Perhaps he had only befriended me to get to her.

"Explain," I said.

"There is no time!" He glanced up the street as if expecting to see someone or something, but the street remained deserted. "My carriage will be here soon. Dress yourself, and be quick about it. We must be ready."

"What does this have to do with the king? You said it involved him."

"Yes, though he does not yet know it himself. But if you come with me now, I promise that the invasion of your world will be over within the week. I can say no more."

*The invasion of your world.* I did not like the sound of that, but I held back a flood of questions demanding to be asked. Somehow, though I didn't understand why, I found I wanted to trust Dworkin.

And if he really knew something that could end our war with the hell-creatures, I owed it to King Elnar to listen. I had never known Dworkin to lie. For the sake of my oath to the king and Ilerium, for my childhood and all the kindness Dworkin had showered on my mother and me, I decided I would take him at his word...for now.

"Very well." I handed him my sword and hurriedly began pulling on my pants.

He remained nervous and apprehensive, glancing up the street every few seconds. He had volunteered little information, I realized, but perhaps I could extract more with an indirect line of questioning.

"Where have you been all these years?" I asked. "I thought you were dead."

"Traveling," he said absently. "My...business took me far from here."

"You could have sent messages."

"You didn't need them. I would have been a distraction for you. Had you known I was alive, you would have given up your commission and come looking for me."

I pulled on my shirt and began lacing the front. "You don't know that."

"Of course I do. I know you, Obere, better than you know yourself."

He shifted slightly, glancing again in the direction of the battlefield outside town. I paused, straining to hear, but even the distant scavenging dogs had grown silent. That seemed an ominous sign.

More slowly, Dworkin went on. "Friends have been sending me reports now and again of you and your career. From raw soldier to lieutenant in ten years is quite a remarkable feat. You have done your parents proud."

"King Elnar rewards deeds more than accidents of birth." I shrugged and began to link my shirt-cuffs. "Less than half his officers have noble bloodlines."

"So I have heard."

"And I owe much to your training."

He nodded slightly. "You were an apt student. But don't discount your own talents—you were born to greatness."

As I buckled on my swordbelt, I found I began to share his apprehension. A strange, almost expectant hush had fallen over the street...over all of Kingstown. Not an insect chirped, not a bat winged overhead, not a single dog howled in the distance. An unpleasant tension hung over everything around us, like the calm before a storm.

"They are near, I think," Dworkin said softly. "Even the animals sense it..."

"Who?"

"The enemy. Those you call hell-creatures."

"You say it like they have some other name."

"They do." He looked at me and smiled. "But in this place, they are merely soldiers, like you or I."

"Not like me! And when have you ever been a soldier?"

He chuckled, a strange gleam in his eye. "You have more in common with them than you realize. We both do."

I gave a derisive snort, not enjoying the idea. That hell-creatures should be here in Kingstown, behind our lines, seemed unlikely. And yet Dworkin certainly appeared to know more about them than King Elnar's own agents. Nobody on our side knew where they came from originally, or how many they numbered—they had swept down from the north a year ago in a vast horde, destroying villages, murdering  men, women, and children alike by the thousands. King Elnar had marched his army against them at once and fought them to a standstill. But slowly, over the months, their numbers swelled and they advanced on us again and again, driving us ever back, until presently they controlled half of Ilerium.

How did Dworkin know so much, when our own agents knew so little? I found it disconcerting to say the least. And it raised more than a few danger flags in my mind.

I tried to take a mental step backward. It was a trick I had taught myself, to try to see more than what was readily apparent. Who was Dworkin, really? What business could possibly have taken him away in the midst of the Scarlet Plague, when every country in the world had shut its ports to our ships?

I suddenly realized then how little I actually knew about my "uncle." When you are a child, you take adults for granted. Dworkin had been a part of my life for so long, I had never thought to question his origins or his business or even his phenomenal skill with a sword, for he had certainly been on par with any master I had trained with in the last decade.

As I leaned against Helda's house and pulled on my boots, I studied him. His strange clothing, his long absence, his swordsmanship, and his ability to keep track of me... I could only reach one conclusion: he had to be a spy. But for whom?

At least he seemed to fear the hell-creatures. No man who has looked into their slitted red eyes, or fought against their wickedly barbed swords and fire-breathing horses, can come away unchanged.

I finally decided that he had to be working for one of the neighboring kingdoms. And they had good cause to fear—if the hell-creatures continued their advance, they would control all of Ilerium within the year, and then they would be free to attack Tyre or Alacia or any of the other Fifteen Kingdoms.

"Where is your carriage?" I asked, taking back my sword.

He looked to the right, down the street. "I hear it coming now."

I loosened my blade in its scabbard and stood straighter. Clearly Dworkin had gone to a lot of trouble to track me down—I had made doubly sure nobody knew where I would be sleeping tonight, from King Elnar to my orderly. And clearly, from his unceremonious pounding on the door, Dworkin truly did fear for my life.

But why should *my* life be in danger? I frowned. I was but one of a dozen lieutenants under King Elnar...a well decorated hero, true enough, but hardly a pivotal figure in the war. It didn't make sense.

The clatter of iron-shod wheels on cobblestones slowly grew louder. Dworkin exhaled heavily and seemed to relax as an odd little carriage sped around the corner half a block away.

I gaped at it. It was shaped almost like a pumpkin, with smooth curved sides that might have been made of milky glass, and it glowed with an eerie phosphoric light, illuminating the whole street. Strangest of all, it had neither horses to pull it nor a driver to steer it, though it had an empty bench on top.

*Magic.*

I'd seen a few itinerant sorcerers visit King Elnar's court over the years, but such were few and far between in this part of the world, and usually their magics were more flash and fancy: parlor tricks and elegant illusions to delight ladies after dinner. For Dworkin to have a sorcerer of considerable power at his disposal showed how important his mission here must be.

I'd had some little acquaintance with magic myself over the years. As a boy, I'd discovered I had the ability to change the features of my face when I concentrated on it, and I'd practiced secretly until I could make myself look like almost anyone I'd ever met. When they found out, both Dworkin and my mother had strongly discouraged this talent. And since such tricks are little use in combat, I'd barely even thought of it for years.

As the carriage neared, white lace curtains at the side windows fluttered briefly. I thought I glimpsed a woman's pale face peering out at us, lips blood red and eyes dark. Could she be steering it from inside?

"Hurry," Dworkin said urgently, taking my elbow and propelling me toward the carriage. I quickened my pace to keep up. "We must—"

At that second, the building behind us exploded. The force of it knocked me flat to the ground, and I scrambled awkwardly to my feet, palms and elbows and knees all stinging from scrapes on cobblestones.

Unbelieving, I stared at what remained of Helda's house. Emerald flames shot a hundred feet in the air. The whole building, from stoop to attic, blazed with an unholy green fire. I had seen its like before on the battlefield— sometimes hell-creatures hurled fiery missiles at us, and they burned with those same green flames.

The heat was incredible. From somewhere inside I heard a woman screaming. Helda—I had to save her!

I started for the door, but Dworkin caught my arm and yanked me to a halt. His grip had iron in it, and I could not wrench away despite my own great strength.

"Obere, no!" He had a crazed, almost desperate look in his eye.

"I love her!" I screamed. "I love her—"

"She is dead!" He had to shout to be heard over the roar of the flames.

Above the conflagration, the roof suddenly fell in with a grinding crash. Green sparks streamed up toward the night sky. The whole building began to sag, threatening to collapse inward as the support beams burned through.

I staggered back, imagining her soul flying up to the heavens. Ash and embers began a gentle, hot rain on our heads.

*Dworkin.* He had known, somehow, that this attack was going to happen. How?

Whirling, I grabbed him by his silk shirt and with one hand raised him a foot off the ground. It's an impressive trick at any time, and over the years I'd taken the fight out of a dozen barroom brawlers by one-handing them into the air, then tossing them out the nearest door or window as though they weighed nothing. "Do you know who is responsible for this?" I demanded, shaking him.

"How did you know the hell-creatures would attack here tonight? Who are you spying for? Is the king in danger?"

He broke my grip with a sudden toe to the stomach that sent me reeling back, gasping for breath. I hadn't been hit that hard since the time a horse kicked me during the battle at Sadler's Mill. Dworkin's blow would have stunned or perhaps even killed most men, but I shook it off and came up growling, ready for a fight. My blade hissed from its scabbard as I drew it and pointed the tip at his face.

"I knew an attack would come against you tonight," Dworkin said warily, staying beyond my reach. "But I did not know what form it would take."

"And the king. How is he involved in this?"

"He is not...yet. The hell-creatures are searching for something. King Elnar is just in the way. Now, do not be a fool, my boy. You are alive because of me. Had I wanted you dead, I could have left you in the house to burn."

I hesitated, looking at the house, unable to deny the truth. She was dead, my Helda, my sweet little Helda—she was dead, and there was nothing I could do about it now, except make an offering to the gods who guard the underworld.

Then Dworkin's head jerked to the side and he stared, tense all over, like a rabbit about to bolt. In that second, I heard the horses too. There were perhaps a dozen, perhaps more, approaching fast. I pivoted, sword ready.

They rounded the corner and came into sight. The moon lay to their backs, but I could see the riders' glowing red eyes and the fiery red breaths of their black steeds. They pounded toward us, swords raised, and let loose wild, gibbering war-cries.

# TWO

We must get our backs to a wall!" Dworkin cried. "Don't let them surround us or we won't last long!"

"Come—over here!"

I sprinted to the house opposite Helda's, a two-story stone building whose owners, like most of the townsfolk, had fled the coming war weeks ago. With the windows shuttered and the doors nailed shut, we couldn't get inside even if we wanted to. Nor could the hell-creatures circle around behind us by going through the back of the house. It was a good place to make our stand.

I tensed, raising my sword, as the riders slowed. How had a band of hell-creatures gotten so far behind our lines? As soon as I returned to camp, I intended to find out, even if it meant stringing up every sentry by his thumbs for sleeping on duty.

Then, remembering Dworkin's carriage and the passenger I'd glimpsed, I glanced up the street. His strange little vehicle had not moved, though its glow had, if anything, increased.

"What about your passenger?" I asked in a low voice. "Won't the hell-creatures attack her, too?"

"No. They won't bother with anything or anyone else until we're dead. And if it comes to that...well, Freda can take care of herself. She will be gone before they get the door open."

*Freda.* The name meant nothing to me.

I turned my attention back to the coming fight. "Use two blades if you have them," I said, "and watch their horses. They'll spit fire in your eyes and blind you if you let them get close."

A year of battling hell-creatures made you wary or dead. I'd lost too many good men to their tricks.

Dworkin drew his own sword plus a long knife, and I pulled a smaller knife from my belt. Then the riders were upon us in a thunder of hooves on cobblestones, still screaming their savage war cries.

With the house to our backs, they ringed us in, but only a few could get at us at any one time. I found myself facing a tall rider on a true devil of a horse. As the rider's flexible sword whipped through the air, trying to catch me with the razored barbs on its end, his mount also lunged, snorting sparks and snapping pointed teeth.

I parried, parried, and parried again, waiting for an opening. It was a weird dance by the light of the burning house across from us and the eerily glowing carriage at the end of the street. On the battlefield, I had seen men beheaded while trying to avoid the horse, or killed by the horse while parrying the swordsman's blows. Fighting with two blades was the best defense for a man on foot. You could keep the horse at bay with the knife while concentrating on the rider.

My hell-creature opponent was a more than able swordsman. He used his height advantage to the full, raining down savage blow after blow, trying to wear me out or beat me down. Such an attack would have worked on a lesser man, but I set my feet and stood my ground. I had little choice—with a house to my back, I could not retreat.

The next few minutes became a blur as I parried, riposted, and parried again. Beside me I heard Dworkin grunt once or twice, and then a horse screamed and fell. In that moment's distraction my blade slipped beneath my opponent's guard and pierced his chest.

With a low gurgle, the hell-creature slumped in the saddle. I ripped my blade free. His horse screamed in anger and reared back, kicking with its front hooves.

I ducked to the side, gave it a good prick with the tip of my blade, and watched as it wheeled and raced back the way they had come. Probably returning him to their camp, I thought. Another hell-creature galloped forward to take his place, red eyes glaring.

His horse didn't wait, but spat a jet of fire at me the second it grew near. I leaned back and batted my knife at its snarling face. Its teeth had been filed to points—a truly hideous creature.

Screaming a warbling war-cry, the rider rained down smashing blows and an intricate slashing attack that only served to strengthen my will. *You will not pass.* That had become King Elnar's rallying cry, and I made it mine now, too.

Giving a roar of my own, I seized the initiative and attacked. He matched me ringing blow for blow. Then, with a quick feint and a nimble thrust, I pierced his right hand with my blade. His sword went flying. As he yanked on his horse's reins with his other hand and tried to wheel away, I closed and struck three quick, sharp blows to the side of his helm.

That tumbled him from his saddle, and his ankle caught in the stirrups. I gave his mount a slap on the rump with the flat of my blade.

"Go!" I screamed at it, waving my sword. "Run!"

Giving an unholy wail, the horse fled. It dragged the hell-creature down the streets, his helm and armor banging and rattling on the cobbles.

I chuckled to myself. If he lived, he certainly wouldn't be fighting for a long, long time.

I enjoyed a second's break as the remaining hell-creatures jockeyed for position to get at me. When I glanced over at Dworkin, I saw with some surprise that he had already dispatched no fewer than six of his opponents. He fought two now, his sword and knife a darting blur as he darted between their horses to parry and stab. I had never seen such speed or swordsmanship before, and it made my own more-than-able defense seem clumsy and amateurish.

No sense letting the break go to waste, I thought. Bending, I pulled a small knife from my boot sheath and flipped it underhand. The tip nicked one of Dworkin's opponents on the chin, just below the helm. I don't think it did more than scratch him, but that was the distraction Dworkin needed to run him through. Then, whirling and with a magnificent double-feint, Dworkin beheaded the other. The body slowly toppled from the saddle, and then both of the horses raced off.

A horn sounded from the end of the street, and distant voices began crying an alarm. The town watch must have finally noticed something amiss, I realized with a snort of amusement. Hundred-foot-tall sheets of green flame and roving bands of hell-creatures with fire-breathing horses battling in the streets hadn't escaped them. Undoubtedly they would show up just in time to claim credit for saving us.

As if realizing they hadn't much time left, the hell-creatures pressed their attack. Dworkin killed another, and I killed two more in quick succession. Six remained. They fell back for a second, steadying their horses and preparing to rush us all at once. This would be the decisive moment in the fight, I realized. Strong as I was, my muscles had begun to tire, and these last six hell-creatures and their mounts were still fresh for battle.

I drifted closer to Dworkin, keeping my sword up.

"Help will be here soon," I said. Not that he needed it. He wasn't even panting. "We just have to hold them off for a few more minutes."

"Wait. I have something here..."

He tucked his long knife under one arm and rummaged around in a pouch with his free hand, muttering softly to himself. Then, just as the six hell-creatures spurred their mounts toward us for their final attack, he pulled out a small crystal that glinted with an inner fire.

"Aha!" he said.

He raised the crystal to eye level, and a beam of dazzling white light shot from the tip, brighter than the sun, brighter than anything I had ever seen before. It sliced through the four closest riders and their mounts like a scythe through wheat. Horses and hell-creatures alike fell, screaming in pain, blood spraying, their various parts flopping on the cobbles like fish out of water. They had been sliced in half, I realized, numbly taking in the horrible scene. Then they lay still, dark blood pooling rapidly.

Cursing, Dworkin dropped the crystal. It had turned black, I saw, and a sharp, unpleasant smoke rose from it. It shattered on the cobblestones, then the bits seemed to turn to dust and disappear like evaporating water. Little remained but a faint black smudge.

"What was *that?*" I demanded, shocked and horrified. It was the most terrible weapon I had ever seen.

"A parlor trick."

"Magic!"

"I suppose you could call it that."

Horns sounded again, much closer now. The two remaining hell-creatures reined in their hissing, spark-spitting horses , hesitated a second, then wheeled, kicked their mounts to a gallop, and fled back the way they had come.

I wasn't surprised. Between us, Dworkin and I had killed fourteen of their band in a handful of minutes. We could easily have dispatched two more. Better to report failure and live to attack another day, especially with the town watch at hand.

Suddenly exhausted, I lowered my sword and stared at the carnage before us, then I stared at Dworkin. By the light of Helda's burning house, he had seemed younger and stronger than I remembered. And now, nursing burnt fingers, blowing on them and shaking them in the air, he seemed almost comical.

"Where did you get that crystal?" I asked in a quiet voice. If I could get more like it for King Elnar, I knew without a doubt that it would turn the tide of war in our favor.

"Never ask a magician his secrets."

"So I'm supposed to believe you're a magician now?"

"Do you have a better explanation?"

"Actually, I do. You're a spy for one of the neighboring kingdoms, one with a wizard. The wizard gave you that"—I indicated the remains of the crystal with my chin—"and your horseless carriage. Other spies warned you about the hell-creatures' coming attack, and you came here to save me either for old times' sake or for reasons I don't yet know."

Throwing back his head, he howled with uncontrollable laughter.

I frowned. Clearly he had no intention of telling me the truth.

"Yes! Yes!" he finally gasped. "Your explanation is much better than mine! Much more believable!"

This wasn't the solemn, serious Dworkin I remembered of old.

"You've gone mad," I said, half believing it.

That sent him howling again.

With the hell-creatures gone, the few remaining townspeople in this neighborhood began to venture from their houses. They stood in small clusters, talking in low voices and pointing at the carnage, Helda's burning house, the odd horseless carriage, and Dworkin and me. The green flames in particular seemed to frighten them; they made no move to form a bucket brigade to try to put out the fire.

I didn't blame them; I wouldn't have gone anywhere near it, either. Luckily the fire didn't seem to be spreading, or all of Kingstown might have been in jeopardy.

Ignoring Dworkin, I bent and cleaned both my sword and my knife on a dead hell-creature's cloak, then sheathed them. A soldier's first duty after a battle is to take care of his weapons, after all. Next I retrieved my throwing knife, cleaned it, and returned it to my right boot.

My movements felt almost mechanical. The whole night's adventure, had taken on an air of unreality, as though it had happened to someone else. The townspeople, the fire, my long-lost mentor...I found myself just standing there, staring into the green flames, remembering. And most of all I remembered Helda, my Helda, who was gone....


Horns sounded again, very close now, perhaps one street over. The town watch would be here soon.

Dworkin touched my shoulder. "We must go."

I focused on him. "I'm not going anywhere until I get the truth."

"Fine. I am a spy. That is as good an explanation as any, for the moment. Come on, we must go before the hell-creatures return in greater numbers. Do not be stubborn about it."

"You think they're coming back?" I demanded, startled. I gazed up the street in the direction the two surviving hell-creatures had fled. *"Tonight?* After the way you cut them in half with that crystal?"

"Of course they are coming back, and I have just about run out of tricks. Now that they have found you, they will not rest until you are dead. They will mount an all-out assault instead of a methodical search."

I shook my head. "That doesn't make sense. Why me? I'm nobody special. They should be going after King Elnar if they want to end the war."

"It is more complicated than that...and this war means nothing to them. They do not want land or slaves. They are searching for you."

"Me? Why?"

It is a long story. I will tell you everything when we are safely away, I promise."

He started for his horseless carriage, then paused and looked back expectantly.

"You had best come, my boy."

I took a deep breath, glanced one last time at the burning house, at the corpse-littered street, then at him. He seemed strong and sure and confident now. Despite all that had happened—or perhaps because of it—my long-seated anger and hurt and resentment over being abandoned began to melt away. I trusted him, I realized, in some deep way I couldn't fully understand.·

And he had claimed he could help end the war. That alone was worth giving him the benefit of the doubt.

A little stiffly, I nodded and started after him. *All right,* I told myself, *you seem to know what you're doing, Uncle. I'll trust you for now.*

I didn't think I had much choice. We could sort out our differences when we were safe. And if he could help save Ilerium from the hell-creatures as he claimed, so much the better. That crystal gave me some idea he hadn't been making idle promises.

## THREE

The pumpkin-shaped carriage looked even more ridiculous now, in the greenish glow of Helda's still-burning house, at the end of a street littered with dead hell-creatures and half a dozen dead horses. As we neared, a little door in its side slowly swung open and delicate steps glittering like spun crystal folded out. A small oil lamp hung from the ceiling inside, and by its pale illumination, I looked upon white velvet seats and cushions, a small ivory-inlaid table, and a passenger—the woman I had glimpsed earlier.

Without hesitation I unbuckled my swordbelt and slid into the seat across from her, balancing my weapon across my knees. My fellow passenger was strikingly beautiful, I found, with long dark hair and a wide, almost familiar face. Thin nose, full lips, strong chin—

*Dworkin,* I realized. *She looks more than a little like him.* Could she be his daughter?

She was dressed in a gold-and-red silk dress, with a round red hat perched atop her head. Heavy gold rings set with large diamonds and larger rubies, if I was any judge, covered her slender fingers. If she had witnessed the battle outside, she showed no sign of concern. She might have been out for a picnic in the country as far as I could tell.

"Hello," I said.

"Not now, Oberon," she said.

Ignoring me, she picked up what looked like a deck of Tarot cards and nimbly shuffled them, then began turning them over one by one on the table between us. Leaning forward she studied intently the pattern made by the first nine.

"Anything?" Dworkin asked from outside the carriage door. I glanced over at him expectantly.

Freda said, "We had best hurry. Time is running out here."

"Time already ran out," he told her. Then he shut the door, and from the way the carriage shook and swayed, I knew he was climbing onto its roof. Probably to steer, I thought, thinking of the bench up there, though the carriage hadn't needed any such guidance before.

"I guess it's just to be the two of us," I said. I gave her a smile, but she didn't look up.

With a slight lurch, the carriage began to move forward. It took me a moment to realize the wheels weren't clattering over the cobblestones. From the smoothness of the ride, we might have been gliding a foot above them. It had been a night of sufficient wonders that I didn't even question it.

Instead, my attention focused on the woman opposite me—Freda, as Dworkin had called her-who seemed intent on ignoring my presence. With deft hands she gathered her cards, shuffled them again, and began methodically turning them over once more, this time forming a circle on the table. She didn't seem the slightest bit interested in me, Kingstown, or the hell-creatures we had just slain.

"I'm Obere," I told her, "not Oberon." Maybe we simply needed an introduction to get off on the right foot. "Oberon is your proper name," she said, still without looking up. "Things must be done properly. I am Freda."

"I know," I said. "Pleased to meet you."

"Yes, you are, dear boy."

"You see that in the cards?"

"No, in you, brother Oberon." She smiled enigmatically, eyes glistening behind long black lashes.

I could play that coy game, too.

Almost teasing, I said, "What man wouldn't be?"

"Indeed," she said solemnly.

"Why are you here?"

"Father does not like to travel alone, and I thought I might be able to help, in my own small way."

"I don't think he needs help from anyone."

"He does from me."

Chuckling to myself, I leaned back. Clearly she thought a little too highly of herself. Dworkin's daughter? Of that there could be no doubt. Apparently hubris was a family trait. I found it more annoying than endearing, however.

I glanced out the little window to my left. To my surprise, what appeared to be daylight glimmered through the lace curtain. Had dawn already broken? How long had we been riding in the carriage? It should have been at least three or four more hours till first light, by my reckoning.

I swept back the curtain and sure enough, the sun greeted me. Low in the sky, it cast a reddish-gold glow across acres of neatly plowed fields. It shouldn't have been there yet, my every sense told me. Had I fallen asleep and not realized it?

No, I thought, shaking my head, that didn't seem possible. I had been awake the whole time. We had just set off from Kingstown a few moments ago...hadn't we?

I rubbed my eyes and, when I took my hand away, suddenly it was night again. I couldn't see anything outside the carriage for the blackness. Even the stars and moon were absent, hidden behind clouds.

I let the curtains drop. Just my mind playing tricks on me, I realized. I *had* been awake too long. Of course it wasn't daytime yet. We couldn't be more than a mile or two from Kingstown.

Leaning back, I noticed a faint light outside through the curtain. Dawn? *Again?* Impossible! Pushing back the lace curtains a second time, I stuck my head close to the window's glass.

No, not dawn...the clouds had parted, and the moon shone down, full and bright, set against a glittering diamond field of stars. By their glow, we sped down a coastal highway, rolling faster than the fastest horse could gallop. Faintly, I could see gentle dunes spotted with clumps of marsh grass. Beyond the dunes lay a pale ribbon of beach where small waves lapped.

Only...we should not have been here. The carriage had taken the south road out of Kingstown, which led to twenty miles of verdant farmlands and then fifty miles of ancient, overgrown forests. This horseless carriage moved quickly, but the nearest beach lay at least four days' hard ride from Kingstown. Over the years, I had surveyed the entire length of Ilerium's coast—and in all that time, I had never seen this beach before. I felt certain of it. So where were we? How had we gotten here?

*Magic,* I thought uneasily. It seemed the only explanation.

I unlatched the window and pushed it open, breathing deeply of the smells of salt and brine. Far off, an owl screeched. The waves shushed against the sand.

It *was* real, not some dream or vision. We really *were* on the coast now...a strange coast not anywhere I knew in Ilerium.

The sky began to grow lighter. The highway turned inland, now cutting through dense sun-bleached grasses whose pale heads rose higher than our carriage. Luminous clouds roiled in the sky, and lightning began to strike all around us. I saw flames shooting through the grass and realized they were dry enough to quickly catch fire. Unless the clouds let loose torrents of rain, and fast, those fires would soon be burning out of control. I knew how fast fires could spread, but somehow, riding in this carriage, I felt perfectly safe. Dworkin's magic would speed us away.

Still the carriage rolled on, faster and faster, leaving the fires behind. The daylight slowly increased, grayish and diffuse now, revealing a drab countryside. Scrub trees replaced the tall grass, dwarf oaks and oddly twisted pines. The carriage turned, climbing sudden hills, then entered a forest of pines, which in turn gave way to more farmlands.

Lightning continued to flash above. The clouds continued to boil and seethe, and the air grew hot and sticky, but no rain fell. I spotted a few small stone houses with thatched roofs among the fields, but no sign of people or animals anywhere...they had probably taken cover to avoid the coming storm.

Peering ahead, I spotted a town of perhaps twenty or thirty low stone buildings just now coming into view. As we rolled through, slowing slightly, men and women dressed in black from head to toe came rushing out from every doorway. All carried swords or knives or axes. Their faces were drawn and pale, and their mouths opened wide to show needlelike teeth and forked tongues.

A thrown axe whizzed by my head, hit the side of the carriage, and much too close for comfort. Gulping, I ducked back inside, peering at them from behind the curtain and the relative safety of the coach's interior. Although they weren't hell-creatures, from their reception, they might as well have been. Whether they wanted to eat us or sacrifice us to some dark god, I couldn't begin to guess. I wouldn't want to pass through here alone and unarmed, I decided with a shiver. And what of Dworkin? If they hit him with an axe—

They gave chase for a few minutes, but Dworkin's carriage outpaced them, and they, too, fell behind in the distance.

The trees around us had begun to grow taller, darker, and more foreboding by the minute. I found myself leaning closer and closer to the window to see. Streamers of a sickly yellow moss and tangled masses of prickly vines draped every branch. Immense bats hung from every available perch by the thousands, and as we passed, they began to open little red eyes and flex leathery wings.

I liked this place less and less the farther we went. Where could Dworkin possibly be taking us? I hadn't minded the coast road, but though I considered myself a brave man, the town and now this forest both sent shivers through me.

Suddenly the bats began to make screechy, chittering noises that sounded altogether too much like kill-kill-kill. They all seemed to be staring hungrily at us now, though none made any move to attack.

I wasn't going to take any chances, though. This time I closed the window and snapped the latch securely. No sense giving them any path inside—though if they decided to attack Dworkin where he rode on top, I didn't know how I'd be able to help him.

Slowly, I fingered the hilt of the knife in my belt, wondering if I should draw it and trying at the same time not to alarm Freda. No sense in worrying her unnecessarily, I thought.

I gave her what I hoped was an encouraging smile. She just stared through me, apparently bored and uninterested.

My gaze kept drifting back to the window, though, and to the dark ruby-eyed shapes perched out there. If anything, they bothered me more than the townspeople. I could defend myself against human—or almost human—attackers. But against swarms of wild animals…

"Father doesn't like to be followed," Freda said suddenly, breaking the uncomfortable silence between us. "He has always been good at laying traps."

"Traps?" I managed to pull my gaze from the window to regard her questioningly. "What do you mean?"

Anyone who tries to follow us will be attacked, of course. That *is* his plan."

"By the bats," I said, realizing what she meant. And the people in that town. And the burning grasslands—"

"Yes." She smiled a bit and smoothed her dress around her, as though we had gone for a pleasant afternoon's ride or a picnic in the country. "Father is awfully clever that way. I never could have thought up those bats."

"But…how—" I frowned, puzzled. Thought them up? She made it sound like he had *created* them, somehow.

"He is a true master at manipulating Shadows," she said with a little shrug. "Far better than me. I like to pick a place and stay there."

"As long as it's safe."

"Of course."

More riddles, I grumbled to myself. Shadows? What was she talking about? She was Dworkin's daughter, all right, and I was sick of their games. Every time one of them said anything to me, it only made my confusion worse.

My attention drifted to the table between us. Apparently she had finished with her Tarot cards; the whole deck sat neatly stacked before her now. I wondered what she had seen in our future. Briefly I considered asking her, but then I thought better of it. Somehow, I didn't think the answers would make much sense to me. And I had never put much faith in fortune-telling.

I turned my attention back to the window. Without warning, the carriage burst into a clearing, and dazzling noontime sun caught me full in the face. I had to shield my eyes and squint to see, and even so, bright spots drifted before my eyes.

A desert...we were riding through a desert of red sand and red rocks now. Heat shimmered in waves, and though I could feel a scorching heat on my face, I felt a chill inside.

*Magic again.* The carriage was ensorcelled, taking us on a nightmare journey where neither day nor night nor landscape held any true form or meaning. Even so, knowing it couldn't possibly be real, as my eyes grew accustomed to the light I found I could not look away.

We turned, crossed a bridge of stone, and entered another forest, this one filled with redwoods of immense proportion, their trunks so big around that it would have taken a dozen men with arms stretched fingertip to fingertip to surround one. High up among the leaves, I glimpsed creatures the size and shape of men leaping from branch to branch. Male and female alike wore skirts of woven grass and carried short wooden clubs hooked to small belts. When they spotted us, they began to shriek and point.

The sky darkened without warning; hailstones the size of peas began to fall, followed by gusts of wind strong enough to shake the carriage. Behind us, I heard a huge grinding, tearing sound like nothing I had ever heard before and a jolt of fear went through me.

Opening the window, I stuck my head out and looked back to see what was happening. A cold, gale-strong wind whipped my hair, and I had to squint to see, but the sight filled me with a terrible awe.

Half a dozen tornadoes writhed and danced through the redwood forest behind us. Trees by the hundreds were falling before the winds, huge knots of root tearing loose from the ground, immense trunks slamming down in an impenetrable maze of wood. I saw hundreds of the manlike creatures sucked up into the black swirling funnels where, still screaming, they vanished.

The road would be impossible to follow on horseback. It had to be another trap for our pursuers, if they made it around the fires, through the townspeople, and past the bats. But how had Dworkin known to come here? How had he known the trees would fall?

They must have been standing for centuries to have grown so huge. For us to pass just as tornadoes blew them over seemed unlikely, to say the least.

No, I thought, Dworkin hadn't *known* the trees would fall, I realized with a growing sense of helplessness. He had *made* them fall. It was the only possible explanation. With such powers as he now commanded, he could have ruled Ilerium. How, in all our years together, had I never even suspected them?

I felt sorry for the tree creatures in that forest who had died because of us, unwittingly giving their lives and homes to protect our passage.

The winds began to drop when we descended into a small valley. Fog came up suddenly, and a dense, dismal gray cloaked the windows for a time. Though I *knew* cliffs stood to either side, somewhere just out of sight, I thought once or twice I heard the sound of gently lapping waves.

I pulled my head in and glanced at Freda, who looked as serene as a cat with a bird in its mouth. I couldn't understand her calm. This journey—and it wasn't over yet!—already had me feeling battle-worn and weary...yet too ill at ease to relax.

"How much longer?" I asked her.

"It depends on Father. He is not taking the fastest or most direct route to Juniper, after all."

Juniper? Was that our destination? I'd never heard of it...and from the name it could have been anything, from castle keep to sprawling kingdom. She expected me to know the name, I thought, from the way she said it, so I simply smiled like I knew what she meant. Perhaps she'd tell me more if she thought I already knew about this Juniper.

Instead of talking to me, though, she settled farther back in her seat and folded her hands in her lap, volunteering nothing.

I did notice that dawn had just broken outside again, burning off the fog with supernatural speed.

After that, everything kept changing, but subtly, never quite while you were looking at it. The sky turned greenish, then yellow-green, then back to blue. Clouds came and vanished. Forests rose and fell to grassland, which gave way to farmland and then back to forests again. Dawn broke half a dozen times.

I had never even heard of magic like this before, which bent time and place to a driver's will, and my estimation of Dworkin—or the people he worked for—grew steadily greater, if that was possible. Whatever wizards had created his crystal-weapon and this carriage clearly had the power to save Ilerium from hell-creatures.

My job would be winning them over to King Elnar's cause.

It seemed our only hope.

Finally, after what felt like hours of travel, we entered a land of rolling green hills. The highway we traveled—at times paved with yellow bricks but for the moment deep ruts with grass in between—curved gently ahead. Brightly plumed birds flitted among the scattered bushes and trees, their cheerful songs strangely normal after all we had been through. Overhead, high white clouds streaked the deep, perfect blue of the sky.

"We are close to Juniper now," I heard Freda say.

I glanced at her. "You recognize the scenery?"

"Yes. A few more hours and we should be there."

Then a dozen horsemen dressed in silvered armor fell in around the carriage.

# FOUR

Instantly my hand flew to the sword lying across my knees, but I didn't draw it. These soldiers seemed to be acting as an escort or honor guard, I thought, rather than a band of attackers. When one turned slightly, I noticed the red-and-gold rampant lion stitched on the front of his blouse. The pattern matched Dworkin's—these had to be his men.

I allowed myself to relax. We should be safe in their care. So close to this mysterious Juniper, what could go wrong?

The carriage slowed enough for them to keep up with us. Trying to appear uncurious, I opened the window again and pulled back the curtain a bit, studying the rider closest to us. Thick black braids hung down behind his rounded silver helmet, and he had a long, thin black mustache that flapped as he rode. His arms seemed odd, I decided—a little too long. And they seemed to be bending halfway between shoulder and elbow, as if they had an extra joint.

Suddenly he turned and looked straight at me. His slitted yellow eyes caught the light, glinting like a cat's with an almost opalescent fire.

Swallowing, I let the curtain fall. Thus hidden, I continued to study him. These might be Dworkin's guards, I thought, but they weren't human. Nor did they have the unpleasant features of hell-creatures. So who—or what were they?

Taking a deep breath, I forced myself to turn away. I'd seen enough. No sense brooding on questions I couldn't yet answer.

My attention now focused on Freda, who had begun to shuffle her Tarot cards and lay them out again. Every few minutes she rearranged them into a different pattern, sometimes circular, sometimes diagonal, once square with a cascading pattern in the center.

"Solitaire?" I asked, trying to get her attention. Perhaps I could learn more from her.

"No."

"I prefer games for two players, myself."

"Games are for children and old men."

I leaned forward, tilting my head and looking at her deck more carefully now. Rather than the standard Tarot cards such as any wisewoman or soothsayer might employ, filled with religious and astrological figures, these showed men and women I didn't recognize and places I had never been—a strange castle, a dark forest glade, even a romantic beach bathed in the warm glow of moonlight...or moonslight, rather, for two moons hung in the sky—the artist's idea of a joke, or a real place? I could no longer be sure.

Freda gathered the cards, shuffled seven times, and dealt out fifteen, three lines of five cards each. Only portraits of men and women came up. Most had features similar enough to Dworkin's to be related to him.

"What do you see?" I finally asked after the waiting became impossible to bear.

"Our family." She pointed to the cards before her. "Nine princes of Chaos, all torn asunder. Six princesses of Chaos, where do they wander."

"I know fortune-tellers are always vague," I said, taking a stab at humor. "But at least it rhymes, almost."

"It is part of an old nursery verse:

*"Nine princes of Chaos, all* torn *asunder;*
*Six princesses of Chaos, where* do *they wander?*
*Fly falcon, stout hart, and unicorn brave;*
*Between the Shadows, to escape your grave."*

I had never heard it before. And yet it did fit.

"A bit grim," I said.

She shrugged. "I did not write it."

With a start, I realized we were no longer speaking Tantari, but some other language, a richer one with a lilting rhythm. It spilled from her tongue like water from a glass, and I understood every word as though I had been speaking it all my life. How did I know it? More magic? Had I come under some spell without even realizing it?

Stammering a bit, unable to help myself, I asked her, "W-what language is this?"

"It's Thari, of course," she said, giving me the sort of odd, puzzled look you'd give the village idiot when he asked why water was wet.

*Thari*...It sounded right, somehow, and I knew on some inner level she spoke the truth. But *how* did I know it? When had I learned it?

My every thought and memory told me I never had.

And yet...and yet, now I spoke it like I'd known it my entire life. And I found it increasingly difficult to recall Tantari, my native tongue, as though it belonged to some distant, hazy dream.

"You *have* been in Shadow a long time, haven't you?" she said with a sigh. "Sometimes it is easy to forget what that can do to you...."

In *Shadow?* What did *that* mean?

Remembering the look she'd given me when I asked what language we spoke, I bit back my questions. I wouldn't appear foolish or ignorant again, if I could help it.

Instead, I said, "Yes, I suppose I have been gone too long." I didn't know what else to say, and I didn't want to volunteer too much and reveal my ignorance. "I hadn't seen Dworkin in many years."

"You still look confused," she said, and then she gave a kinder laugh and reached out to pat my hand. Her skin, soft as silk, smelled of lavender and honey. "It does not matter."

I smiled. Now we were getting somewhere.

"Wouldn't you be confused, too?" I asked. "Pulled from my bed in the middle of the night to fight hell-creatures, trundled off in this ludicrous carriage, then thrown in here for a frantic midnight ride—all with no questions answered?"

"Probably." She cleared her throat. "Thari is the primal tongue," she said matter-of-factly, as though lecturing a small child who hadn't learned his lessons properly. "It is the source of all languages in all the Shadow worlds. It is a part of you, just as everything around us is part of Chaos. You *do* remember the Courts of Chaos, don't you?"

I shook my head, once again feeling foolish and ignorant. "Never been there, I'm afraid."

"A pity. They are lovely, in their way." Her eyes grew distant, remembering. I could tell she liked that place...the Courts of Chaos, she'd called it.

Hoping for more answers, I said, "It's been quite a night. Or day now, I suppose. What do you think of all this?" I made a vague, sweeping gesture that covered the carriage, the riders, her cards. "What does it portend?"

"War is coming. All the signs are there. Everyone says so, especially Locke. He has been playing general long enough, he is bound to be good at it. But we will be safe enough in Juniper, I think. At least for now."

"And this Juniper?"

"You have never been there, either?"

I shook my head. So much for my plan to keep my ignorance to myself.

"It is nothing like the Courts of Chaos, but for a Shadow, it is really quite lovely. Or used to be."

That didn't really help. So *many new questions...* Juniper...Shadows...the Courts of Chaos—what *were* they?

I glanced at the window again, thinking about Chaos. At least that name sounded familiar. Reading from the Great Book was part of every religious holiday in Ilerium, and I had heard some of the most famous passages hundreds of times over the years. Our most sacred scriptures told how the Gods of Chaos wrought the Earth from nothingness, then fought over their creation. They were supposed to be great, magical beings who would someday return to smite the wicked and reward the pious.

As a soldier, I had never put much faith in anything I couldn't see or touch. Deep down, I had always believed the stories set forth in the Great Book were nothing more than parables designed to teach moral lessons to children. But now, after all I had seen and done this night, it began to make a certain amount of sense. If the stories were literally *true...*

I swallowed. The Gods of Chaos were supposed to return with fire and steel to punish those who didn't believe. Perhaps the hell-creatures marked the beginning of their return. Perhaps we had been working *against* the Gods of Chaos all along and hadn't realized it.

*For they shall smite the wicked...*

No, I decided, I had to have misunderstood. The scriptures didn't fit. The hell-creatures killed everyone, from priests to tradesmen, from doddering crones to the youngest of children. No gods could have sent such an army.

What *were* the Courts of Chaos, and where did Dworkin fit into all of this?

Freda seemed to sense my confusion. Smiling, she reached out and patted my hand again.

"I know it's a lot for you," she said. "Father did you no favors in letting you grow up in a distant Shadow. But on the other hand, that may be why you are still alive when so many others are not. I think he means you for something greater."

I frowned. "You think so? What?"

"We can try to find out."

In one quick motion, she gathered her deck of Tarot cards into a neat stack and set it in front of me. She tapped the top card once with her index finger.

"This deck has forty-six Trumps. Shuffle them well, then tu the top one. Let's see what they tell us."

Chuckling, I shook my head. "I don't believe in fortune telling."

"I do not tell fortunes. As Father says, even in Chaos there is a grand pattern emerging, truths and truisms if you will. The Trumps reflect them. Those who are trained—as I am—can sometimes see reflected in the cards not only what *is,* but what *must be.* Since the whole family is gathering in Juniper right now, it might be best for us to know where you stand...and who will stand with you."

Giving a shrug, I said, "Very well." I didn't think it could hurt.

I picked up the cards. The backs had been painted a royal blue, with a rampant lion in gold in the middle. They were a little thicker than parchment, but hard and chill to the touch, with a texture almost like polished ivory.

I cut them in half, shuffled them together a couple of times, then set them down in front of Freda. The palms of my hands tingled faintly. A light sweat covered my face. Somehow, touching the cards had made me distinctly un, comfortable.

"Turn the first Trump," she said.

I did so.

It showed Dworkin, but he was dressed as a fool in red and yellow silks, complete with bells on his cap and long pointed shoes that curled at the toes. It was the last thing I had expected to see, and I had to choke back a laugh.

"That's ridiculous!" I said.

"Odd..." Freda said, frowning. "The first turned is usually a place, not a person." She set the card to the side, face up.

"Meaning...?" I asked.

"Dworkin, the center of our family, who is now or will be the center of your world."

I said, "Dworkin is no fool"

"What matters is the person pictured on the card, not his clothing. Aber made these cards for me. Everyone knows he's a bit of a prankster."

Suddenly I had a new name to remember: *Aber. Aber the prankster.* I thought I might like him. And she seemed to assume I knew who he was.

"Turn another card," she told me.

I did so. It depicted a younger man, fifteen or sixteen years old at most, dressed in yellows and browns. Without a doubt, he had to be another of Dworkin's children—they shared the same eyes and strong chin. He wore a hat adorned with a set of preposterously large elk antlers and looked slightly bored, like he wanted to be off on adventures instead of having to sit for this miniature portrait. He held up a broadsword with both hands. It looked too long and too heavy for him. Somehow, he struck me as familiar, though I would have sworn we had never met—or had we?

Freda sucked in a surprised breath.

"Who is he?" I asked.

"Alanar," she whispered.

Again, the name didn't sound familiar, but I couldn't rid myself of the feeling he and I had met somewhere before. I could half picture him lying in a pool of blood...but where? When?

"Maybe he's coming back," Freda said.

"No," I said with certainty. "He's dead."

"How do you know?" she asked, searching my eyes with her own. "You haven't met him."

"I—don't know." I frowned, fumbling for the memory, finding it elusive. "Isn't he dead?"

"He's been missing for more than a year. Nobody's heard from him or been able to contact him, even with his Trump. I thought he was dead. Everyone does. But none of us has any proof."

Contact him...with his Trump? I looked down at the card, puzzling over that odd turn of phrase. Stranger and stranger, I thought.

"If you haven't seen a body," I said, trying to sound comforting though I knew it was a lie, knew that he *was* dead, "there is reason for hope."

She shook her head. "Our enemies do not often leave bodies. If he is dead, we will never know it."

I found myself agreeing. After battles, we had seldom been able to recover our dead comrades from lands the hell-creatures controlled. What they actually *did* with the corpses remained open to conjecture—and the guesses were never very pleasant.

Eyes distant, Freda shook her head sadly. I realized that she had cared deeply for young Alanar. We had something in common, then; I had lost Helda...she had lost her brother.

Swallowing, I reached out and gave her hand a sympathetic squeeze. "Best not to dwell on it," I said softly. "These have been hard times for everyone."

"You are right, of course." Taking a deep breath, Freda placed Alanar's card on the table, a little below Dworkin's jester and to the right. Next to each other, their resemblance was even more striking. Clearly they were father and son.

"Pick again," she said, indicating the Trumps.

Silently, I did so. It was another young man, this one dressed in browns and greens, with a wide pleasant version of Dworkin's face. A faint dueling scar marked his left cheek, but he had a genial smile. He carried a bow in one hand and what looked like a wine flask in the other. A trickle of wine ran down his lips and beaded underneath his chin.

A young drunkard, the card seemed to suggest.

"Taine," Freda announced, keeping her expression carefully neutral.

"I don't know him," I said.

"I think he is dead, too."

"I'm sorry."

We went through four more cards rapidly. Each showed a man between the ages of twenty and forty. Most bore some resemblance to Dworkin—either the eyes, the shapes of the faces, or the way in which they held themselves. His offspring almost certainly, I decided. It seemed he'd kept busy with a number of women over the years. How many children had he sired? And with such a large family, how had he still found so much time to spend with me during my own youth—all the while pretending to be unmarried? The next time I had him alone, I intended to ask.

Each of these cards Freda placed below Dworkin's, circling the edge of the table. In all, counting Alanar and Taine, she thought four of Dworkin's sons were dead. I didn't recognize either of the other two.

Then I turned over a card that showed a man with my face, only his eyes were brown to my blue. He dressed all in dark browns and yellows, and he held a slightly crooked sword almost defiantly. I didn't know if it was a private joke, but certainly the crooked sword seemed to imply one.

"Who is he?" I asked hesitantly. He looked familiar, too. Where had we met? And when?

"Do you know him?"

"He looks a lot like me…"

I held the card a minute, just staring at it, until she took it out of my hand and placed it below the others.

"Mattus," she said. "His name is Mattus."

"He's dead, too," I said numbly.

*"How* do *you know?"* she demanded, voice rising sharply.

I shrugged helplessly. "I don't now. It's like…like an old memory, distant and hazy. Or maybe a dream. I can almost see it, but not quite. I only know he was in it, though, and I saw him die."

"What happened to him?" she went on. "How did he die?"

I shook my head. "I'm sorry. I can't quite remember." But I felt certain it hadn't been pleasant, though I couldn't bring myself to say so to Freda. I didn't think she'd take the news well. Clearly she had cared for Mattus.

She sighed.

"Maybe it *was* only a dream," I told her, trying to sound a little reassuring, a little hopeful, though deep inside I knew it for a lie. "Perhaps they are both still alive, somewhere."

"Do not dismiss your dreams so easily. They are often powerful portents of the future. Over the years, I have had hundreds of dreams that proved to be true. If you say both Alanar and Mattus are dead, and you saw them die in a dream, it may very well be so."

"It was only a dream."

"Perhaps I believe *because* you saw it in a dream."

"As you say," I said with a small shrug. Most of the time, I put as little stock in dreams as in fortune-tellers.

Sitting back, I regarded her and her cards. It seemed she shared Dworkin's strengths as well as his flaws. He had never been one to shy away from bad news, no matter how terrible. It was one lesson I had learned well from him.

I said, "Tell me about Mattus."

"Like Alanar, he has been missing for about a year. Nobody has been able to contact him. He always had a quick temper, though, and one night he stormed off after a shouting match with Locke...and that was the last anyone heard of him."

Locke was a disagreeable-looking, puffed-up man on one of the other Trumps I had drawn. She had mentioned him earlier, I recalled, with a disparaging note in her voice. Clearly they were at odds.

She added, "I *had* hoped Mattus would get over his sulk and simply show up one day, forgiving Locke and taking up where we had all left off, before..." She smiled wistfully and blinked back tears. "But that is not your concern right now, Oberon. Please, go on. Draw again."

Quickly, I turned the next card.

"Aber," she said. She added him to the other eight Tarot cards to form a circle around the top of the table.

I leaned forward for a better look at this prankster who painted cards so well. He was ruggedly handsome—at least as portrayed on the card—and he dressed all in deep reds, from his leggings to his tunic, from his gloves to his long, flowing cape. It was hard to tell, but I thought we looked about the same age. He had short brown hair, a close-cropped brown beard, and steady gray-green eyes. In his portrait he struck a valiant pose, but instead of a sword, he held a long paint brush. I gave a mental chuckle. Truly, he had a sense of humor that appealed to me.

I also saw a bit of Dworkin in him, the oddly whimsical side that only came out on rare occasions, usually at high holidays or festivals when he had drunk too much wine. Then he would delight one and all with small tricks of the hand, making coins appear and disappear, or recite epic tales of ancient heroes and their adventures.

It must have been a trick of the light, but as I studied Aber's card intently, I would have sworn that it took on an almost lifelike appearance. It seemed to me that the tiny image blinked and started to turn its head—but before anything more could happen, Freda reached out and covered it with her palm.

"Do not!" she said in a warning tone.

I raised my eyes to her face, which had suddenly gone cold and hard. Perhaps, I thought, there was more to her than I first suspected. This was no mere fortune-teller, but a strong woman who had suddenly moved to action and taken charge of the situation. I admired her for that; I had never found much to like in weak-willed females. A woman of fire and steel added extra passion to a love affair.

"Why?" I asked blankly.

"It is already cramped in here. We do not need his company right now. And Father would be quite annoyed with me if I let him drag you away."

"Very well," I said, confused. For now, I had to trust her to look out for my best interests. Leaning back, I folded my arms and gave her my most trustworthy look. "I wasn't trying to cause you trouble."

She sighed, her manner softening. "No, not...*trouble*. Aber can be a...a *distraction*. That's a good word for it. And a distraction is *not* what we need right now."

I tilted my head and studied her cards from what I hoped would prove a safe distance. The more I thought about it, the more certain I became that Aber's picture *had* moved. But cards couldn't come to life, could they?

After all the magic and wonders I had witnessed over the last few hours, suddenly I wasn't so sure.

## FIVE

I focused my attention on the pattern of cards around the table, trying to see them as Freda did. Was there a pattern? All the subjects were male, five probably dead, four definitely alive. Somehow I had recognized two of the dead men—recognized them and knew without a doubt that they *were* dead. And yet I had never met them. Of the four still living, I knew only Dworkin. As I studied their features, I was fairly certain I had never seen Aber, Locke, or Fenn before.

"You're the fortune-teller," I said to Freda. "What do you make of this pattern?"

"I'm not sure." She bit her lip, gazing from one miniature portrait to the next, not letting her gaze linger long. "It's only people, thus no clues as to past, present, or future destinations. Clearly the whole family is tied up with you in events to come, but with war on the horizon, that may not be much of a surprise. Father and the others, dead or alive, all playa part in it-but what part?"

"You tell me." Leaning back, I studied her.

She seemed truly puzzled. Her brow furrowed; she drummed her fingertips on the tabletop. Clearly she took her card reading quite seriously. Finally she leaned back with a sigh.

"I see more questions than answers," she admitted.

"Do you want me to turn another card over?"

"Just one. That is more than I usually use for a personal reading, but in this case…"

I turned over the next Trump. This one showed a place I'd never been before—a gloomy keep half lost in night and storm, half illuminated by dazzling light. I say half because the sky seemed to be split almost in two, with star-pocked darkness to the left and a dazzling orange-yellow-red sky on the right, like a bottle of differently colored sands that had been shaken so that you could still see individual grains, but no one color ruled.

My palms itched. I could not look at it for more than a second or two without glancing away. I had the sensation that this mad picture was no artist's whim, but an actual place...a place at once dark and light, night and day, cold and hot, without season, shapeless and changing. I did not like it.

"The Grand Plaza of the Courts of Chaos!" she said. "That *is* odd. It should not be there. I did not even know I had that particular card with me...I had not meant to bring it!"

There it was again—Chaos.

Wherever the Grand Plaza was, it didn't look welcoming, I decided with a little shudder. The buildings, the lightning-shapes in the air, the very *essence* of the place—it all made the hair on the back of my neck stand on end and gooseflesh rise on my arms.

On impulse, I reached out and turned the card face down. The instant I no longer looked upon it, with its unnatural angles and weird geography, I began to feel better. I realized I'd begun to sweat all over just from having the Trump where I could see it.

"Why did you do that?" Freda asked. Luckily, she made no move to turn the card back over.

"I don't know," I said truthfully. "It felt like the right thing to do. Somehow, I didn't want to look at it."

I don't think I *could* have looked at it any longer. Just thinking about it made my head ache.

"I see." Again her brow furrowed. "Mattus felt the same way," she said. "We had to all but drag him there when..."

"When what?"

She hesitated. "When he came of age."

I gestured toward the face-down card. "Does it mean anything? My finding the Courts of Chaos?"

"Every action has meaning with the Trumps. They reflect the world around them."

"What is the meaning this time?"

"I...cannot say."

I swallowed, suddenly uneasy again. *Cannot say—or won't?* Her choice of words left me wondering, and her suddenly nervous manner gave me the distinct impression that she hadn't told me everything she'd seen.

An unsettling thought came to me. I tapped the back of the Chaos card.

"This isn't where we're headed, is it?"

"No, Juniper is about as far from the Courts of Chaos as you can get. Hopefully far enough to keep us safe."

Safe from what? Hell-creatures? Someone or something else?

I bit back my questions, though—call it pride or my own obstinate nature, but I thought it prudent to watch and learn. I would keep my queries to a minimum, and try to make them brief and unassuming.

Freda scooped up her deck of Trumps and sorted through them, finally pulling out a card that showed a sleepy, moss-draped castle atop a distant hill. She passed the card across to me.

"This is Juniper," she said. "At least, as it used to be. Aber painted it about two years ago."

In front of the hill sat a small, peaceful looking village, with perhaps seventy or so brick-and-mortar buildings with yellow-thatched roofs. Before and beyond stretched verdant acres of farmland and rich pastures, dotted with houses and barns, small ponds and even a broad blue stream. Juniper looked like any of a dozen small keeps in Ilerium, and unlike the Courts of Chaos, it didn't make my skin crawl. That alone made me feel a lot better.

"A lot can change in two years," I said.

"It has."

As I stared, the tiny cows, sheep, and horses sketched with unerring skill began to move across the fields. I swallowed and forced my attention back to Freda. She took the card when I offered it.

"What's different now?" I asked.

"An armed camp surrounds it—Father's troops, of course. Juniper is not under siege, at least not yet, but it has grown loud and dirty. I do not think it will ever be the same again."

I nodded. Wars did that. A year of battling hell-creatures had forever changed Ilerium, and not for the good.

"Since Juniper has changed so much," I said slowly, hoping to get another clue as to the nature of these mysterious Tarot cards, "will your Trump still work?"

"Yes...after a fashion. It just takes longer. The essence of the place remains the same even as the landscape changes."

I handed back her Juniper card. With a sad little sigh, Freda put it with the rest of her cards, shuffled them once, and stashed them away in a small wooden box. It looked like teak, inlaid with an intricate mother-of-pearl pattern of a lion.

"You said Aber made all your cards?" I asked. Might as well try to gather as much information as I could since she seemed to be in a more talkative mood now.

"Yes." She smiled, eyes far off, and I could tell she liked her brother. "He is good at it, too...almost as good as Father, though Aber tends to make fun of everyone when he draws them." She focused on me. "I wonder how he will draw you...nicely, I hope. I do think he will like you."

I snorted. "Why should he bother drawing me?"

"Why not? He draws everyone and every place he thinks might be useful. He must have hundreds or even thousands of Trumps stashed away in his rooms by now. I do not know where he possibly keeps them all."

I glanced out the window. Still rolling green hills, still a dozen odd horsemen with extra joints in their arms. We had to be nearing our destination, I thought, since the landscape hadn't changed much. Either that, or Dworkin was now resting up from all his magics.

"Do you know how much longer we'll be traveling?" I asked.

"Father did not tell you?"

"He was...vague."

"It *is* wise to be careful when traveling," she said with a slight incline of her head. "I am sure it is for our safety."

"Then tell me more about Juniper."

"What is there to tell? It is a remote Shadow. I think Father once hoped to retire there to a quiet life of study and reflection, but all these attacks have forced him to be a man of action. It is against his nature, but he can be a man of action...a hero...when he chooses. Or when he is forced to be." She peeked out the window. "We are close now. I do recognize this land."

"All things considered," I said, "this has been one of the worst nights of my life." Only my mother's death seemed more terrible. "All told, I'd rather be home. At least I knew where I stood there...or thought I did."

A look of profound sadness crossed her face as I said that, and I realized I'd unintentionally touched upon a sensitive topic—home.

"I'm sorry," I said, the truth suddenly dawning on me. "Your home...it's gone, isn't it? Was it attacked by hell-creatures, too?"

She nodded. "I called it Ne'erwhon," she said. "It was...beautiful. And peaceful. And *they* destroyed it when they tried to take me. Father rescued me just in time."

Her story sounded disturbingly similar to mine, and I said as much.

"Father has been rounding up a lot of people," she said.

"As soon as he discovered his friends and relatives were being hunted down, he set out to rescue every one of us. That is why there is such a gathering at Juniper now."

"I had no idea," I said.

"None of us did." Freda forced a yawn. "It has been a long trip for me, and I am growing tired. I hope you do not think it rude, but..."

She leaned back and closed her eyes.

"Not at all," I murmured.

She'd found the perfect way to escape my questions. And just as the answers were getting interesting, too.

I sat back, waiting patiently until her breathing grew steady and I saw her eyes start to dart beneath their lids. Let her dream of better days; work remained.

Making as little noise as possible, I gave the carriage a quick search. No papers, no scrolls or books, no magical crystals that shot lines of fire. A small lever to the side operated some hidden mechanism—probably to open the door.

Then I discovered the seat beneath me moved. I swung it up, revealing a storage compartment. Inside lay a stack of soft white blankets...nothing else.

Sighing, I covered Freda with a blanket. Might as well make her comfortable. She stirred for an instant, murmured a thank you, then lay still.

A little disappointed at not having found something more worthwhile, I sat back to ponder my situation. Freda, I noticed, had left her box of Trumps on the table between us. It could have been an invitation to look through them...but somehow they seemed foreboding. I had seen enough of them to know they didn't mean much without an expert to name the portraits and places. And what if they started to move? I wouldn't know what to do, short of turning them over or covering them with my hand, as Freda had done. Better to leave them alone.

Other than that, the carriage had no furnishings, no clues for me to puzzle over. It had been cleaned so thoroughly that not a smudge remained to tell of any previous passengers.

Turning back to the windows, thinking of all I had seen, all I had done in the last day, I stared out once more as mile after mile of greenery rolled past. Trumps...Shadows...this magical journey...Juniper...The Courts of Chaos...it made a confusing hodge-podge in my mind.

I felt grateful that Uncle Dworkin had come back to rescue me, after so many years of abandonment, but somehow I thought he must have other motives. What? Where did I fit into his plans?

Somehow, I didn't think I'd like the answers.

## SIX

It turned out Freda really *was* exhausted. A few minutes after I covered her with that blanket, she began to snore. Perhaps magic took more out of her than I realized—though I still didn't put much trust in her future-telling skills. When she'd read her Trumps, she hadn't revealed more than crumbs of information...a few names, a few hints of dire things to come, which might or might not involve Dworkin and his various children.

Still, I *had* seen a picture of Juniper, so I didn't count it as a waste of time. And I had learned I didn't want to go to the Courts of Chaos. Something about the place made my skin crawl.

After a few more minutes of staring out the window and finding nothing but more questions, I gave up. Maybe Freda had the right idea, I decided, leaning back in the comfortable padded seat and stretching out my long legs. It had been an exhausting night, and I'd only had an hour or two of sleep. Might as well try to catch up.

I closed my eyes. Exhaustion flooded over me, but for the longest time I found myself twisting and turning, trying to get comfortable. My thoughts kept racing through the events of the day, turning over all the questions I'd already asked myself, but finding no more answers.

Finally, sleep did come, but it was not the sleep of the dead. It was anything but refreshing. Dreams of Helda and the hell-creatures haunted me, of burning buildings and green fires and horses that spat sparks, and towering over it all, a fairy tale castle grown to nightmare proportions—the legendary Juniper.

Some time later the carriage began to slow. I sensed the change in our pace and came awake instantly, yawning and stretching the kinks from my muscles.

Opposite me, her chin on her chest, Freda snored softly. No sense in waking her yet, I decided. Better to wait till we actually reached our destination.

I pushed back the lace curtain and peered out.

Morning had given way to late afternoon, if the fading light of the sun proved a true indicator of time. The verdant green forests had been replaced by open fields-and a sprawling army camp that stretched as far as the eye could see. Long rows of tents, pens of horses, sheep, and cattle, hundreds of cooking fires, and countless thousands of soldiers-some with the extra joints in the arms, some fully human-filled my view. I couldn't hear much through the carriage walls, but my imagination filled in the sounds of a camp life, the boasting talk of soldiers at work and leisure, the tramp of boots, the squeak of leather and the jingle of chain mail.

We passed a large open field where dozens of squads marched and drilled, and in the distance I saw more sol, diers paired *off* to practice swordsmanship. It was a familiar enough scene, but on a larger scale than I had ever witnessed before.

King Elnar had raised an army of eight thousand against the hell,creatures, and I had thought he commanded a huge force. This one dwarfed it. There had to be tens of thousands of soldiers here, I thought with awe. Again we rolled past row after row after row of tents.

But whom did they serve? No small keep like Dworkin's could possibly support this many soldiers. He must have allies-powerful ones. None of the Fifteen Kingdoms could have summoned up and sustained a force like this one.

Opening the window, I leaned far out and craned my neck. At once I spotted what had to be our destination: Juniper, just as Aber had painted it. But he hadn't done it justice.

An immense moss-and-ivy draped stone castle set high on a hill, its ancient walls had to be eighty feet high. Even at this distance I could clearly see half a dozen men patrol, ling the battlements.

When the road turned and headed straight toward Juniper, our horsemen, escort peeled off. The castle's huge stone walls had been built of massive blocks nearly as tall as me-an impressive feat of engineering, I thought. It would be hard to take this place by siege.

Without slowing, the carriage mounted a long ramp overlooked by battlements on our right and entered a massive gatehouse, emerging after a right turn in a courtyard paved in red flagstones. It stopped, then swayed a bit as Dworkin climbed down.

Leaning forward, I touched Freda's arm.

"Mm?" she said.

"We're here."

Yawning, she sat up. "Juniper?"

"I believe so."

Reaching to her left, she pulled a small lever by the door. Instantly it swung open and those delicate-looking glass steps folded out.

I went down first, staring at the crowd that had begun to assemble. It included army officers as well as servants in white-and-red livery bearing water and other refreshments. I also recognized two of Dworkin's sons from Freda's Trumps—Locke and Davin. It seemed everyone wanted or needed to talk to Dworkin urgently, for they surrounded him, a dozen voices speaking at once. Locke paid me no heed; Davin gave me a curious glance, but did not address me. Clearly I wasn't important enough to warrant their attention.

When Freda appeared in the carriage's doorway, I offered her my hand and helped her to the ground.

Dworkin seemed to have forgotten us. He was busy giving orders—where to move troops, what supply stocks to draw upon, training and patrol schedules-as though he were the general who commanded this army.

"Come," Freda said, "he will be busy for hours."

Linking her arm through mine, she steered me toward a set of large double doors opened wide to the warm afternoon air. A steady stream of servants moved through them.

"But if he wants me—" I began.

"If he wants you, he will find you when he is ready. He always does."

I didn't argue. I still didn't know enough about the situation to make a decision. But I *did* know enough to realize that Freda was my sole key so far to learning more Dworkin's surprising double life. I'd have to get her alone and work on charming information out of her, I decided, before my uncle came looking for me. I was more handsome than most men, after all, and I'd always had a winning way with women. Romance might well be the key....

The double doors led to a large audience chamber. Tall, narrow stained-glass windows showing hunting and battle scenes filled the right wall. Similarly themed tapestries lined the other walls. Ahead, on a low dais, stood what could only be a throne, with half a dozen lesser chairs set slightly lower to either side. All sat empty now, but the room was far from deserted-at least a dozen servants scurried about on errands, carrying boxes, bundles of scrolls and, parchments, trays of food, and additional items. Other servants had lowered the immense crystal chandelier from its mount on the central roof beam and were busily cleaning it and replacing candles.

"This way," Freda said, 'starting for a door to the left of the dais. I hesitated a second, then followed.

Behind us, Dworkin and his entourage swept in, several voices still talking at once. I thought I heard Dworkin called "Prince" by at least one of the officers, which shocked me, but when I glanced back they were heading toward a different door.

As we entered a wide hallway, I noticed how Freda seemed changed here, inside the castle. She smiled constantly, nodding to servants and soldiers who passed us in the hallway. All called her "Lady" and bowed. They all gave me curious looks, but no salutations. And Freda offered them no hint as to my identity.

We turned, turned again, and went up a broad winding staircase to a second floor. I saw fewer servants here, but they seemed .older and more polished. They too bowed, and they greeted Freda as "Lady Freda," as though they were accustomed to dealing with her personally.

At the end of the last hallway we came to a large salon, richly carpeted and filled with comfortable looking chairs and sofas. A stained glass window of yet another hunting scene filled most of the west wall, and the lowering sun gave everything inside a warm, comfortable glow.

"Freda!" cried a woman from one of the sofas.

I studied her. She looked older than Freda, but they might have been sisters. Both had Dworkin's unmistakable features.

"Pella, you're back!" Freda said with clear delight. "When did you get in?"

"Last night."

"Any trouble?"

"Nothing to speak of."

The two embraced warmly, then Freda pulled me forward. "This is Oberon."

Pella raised her delicate eyebrows. "The long-lost Oberon? I though Father—"

"*No,*" said Freda pointedly. "Oberon, this is my full sister, Pella."

*The long-lost Oberon?* I wasn't sure quite what she meant by that. It seemed as though she'd heard stories about me. But how could that be-unless Dworkin had told them? But why would he bother?

Putting on my charm, I took Pella's hand and kissed it. "Call me Obere," I said with my most winning smile.

"He *is* cute," Pella said to Freda. "I can see he's destined to give Aber a run."

"Aber?" I said. "Is he here, too?"

"Of course," Pella said.

Freda added, "I do not think he has ventured outside Juniper's walls in at least a year."

"Not at all?" I asked, puzzled. The castle seemed nice enough, but I wouldn't want to hole up in here. If not training in the field with the soldiers, I'd want to be off hunting, patrolling the forests, or simply exploring new territory.

"He has been busy chasing the kitchen maids."

"Oh." I blinked, somewhat surprised.

Freda said to Pella, "He is such an innocent. He was raised in Shadow, you know. He knows next to nothing of Father or our family."

"Not so innocent!" I protested.

They both laughed, but it was done in such a kindly way that I couldn't possibly take offense.

A throat cleared behind us, and I turned to find a new woman leaning almost seductively against the doorway. She wore a low-cut gown of shimmering white, showing off ample cleavage. She was younger, a tad shorter, and far more attractive than either Pella or Freda. She wore her dark brown hair up, and makeup accentuated her high cheekbones, pale complexion, and perfect white teeth. She was beautiful and knew it.

When she gave me an almost predatory boots-to-eyes appraisal, I took an instant dislike to her.

"Oberon, this is Blaise," Freda said. I couldn't help but notice the chill that had crept into her voice. Apparently she shared my feelings about this woman.

"Introductions?" came a man's cheerful voice from behind Blaise. "Someone new here?"

The man goosed Blaise, gave a grin at her indignant glare, and ducked around her with a swirl of red.

"Aber?" I said, staring. He dressed as he had in his card: red from head to heel.

"That's right!" He gave a laugh, stepped forward swiftly, and seized my arm in a firm grip, pumping it. "And you, I gather, must be the long-lost Oberon."

"That's right. Call me Obere."

"Let me save you from these old hens, brother."

He pulled me toward the back of the wall, where a cart filled with several dozen bottles of liquor sat. "Care for a drink?"

"Gladly!" I glanced back at Freda and Pella, and beyond them to Blaise. "Care to join us?" I asked politely.

A little sulkily, Blaise said, "Aber knows what I like."

"Apple brandy," he said with a grin and a wink at me. "Red wine for Freda and Pella. And you, brother Oberon?"

Brother again. Why did he call me that? I wanted to ask, but what I said was, "Whatever you're having is fine."

"Whiskey, neat?"

"Perfect. It's been quite a day."

He poured quickly and I got to pass out the drinks. The five of us formed a little semicircle around the liquor cart, Pella and Freda chatting about people I had never heard of, Blaise pretending an interest in them, Aber sizing me up be, hind his drink. I sipped my whiskey and returned his inquiring stare with one of my own.

"Good whiskey," I said.

"It's imported from a distant shadow at great risk and effort...my own. Best I've ever found."

"Believe him," Pella said to me. "He used to roam farther through Shadow than any of us. And he always seemed to turn up something delicious to bring back."

"All for you, dear sister!" he said with a laugh. Then he raised his glass in a toast. "To king and family," he said.

The others raised their glasses, too.

"To Dworkin," I said, "for rescuing me."

It was only then that I caught a glimpse of the five of us in a long mirror hanging on the far wall. I was the tallest by a head, then Aber and Pella. But what truly caught my eye was the similarity between Aber and me. Our eyes were different colors, the shape of our faces and noses not at all the same—but there was something about us that struck a familiar chord. Our cheekbones, I thought, high and broad—and the similarities had to be more than coincidence.

We looked like brothers.

I had been denying it all along, but suddenly I realized how the women and I also shared many traits. Just as we shared them with Dworkin.

Almost choking, I set my drink down. *But my father is dead. He was a naval officer.*

So I had been told all my life.

But now, faced with overwhelming evidence, a different truth suddenly made sense.

I *was* Dworkin's son.

I had to be.

It all fell neatly into place. Dworkin's interest in my mother and me. All the lessons he taught me during my childhood. His unexpected return last night to save me from the hell-creatures, just as he had saved Freda and his other children.

I *was* a part of his family. Just as these strangers were now a part of mine.

Both Freda and Aber already knew. They had both called me "brother." I assumed Pella and Blaise knew as well. Apparently I was the only one who had been kept in the dark, too blind or stupid or naive to guess my true heritage.

Why *hadn't* Dworkin or my mother ever told me? Why had I been forced to think of myself as an orphan all these years? It wasn't fair! All through my childhood, I had longed for a father and brothers and sisters, longed for the sort of family everyone else had. Now it turned out I'd had brothers, sisters, and a living father all the time-only I'd never known it. I had been robbed of the family I could have had.

Why had my mother hidden the truth from me?

Why had I spent my childhood lonely and alone?

The next time I saw my new-found father, I intended to ask some hard questions. For now, though, I tried to hide my sudden realization. My siblings all acted as if I should have known the truth about my parentage. Well, let them continue to think so. I seemed to get more information when people assumed I knew more than I did, as with Freda in the carriage.

Suddenly I realized I'd missed an important thread of conversation. My attention snapped back to Aber.

My new-found brother was saying, "...and that's what Locke claimed. I'm not sure he's right, though."

"Time will tell," Blaise said.

Pella laughed. "That's what you always say, dear. It hasn't been true yet."

Blaise, bristling like a cornered wolf, opened her mouth to say something I knew she'd regret, so quickly I jumped in with, "It's nice to finally meet you all. How many more of us are here in Juniper now? Freda said something about a family gathering."

"Nicely done, brother," Aber said with a grin. "To answer your question and ignore the bickering"—he looked pointedly at Blaise and Pella— "there are fourteen family members present, including all of us."

"Fourteen!" I exclaimed, unable to help myself.

Freda said, "I know it seems like a lot, but I'm sure you'll have no trouble remembering all the names."

"When will I see them?"

"Tonight at dinner, I'd imagine," Aber said. "Fresh blood brings them out of the woodwork."

"Aber!" Freda gave him a sharp look.

"Out from under the rugs?" he amended.

With a sigh, Freda said, "There is Anari." She raised her hand and beckoned, jeweled fingers glittering, and an elderly man in red, and, white livery hurried to her side.

"Lady?" he asked.

"Take Lord Oberon upstairs and find him appropriate rooms," she said. She fixed me with her brilliant smile. "I am sure he wants to rest and freshen up before dinner."

"Yes, please," I said. Much as I hated leaving the liquor cart, a nap and a wash basin sounded more appealing right now. It sounded like I'd need to be ready for a long evening tonight, with fourteen new-found relatives waiting to inspect my every word and gesture.

And Freda had called me "Lord Oberon," I noticed. It was a title I knew I could get used to.

"This way, Lord," Anari said, heading toward the door.

"Until dinner, then." Giving my four siblings a polite wave, I turned to follow Anari.

Behind me, I heard Blaise's tittering laugh and an almost breathless exclamation of, "Isn't he *precious?*" that made my cheeks burn. No one had ever called me "precious" before. I wasn't sure I would have liked it coming from a woman I'd bedded, and I certainly didn't like it coming from my sister—or half-sister, since we could not possibly have shared the same mother.

Still, precious or not, I had done my best here. I had been raised a soldier, after all, and I wasn't used to niceties of polite society or court life, whether they were mine by blood-right or not. As always, I'd do the best I could and they could either accept me, rough edges and all, or not. Either way, we would still be a family.

"Please follow me, Lord," said Anari, turning to the left and starting up a wide set of stairs at a slow, deliberate pace.

"What's your job here?" I asked.

"I am chief of the domestics, Lord. I manage the house and servants."

I nodded. "How long have you served my father?"

"All my life, Lord."

"No, not my family...just my father, Dworkin."

"It has been my privilege to serve Lord Dworkin all my seventy-six years, as my father and my father's father served him before me."

"That would make him..." I frowned, trying to add up the years. "More than a hundred and fifty years old!"

"Yes, Lord."

I shivered, suddenly and inexplicably unsettled. I must have misheard, I thought. No one lived a hundred and fifty years. But Anari had said it so matter,of,factly he clearly believed and accepted it as a matter of course.

Although Dworkin hadn't looked more than fifty when he first came to Helda's door, now that I thought about it, he had looked distinctly younger than that when we had fought the hell-creatures.

*More magic,* I thought. Would it never end?

Anari led me up two flights of steps to a wing of the building devoted to, as he said, my family's private quarters. All around me I saw symbols of great wealth and power: Not just paintings and tapestries of the sort I'd seen below, but intricate mosaics set in the floor, beautifully carved statues of nymphs and nude women in alcoves, crystal chandeliers and wall sconces, and gilded woodwork everywhere. Over the decades—or centuries—of his life, Dworkin had accumulated treasures enough for a dozen kingdoms.

"These will be your rooms, Lord," Anari said, stopping before a large double door. "I trust you will find them acceptable."

He pushed them open—and I found myself standing before what seemed to me a private palace.

Rich red-and-gold carpets covered the floors in thick, luxurious layers. Beautiful paintings and hanging tapestries covered the walls, showing fairy tale scenes with mythical creatures. Overhead, gilded columns and crown moldings supported a ceiling painted in pastel blues, with high clouds and even a few swooping hawks in one corner. Three elegantly upholstered chairs clustered around a small table to the far right. To the left, on the other wall, sat a small writing table complete with pens, ink, paper, sealing wax and seals, and a blotter.

"Your bed chamber is through here," Anari said, stepping into the room and opening another set of doors set in an arched doorway. Through it I could see a high canopied bed and a full-length looking glass, plus a wash stand with pitcher and basin. "There are two wardrobes and a changing room as well."

"Thank you."

"My pleasure, Lord. Do you have baggage?"

"Nothing but my sword and the clothes on my back."

He stepped back and looked me over critically. "I believe I can find you suitable garments for tonight," he said. "I will make an appointment for one of the castle tailors to measure you tomorrow morning. We cannot have a man of your stature improperly furnished, after all."

"Indeed," I said agreeably, as if I had this sort of conversation every day. "I'll leave the appointment up to you. Schedule it as late in the morning as possible."

"Thank you, Lord." He bowed slightly. "I will endeavor to live up to your faith in my abilities. In the meantime, with your permission, I will order a bath drawn and heated."

"Please."

"Is there anything else you require at this time?"

I almost laughed. Anything else? I needed *everything* else, starting with explanations to dozens of questions about my newly discovered family. But I merely smiled and shook my head.

"The bath will do," I said. "Now, where—?"

"A boy will summon you when the water is ready."

"All right. That will be all."

"Very good, Lord." He shut the doors on his way out, and as he did, I noticed how the heavy old hinges gave a faint squeak. At least nobody would be able to sneak up on me, I thought, the soldier inside taking over for the moment.

Unbuckling my swordbelt, I draped it across the back of the nearest chair, then sat down and pulled off my boots. It felt good to be alone. I tossed my boots into the corner by the door, then wandered through the suite, admiring all the little decorations, the gilding on the moldings and woodwork, the paintings and tapestries on the walls. Finally I flopped onto the bed, spreading my arms and feeling the goosedown yield beneath me. Soft...softer than I had felt in a long time. Not even Helda's bed had been this comfortable.

I just needed a woman's warmth beside me, I decided while stifling a yawn, and I could easily call this place home. But a trace of guilt crept into my pleasant thoughts.

King Elnar and Ilerium remained besieged, and I remembered Dworkin's promise that he could help end the attacks. I would have to press him for an explanation the next time we met. Duty called.

An hour and a half later, after a long hot bath had soaked many of the day's accumulated aches from my bones, I returned to my rooms for a quick nap.

The castle's staff had been busy in my absence, I discovered. My boots had been cleaned and polished to a shine that would have made my orderly green with envy. Not even my sword had escaped their attention—the gold and silver inlay on the hilt had been polished to perfection. When I pulled half the blade's length from its scabbard, I discovered it had been freshly oiled. I couldn't have done a better job myself.

I could definitely get used to this sort of life, I thought, yawning widely.

The bath attendants had made off with the blood-and-sweat stained clothing I'd been wearing, replacing it with the long black robe I now wore. Anari had not yet produced the clothes he'd promised...not that I found fault—he hadn't had much notice, after all.

With nothing to wear and nothing to do before dinner, I crawled into bed. Almost immediately I grew dead to the world.

Some time later, when the afternoon light had begun to fade, I came awake with a start.

I'd heard a noise. Something just wrong enough to sound an alarm and wake me.

A light knock sounded again from the other room, so softly I almost missed it. Then the hinges squeaked slightly as the door opened slowly...stealthily.

Someone trying to sneak up on me? No hell-creatures could possibly get in here, I thought.

I sat up, instinctively reaching for my sword. It was gone—I had left it on one of the chairs in the next room, I realized.

Lord?" I heard an old man's voice call. It wasn't Anari. "Lord Oberon?"

"I'm here." Rising, I found I still wore the robe I'd donned after my bath. I tightened the belt and wandered out into the main room of my suite, stretching the kinks from my muscles. "What is it?"

A man in his late years, dressed in castle livery, stood in the doorway to the hall. He held a large silver tray laden with towels in his age-spotted hands. He had to be at least seventy years old, I guessed. Undoubtedly, he had been serving my father as long as Anari. He had a warm, gentle smile.

"Your pardon, Lord Oberon," he said. His voice quavered slightly. "I am Ivinius, the barber. Lady Freda said you required a shave and haircut before dinner."

I ran my fingers over the thick stubble on my chin. "Thoughtful of her."

"Her ladyship *is* most kind," he murmured. "I've known her since she was a babe in her mother's arms, bless her."

He set his tray down on the table. In addition to the towels, I saw that it held two small blocks of shaving soap, plus several cutthroat razors of varying lengths and a selection of tiny glass bottles: probably lotions and perfumes. Without asking, he began to drag one of the armchairs toward the window.

"I'll get that," I said, starting forward to help. He looked too frail to be moving furniture.

"No need, Lord," he said. He gave the chair one final tug and swung it into the last of the afternoon sunlight, exactly where he wanted it. "Please sit, Lord."

As I did so, he went into my bedroom, picked up the small table with the wash basin and pitcher of water, and lugged them slowly over to my chair.

"Do you need help?" I asked, half rising.

"No, Lord." He gave a low chuckle. "It is kind of you to ask, but I have been doing my job since before you were born. Please relax. I will be ready for you in a moment."

He might look doddering, I thought, settling back in my seat, but he obviously had his pride. And he obviously knew his own strength. With a slight grunt, he set the table down beside the chair. He hadn't spilled so much as a single drop of water from the pitcher.

I loosened my robe around my neck and took a deep contented breath, stretching out my feet and clenching and unclenching my toes. It would be nice to get a decent shave and haircut, I thought. I'd made do with battlefield barbering for most of the last year, and I'm afraid it showed.

With deft hands, Ivinius poured a small measure of water into the basin, took a block of shaving soap from his tray, and expertly lathered it with a brush. He spread towels across my chest and shoulders, then liberally foamed my chin, cheeks, and neck. While my beard softened, he selected the longest straight-edge razor from his tray—one almost as long as his forearm—and began stropping it across a long piece of leather tied to his belt.

To my surprise, I realized I could easily have gone back to sleep. I half closed my eyes, the clean scent of the shaving soap in my nostrils, the *shup-shup-shup* of the stropping blade a lullaby to my ears. *The joys of civilization*...yes, I could easily get used to life in Juniper, I thought with a half smile.

Silently, I gave thanks to Freda's thoughtfulness for sending Ivinius. The closest thing to a real barber I'd seen in the last year of campaigning against the hell-creatures had been my own orderly, who had more thumbs than fingers. He managed to trim my hair with a minimum of blood loss, but after his first stab—and that was the word—at shaving my face, I told him to get out and reclaimed my razor. My instincts for self-preservation demanded it.

In a near monotone, Ivinius kept up a steady murmur about his years in the service of Lord Dworkin. He mentioned his wife of sixty-two years, a cook in the kitchens; his five boys, who all served as valets in the castle; and his twenty-six grandchildren and great-grandchildren. one of whom would soon be of age to join the army. I made appropriate noises whenever he paused— *"uh-huh,"* *"yes,"* *"go on"*—*but* really I heard only every second or third sentence.

When I turned my head slightly, I could see us both in the looking glass. At that moment I knew why Freda had sent him: my hair was a wild tangle that not even a dunking in bathwater could tame. Dark circles lined my eyes, and I looked ten years older than my actual age. Everyone had been too polite to tell me I was a mess...certainly unsuitable to bring to dinner without being cleaned up.

Ivinius finished working on his razor and turned to me once more. Gently touching the bridge of my nose with two fingers, he tilted my head to the side. He didn't realize I could see our reflection, and with sudden alarm I noticed how he shifted his grip on the razor's handle. Now he held it like a butcher's knife poised to joint a leg of lamb.

With my right hand I caught his wrist barely an inch from my throat. "That's not how you hold a razor," I said, voice hard, turning to look at him.

"Lord," he said in the calm tones one uses to gentle a spooked horse, "I am a barber. I know my job. Let me do it."

"I'd rather shave myself, if you don't mind."

"*I do* mind," he snarled.

I pushed back the hand holding the razor. Or tried to—for he suddenly bore down on me with all his weight and strength. Much, much more strength than an old man deserved.

## SEVEN

I am a strong man—stronger than any human I've ever fought. It should have been an easy thing for me to push an old man's arm away from my throat.

But it wasn't.

Ivinius, despite his age, was at least as strong as me—certainly stronger than any seventy-year-old servant ought to be.

It became a struggle of wills and brute force. I felt my bones start to creak; the muscles in my arm stood out like bands of iron. Grunting from the strain, I gave my every effort to throw him off.

It wasn't enough. Standing, he had the better position. He threw not only his strength but his full weight against me, and steadily the razor drew closer to my throat. I gulped, suddenly realizing I couldn't win.

Out of desperation, I kicked off against the floor with both feet, throwing my shoulders back as hard as I could and rolling. The chair tipped and went over backwards. Instead of pushing, I tightened my grip on Ivinius's hand and pulled to the side. The razor's blade sliced air just beyond the tip of my nose, then went past my right ear. I heard the dry snap of a bone.

Ivinius howled with pain and dropped the razor, clutching his wrist. I released him and continued my backwards roll. Coming up on my feet, legs spread, arms and fists ready, I began to back away, looking for a weapon anything. Unfortunately, my sword lay on the other side of the room, still draped across the back of the chair where I had left it.

"Get out," I said to him, stalling for time. "Run. You might make it out alive. I'll give you fifteen seconds before I raise the alarm."

Glaring, Ivinius bent and scooped the razor up with his good left hand.

"It would have been an easy death for you," he said in a low growl. Then he rushed at me.

I bumped into the writing desk. It would have to do, I thought.

Seizing it, muscles straining, I lifted it and threw it at him. Paper, blotter, inkpot, and quills went flying in all directions. Ivinius couldn't quite duck in time, and one of the legs struck him across the forehead and sent him sprawling. Luckily he lost his grip on the razor, which clattered on the floor.

I threw myself on him, fingers closing around his throat, and noticed that the blood gushing from his forehead wasn't red. It was a sickly yellow, the color of a squashed bug, the color of vomit. He wasn't human, despite his appearance. That explained his extraordinary strength.

"Hell-creature!" I snarled.

I saw no human emotion in his eyes, no regret, no wish for mercy. Just a cold hatred.

I felt no desire for mercy, either. His kind had killed Helda. His kind has destroyed Ilerium with a year of war and terror.

"Die!" I said.

I squeezed his throat shut. His eyes began to bulge; he made a desperate gurgle. Still I tightened my grip, pouring a year's worth of hate and anger toward the hell-creatures against this *assassin* sent to murder me in my own room.

Then he began to struggle desperately, trying to buck me off, but with a broken wrist he could do nothing to stop me. Finally, with a sudden wrenching motion, I broke his neck.

His body seemed to sag, like a wineskin whose contents had suddenly run out. His skin changed, turning a mottled yellow-gray. In a few heartbeats, he was a man no more, but something else...something hideous and distorted, with solid black eyes that continued to sink deep into sharp, bony cheeks. Talons had replaced those age-spotted fingers, and two rows of narrow, slivered teeth suddenly lined a tiny round mouth at the end of a pointed jaw.

*Magic.*

Whatever he was, this *thing* who had looked so much like a man, he had been cleverly disguised. And he had known enough about life in Juniper Castle to get to my rooms and nearly kill me.

Of course, I *was* a stranger here, but nothing he had said in all that old-man prattle had put me on my guard. If it hadn't been for the looking glass, I felt certain, I would now be dead. I swallowed and touched my throat.

Still his transformation continued, as whatever sorcery had disguised him unraveled. His prominent nose dwindled to mere nostril slits. His skin shimmered with faint iridescent scales. And then his transformation seemed to be complete.

I beheld a monster like none I had ever seen before. Clearly this wasn't one of the hell-creatures I had fought in Ilerium...so what was it? And why would it want me dead enough to risk murdering me in my own rooms?

My battle-rage had begun to fade, and I took a deep cleansing breath, muscles suddenly weak. I felt like I'd lost control of my life, and I didn't like the sensation.

So, yet another mystery faced me. What had this creature been doing here, inside Dworkin's castle? How had he slipped past all those guards—past an entire army on the lookout? And most of all, how had he known to come to me posing as a barber?

I frowned. Clearly he must have had help. Someone had sent him—and set me up to be killed. Much as I hated the thought, I knew what it meant: Dworkin had a spy in his castle, someone in a fairly high position who knew our family's comings and goings. Someone who could smuggle a hell-creature into the castle, get him the clothes and tools of a barber, and give him enough information to get him safely into my rooms and make me lower my guard.

Rising, I paced for a second, trying to work through the problem, trying to decide what to do next. Should I call Dworkin's guards? No, I wouldn't know whether to trust them. Any of them might be another hell-creature in disguise, and I didn't want to reveal how much I knew yet. Freda, maybe? She seemed to have her own plots. Aber the prankster? I wasn't sure what help he could be; I needed solid advice, not Trumps.

That left only Dworkin, and I certainly couldn't go running to *him* at the first sign of trouble. It would make me look weak, helpless, unable to protect myself...in short, a perfect target.

Another problem worried me more. If assassins roamed Juniper's halls disguised as servants, I reasoned, they might just as easily pose as family members. Since I didn't know anyone in Juniper well enough to tell real from fake, except perhaps Dworkin, I knew how easily I could be fooled by another assassin. Ivinius had come close to succeeding; I didn't want to give his masters a second chance.

Taking a deep breath, I rose. *When in doubt,* do *nothing you know is wrong.* That was one of the lessons Dworkin had always stressed throughout my childhood. I wouldn't report this attempt on my life just yet, I decided. Perhaps whoever had set me up would reveal himself if I simply showed up alive and well, like nothing had happened. Surely *someone* would be curious as to what had happened. I'd have to be doubly watchful.

One problem remained: how to proceed?

Clean up, I decided. I'd have to hide the body somewhere and get rid of it after dark. Perhaps it could be dumped into the moat, or smuggled out into the forest. Though exactly how I might do so, when I knew none of Juniper's passageways—let alone the safest, least guarded path to the forest—escaped me at the moment.

Details could come later, I decided. For now, it was enough to have a plan.

I dragged the corpse into the little sitting room and positioned it behind a heavy tapestry where it couldn't be seen from the main room. Hopefully, servants wouldn't stumble across it before I was ready, and hopefully it wouldn't begin to stink too much. Then I began tidying up, setting the chair I'd knocked over back where it belonged, picking up Ivinius's razor and returning it to the tray with the towels, straightening the table with the basin, retrieving the desk and restoring its papers and blotter to their proper order—generally putting everything back the way it had been before the fight. To my surprise, the hardest part came last: mopping up the spilled ink. I cleaned it up as best I could with one of the towels, then covered the spot on the carpet with a smaller rug.

Not a bad job, I finally decided, standing back and studying my work critically. The room looked more or less normal. You couldn't tell there had been a fight or that I'd hidden a corpse in the next room.

Then I spotted my reflection in the mirror that had saved my life, and I sighed. I still had the residue of a full lather on my face and neck, and it had begun to dry and flake off. Well, I needed to get cleaned up for dinner anyway—no sense in wasting a sharp razor, even if it had been meant to slit my throat.

I returned to the basin and the block of soap, lathered up again with the brush, pulled the mirror over to the window's light while my beard softened, and began to shave myself with one of the smaller razors, which had a blade about as long as my hand. It gave me something to do while I continued to think things through.

A plan...that's what I needed right now. Some way to sort friend from foe, hell-creature from servant or relative...

Behind me, a floorboard suddenly squeaked. I whirled, razor up. I should have buckled on my swordbelt, I realized. More assassins, come to finish the job—?

No, it was only Aber, grinning at me like a happy pup who'd found its master. I forced myself to relax. He held what looked like one of Freda's Trumps in his left hand, I noticed, and he carried a small carved wooden box in his right.

"A present for you, brother," he said, holding out the box. "Your first set of family Trumps!"

I took them. "For me? I thought Freda was the expert."

"Oh, everyone needs a set. Besides, she already has all the Trumps she wants."

"I didn't hear you come in," I said, glancing pointedly at the door. The hinges most definitely had *not* given their telltale squeak. "How did you get in here? Is there another way—a secret passage?"

"You've been listening to too many fairy tales," he said with a little laugh. "Secret passages? I only know of one in the whole castle, and it's used all the time by servants as a shortcut between floors. Not much of a secret, if you ask me."

"Then how did you get in here?"

Silently he raised the Trump in his hand, turning it so I could see the picture: my bedroom. He had drawn it perfectly, right down to the tapestries on the wall and the zigzag quilt on the bed.

Suddenly I remembered how the trump with Aber's picture on it had seemed to move, almost to come alive, when Freda and I were in the carriage. Her cryptic comment about not wanting Aber to join us came back to me, and now it made sense. He had to be a wizard. One who used Trumps to move from place to place. That's how he had gotten in here without opening my door.

"It's a good drawing," I said, taking the card and studying it. He had caught not just the look, but the feel of my bedchamber. As I stared at it, the image seemed to grow lifelike and started to loom before me...I had the distinct impression that I could have stepped forward and *been* in the next room. Hurriedly I pulled my gaze away and focused on him.

"I'm glad you like it," he said, chest swelling a bit with pride. "Art is but one of my many talents, if I do say so myself."

"Are there any more cards like this one?"

"No, that's the only one I've done so far."

Instead of handing it back, I tossed it atop the pile of dirty towels on the tray.

"You don't mind if I keep it." Deliberately, I made it a statement instead of a question. I didn't need him—or anyone else—popping in on me unannounced.

"Not at all." He shrugged. "I made it as part of your set, so it's yours anyway. You should always have a few safe places to fall back on if need arises."

"Then...thank you."

"Don't mention it." He gestured toward the box I still held. "Go ahead, take a look at the others."

I took a moment to admire the mother-of-pearl dragon inlaid on the top of the box—also his work, it turned out—then unlatched the clasp and swung back the lid. Inside, nestled in a velvet-lined compartment, lay a small stack of Trumps, all face down. Their backs showed a blue-painted field with an intricate gold lion in the middle, exactly like Freda's.

I pulled all the cards out and fanned them-about twenty-five, I judged. Most showed portraits done much like the ones in Freda's set. I pulled out Aber's. He looked even more heroic than in Freda's set, if possible; here, he held a bloody sword in one hand and the severed head of a lion in the other. Clearly he had no problems with his own self-image.

"They're terrific," I said.

"Thanks."

"You'll have to show me how they work later, when we have more time." I put them back in the box, adding the one of my bedroom to the top of the stack.

"You don't know…" he began. "Sorry! I thought you knew. This morning, someone used my card. Just for a second, I thought I saw you and Freda inside a carriage."

"That was me," I admitted. "But it was an accident. I didn't know what I was doing."

He shrugged. "It's not hard. Take out a card and concentrate on it. If it's a place, It will seem to grow lifesized before you, like a doorway. Just step through and you're there."

"And the people?"

"You'll be able to talk to them," he said, "but only if they want to talk to you, too. After contact is made, either one can help the other pass across."

"It works both ways?"

"That's right." He nodded. "Just stick out your hand, the person you're talking to will grasp it, and you step forward. Fast and easy."

"It almost seems too good to be true!" I said, a trifle skeptical. Why would anyone bother with horses or carriages if a single card could make traveling quick and painless? "Freda said you liked pranks. You're pulling my leg now, aren't you?"

"No," he insisted, "I'm telling the truth. I *always* tell the truth. It's just that half the time nobody believes me!"

I gave a snort. "That's what the best liars say."

"You don't know me well enough to say that. Give me the benefit of the doubt, Oberon."

"Very well—explain to me again how you got in here."

"I used that Trump of your bedroom," he said solemnly, indicating the one I'd put in the box. "I left Dad in his study just a minute ago. Which reminds me, I'm here because he wants to see you. So you'd better hurry up. He doesn't like to be kept waiting."

I had to smile. "Some things never change."

Throughout my childhood, Dworkin had hated waiting for anything, from lines at the baker's to finishing my penmanship lessons so we could get on to more important things, like swordplay and military tactics.

"So," I went on, "if I concentrated on Dad's card right now, he'd pull me into his study? Just like that?" I'd never be able to master such a trick, I thought. It sounded impossibly hard, somehow.

"Sure. But I wouldn't do it with Dad, ever, unless you haven't any other choice...he doesn't like to be distracted when he's working. Sometimes he has delicate experiments going on, and if you accidentally mess one up...well, let's just say he has quite a temper."

"Thanks for the warning;" I said. I knew what he meant about our father's temper, all right. Once in the marketplace, when a soldier twice his size had insulted my mother, Dworkin had beaten the fool senseless with his bare hands. It had taken four of the city watch to drag him away, or he surely would have killed the fellow. I hadn't seen him that angry very often, but it was a terrible thing to behold.

Some things, it seemed, never changed.

"Let me finish getting ready," I said, turning back to the mirror and picking up the razor. "Then maybe you can show me the way down."

"Sure, glad to."

"Anari was supposed to find me some clothes. Maybe you can hurry him up."

"What about those?" He pointed through my bedroom door, and to my amazement I saw brown hose, a green shirt, and undergarments laid out on the chair next to the bed where I'd been sleeping.

"I must be going blind," I said, shaking my head. "I would've sworn they weren't there five minutes ago!"

He chuckled. "Okay, you caught me. I put them there. After I saw Dad, I went to my room first to pick up your set of Trumps. Ivinius was in the hall, and I told him to let you know I'd bring in some clothes for you. I guess he forgot to mention it."

I laughed with relief. "So I'm not crazy!"

"No...at least, I hope not! Say, why didn't you let him shave you?"

"The way his hands were shaking? Never!"

"Well, he *is* getting old." He gave an apologetic shrug.

"Someone ought to tell Anari to find us a new barber."

"I think that would be a good idea. I wouldn't want to have my throat cut."

I finished shaving quickly. All the while I studied my brother. He stood by the window, gazing out across the castle grounds. He didn't seem at all surprised at finding me alive. If anything, he seemed to like my company; I thought he must be lonely. It was easy to rule him out as a suspect in a conspiracy to have me killed—you didn't kill friends, especially ones with as little power here as I had.

And that, I thought, made him my first potential ally.

I splashed water on my face, then toweled dry. Not the best job, I thought, studying my reflection and rubbing my chin, but it would do for now. I'd get a haircut tomorrow, if I could find a real barber.

I began to dress quickly. Anari had a good eye for clothes; these fit me almost perfectly. A tiny bit too narrow in the shoulders, a little too wide in the waist, but with a belt, they would do nicely.

"You look a bit like him," Aber said suddenly as I pulled on my boots.

"Who?"

"Taine. Those are his clothes."

Taine...another of my missing half-brothers. I studied my reflection more critically...yes, I thought, dressed in his colors, I looked a lot like him in his Trump.

I said, "Freda thinks Taine is dead. Do you?"

He shrugged. "I don't know. He has Dad's temper, and he left after a fight with Locke. I suppose he could be off somewhere, brooding and planning his revenge."

"What did they fight about?"

"I don't know. Locke has never said."

I finished dressing and reached for my sword, but Aber shook his head. "Leave it," he said. "Father doesn't allow swords in his workroom."

Shrugging, I did so. Ivinius's impersonator was dead...there probably wouldn't be another attempt on my life tonight. And walking around without a sword clearly showed my lack of fear...I couldn't let my enemy or enemies know how much my nerves had been shaken.

"Lead on!" I said.

"Want to try a Trump down?" he asked suddenly.

"I thought you said—"

"Dad doesn't like to use them. But I've made Trumps of every interesting room in the castle...and many of the uninteresting ones, too." He chuckled. "Those can be even more useful, you know."

"I can imagine. And I suppose you know an uninteresting one near Dad's workshop?"

"There's a cloakroom just off the main hall...and it's about thirty feet from there to his workshop door."

"No," I said, shaking my head. Much as I liked the idea of trying out some magic, this wasn't the right time. "Juniper is huge. I'll never get a feel for its layout if we jump around like spring hares. Let's walk. That will give us a chance to get to know each other, and you can tell me about the castle as we go."

"As you wish." With a little shrug, he led the way out to the hall. "Those are my rooms," he said, pointing to the double doors directly across from mine. "Then Davin's to the left, then Mattus. Locke, Alanar, and Titus have the rooms to the right, and then Fenn and Taine and Conner opposite. Our sisters have the floor above."

We started down a broad stone stairway, heading back toward the salon in which we'd had drinks earlier that afternoon. As we walked, servants quickly stepped aside to let us pass, bowing their heads. I thought I recognized a few from my last trip through here, and several of them called me "Lord Oberon" as we passed. Clearly news of my arrival was spreading.

I still regarded them with veiled suspicion. Any might be another hell-creature spy or assassin in human guise. And yet I couldn't allow myself to become *too* fearful or paranoid. If Juniper had to be my home now, I would accept it, even if it came with a measure of danger. I couldn't brood on Ivinius and the possibility of assassination attempts or the assassins would have won...they would rule me.

No, I vowed, I would ferret them out in due course. But I wouldn't let them change how I lived my life—heartily, savoring the pleasures and passions.

Where to start, though? Best to get Aber talking, I decided. He might reveal more information about our family and the military situation here—what I needed most at this point was information. With so many soldiers stationed around Juniper, and hell-creatures infiltrating the castle, the war Freda had mentioned must be imminent.

I decided to start with a comfortable topic before working our way to more sensitive matters, something to loosen his natural reserve. What Freda had said about him in the horseless carriage came back to me: *Aber the prankster, Aber the artist, Aber the distraction who could not be trusted* to *join us.* Art seemed one of his main interests.

I said, "So, you make your own Trumps?" Most people enjoyed talking about themselves, and his talent for art seemed a natural place to begin.

"That's right!" He grinned, and I knew my question pleased him. "Everyone says I inherited Dad's artistic tendencies, just not his temperament. Apparently he used to make Trumps all the time when he was my age, but I don't think he has in years. There are more interesting things, he keeps saying. He's always got dozens of experiments going on in his workshop."

Experiments? A workshop? I had never seen this side of Dworkin in Ilerium...or perhaps I'd been too young to notice.

"I've been impressed by everything he's made," I said. "That horseless carriage—"

He snorted derisively.

"You don't like it?" I asked, bewildered. I'd found it the finest means of transportation I'd ever used, except perhaps horse and saddle.

"Not really," he said. "It's too slow, and you can't see anything if you're riding inside. I told him it should be open on top so passengers can take in the sights."

A good idea...until it rains!" I also thought of those monstrous bats, who could have swooped down on Freda and me had we been riding in the open.

"It never rains in Shadows unless you want it to."

"I suppose," I said nonchalantly, unwilling to expose my ignorance of exactly what *Shadows* were in the context of my new-found family.

We turned down another hallway, heading away from the salon. The topic changed back to Juniper Castle—the fastest way to get to the kitchens, where to find guard stations on this level (which also housed the weapons room, the main dining hall, and even the servants' quarters)—so many places and directions that my head swam. I didn't think I would be able to find any of them on my own.

Finally we reached a short windowless corridor. Two guards posted at its mouth held pikes. Down the corridor, small oil lamps set in wall sconces revealed plain stone walls and a red-and-white checkerboard slate floor. They didn't challenge us, but nodded to Aber as if expecting him.

We went up the corridor in silence and halted at the heavy oak door at its end. The hinges were thick iron bands. It would have taken a battering ram to get through.

"Look," Aber said softly, giving a quick glance back at the guards. We were clearly out of earshot, and he kept his voice low. "There's one more thing I should tell you about your family. We're all on our best behavior now, with war coming. But it won't last.

It never does. You'll going to have to choose sides, and choose soon. Freda likes you, which counts for a lot as far as I'm concerned. I hope you'll throw in with us."

I paused to digest this.

"It's you and Freda and Pella?" I guessed at one faction.

"Yes."

"And the others...Davin and Locke, of course."

He pulled a sour face. "The boors stick together. Yes. Locke and Davin-and also Fenn and Isadora, the warrior-bitch from hell."

I arched my eyebrows at that description.

"You haven't met her yet," he said with an unapologetic laugh. "You'll see *exactly* what I mean when you do. Be warned, though—tell one of them anything and they'll all hear it. But none of them will ever act unless Locke says so."

"What about Blaise?" I said.

He gave a dismissive wave. "She's got her own interests. For now, she's too busy seducing army officers and playing court with Leona and Syara—I don't think you've met them yet, have you?—to be a real concern to anyone but Dad, who generally disapproves but doesn't know how to tell her to grow up. She wants to wield power inside Juniper, but she doesn't have any way to support her ambitions. Of all our family, she's probably the most harmless...or least harmful might be a better way of putting it."

"I'm sure she'd be hurt if she heard you'd said that!"

Aber clapped me on the shoulder. "Right you are! So keep it between the two of us, okay? If something terrible happens and she does end up running everything, I still want to be on her good side."

"How...politic of you."

"I would have said self-serving."

I had to laugh at that. "Don't worry, I know when to keep my mouth shut." I glanced at him sidewise. "I'm a soldier, you know. What makes you think I won't throw in with Locke? After all, he and I seem to have the most in common."

"The fact that you're asking means you've already decided not to."

"It never hurts to know all your options. And Locke would seem to be a good one."

He hesitated. "I'll probably regret saying it, but...I like you, Oberon. I know it sounds simple-minded, but it's the truth. I don't know why, but I've liked you since the moment we met. You're not like anyone else in our family."

I knew exactly what he meant. "They're all stiff and formal, afraid to say or do the wrong thing." I'd seen it in Ilerium, among the bluebloods in King Elnar's court.

"From what Dad told us, Freda and I expected you to be another Locke. You know, all soldier, dedicated to war and politics. But you're not like Locke at all. I wouldn't trust Locke to clean my paint brushes. You, dear brother, I just might."

I scratched my head. "I'm not quite sure how to take that," I admitted. Clean his paint brushes?

He laughed. "As a compliment, of course! Good brushes are a painter's best friend. More valued than wine or women—and twice as expensive."

"Surely not more valued than women!"

"Well, the available women in Juniper, anyway."

"Then thank you for the compliment."

"You *feel* like a friend, somehow," he went on, eyes far away suddenly. "Like I've known you all my life and we've just been apart for too long and need to catch up with each other. Does that make sense?"

"Sure," I said. I knew exactly what he meant—I already felt the same way about both him and Freda: comfortable.

I changed the subject. "So Locke's not a friend?"

"When it's convenient for him—and that's usually when he wants something. He took me out drinking a month ago when he wanted me to make him some new Trumps, and I haven't had two words from him since. Well, that's not true. He said 'pass the wine' last night at dinner, and that's three words."

"I see the real problem."

"Really?" He looked startled. "What?"

"If you have to pass the wine, there aren't enough bottles on the table!"

That got a snort of amusement.

"See? This is what I meant...and why I like you. Nobody else in our family has a sense of humor. Not even Freda."

"It can't be that bad."

"To Locke, we're all tools to be used toward his own ends. Davin doesn't mind being a tool. That's the height of his ambition, to be second in command. The others ..." He shrugged. "Nobody really wants to serve under Locke. He's a bully when he wants his way. If not for Dad pulling us all together here, we'd scatter to the winds again."

I found myself agreeing with his assessment. Every word he'd said rang true.

Over the years, I'd known quite a few officers like Locke. They were always noble-born, and their only interest lay in yoking those beneath them to their own political and military advancement. Oddly enough, they always found eager followers. Sometimes a lot of them.

And I had invariably ended up at odds with them.

Aber said, "I still remember the first time Locke and Freda met as adults!" He shook his head. "He ordered her to fetch him and his men wine__he treated her like a common servant. Freda!"

"Did she do it?"

"Of course, like any prim and proper hostess. And then she dumped the whole tray in his lap."

I smiled at that.

Aber said, "She still hasn't forgiven him...nor has he forgiven her."

"Well, I *can* see both of their positions," I said, picturing the scene with some amusement. "And yet, part of me still thinks I'd be better off throwing in with Locke. After all, as the general in charge of Juniper's army, and the first-born son, he seems poised to take over after our father. And I'm a soldier. I'd fit in with Locke. We'd...understand each other."

"You're wrong, brother." He said, voice firm. "Locke sees you as a threat. If you try to make friends with him, you won't live long enough to stand a chance to replace him."

"He'd kill me?" I said uneasily. "His own brother?"

"Half brother. And not directly, no...but he grew up in the Courts, where fighting and treachery are a way of life. His rivals never lasted long."

"Murder?" I wondered aloud, thinking of Ivinius the demon-barber, sent to kill me in my chambers. Locke could easily have told him all he needed to know.

"Let's call it a series of convenient accidents. Locke is careful, and no one has any proof of his involvement. But over the years, there have been too many hunting accidents, a drowning, two convenient suicides, and half a dozen mysterious disappearances in our family alone. That's not counting other rivals."

"Coincidences, I'd say."

"So many? I think not." He looked away. "When Dad turned the army over to him, I knew it was a huge mistake. He'll never surrender command now. And he won't welcome any rivals in the ranks."

"I've served kings and generals my whole career. I'm used to taking orders, and I'd probably make a good lieutenant for Locke."

"You don't have ambitions?"

"Of course. But I'm not going to stroll in and try to wrestle away Locke's position. That's a fool's errand. He has his command, and he's welcome to it."

"But—it can't be that way!" he blurted out.

"Why not?"

"Freda said—"

Aber hesitated; clearly he didn't like the direction our conversation had taken...and I took some pleasure in shaking apart his all-too-cozy view of our relation ship. He had revealed a lot to me already—more than I had dared to hope, in fact—but I wanted more. And I thought I could get it.

"I can imagine what she said." I lowered my voice to a more conspiratorial whisper. "I was just jerking your chain about Locke. Did Freda tell you...*everything?*"

He relaxed, his relief obvious.

"She told me enough," he admitted. "The cards were a surprise. I didn't think anyone could ever oppose both Dad and Locke."

*So, Freda* did *leave something out when she read my future,* I thought. Oppose Dworkin and Locke? That had an ominous sound. Oppose them in what?

With deliberate mildness, intrigued despite my skepticism about Freda's talents, I said: "Freda didn't mention anything to me about opposing Locke and our father."

He gulped suddenly, eyes wide with alarm. "No?"

"No."

I folded my arms, waiting patiently as an awkward silence stretched between us. He shifted uneasily from foot to foot, not looking at me, gazing back down the corridor like he wanted to go haring off to his rooms.

I saw it now. Freda had put him up to befriending me, feeling out my loyalties, and trying to win me over to their side. Despite that, I liked Aber, and I had the feeling he genuinely liked me.

Now he desperately wanted to take back his words and start on a different tack. It was something Freda could have done, I thought: just switched. subjects and kept going, or announced she was tired, closed her eyes, and gone to sleep. Anything to get out of a cat-and-mouse game of questions-and-answers that couldn't be won. Poor Aber made an excellent mouse.

"And?" I prompted, when I'd waited long enough. Like most questions, the benefit was in the asking, not the answering. "What did she see?"

He just stared at me wonderingly. "You *are* good," he said suddenly. "Honestly, I thought you were just a soldier. But Freda saw truly."

*"I am* just a soldier."

"No. You're better at these games even than Freda. She was right about you. I thought she was crazy, but I see it now. You *are* a threat to Locke. And to our father. Maybe to all of us."

"What did she say?" I asked again.

"I guess it can't hurt." He sighed, looked away. "You and Locke are going to be at odds. And you will win."

"And our father?"

"Him, too."

"She saw all this in her Trumps?"

"Yes."

"Rot and nonsense."

"It's not!"

"You're saying exactly what you think I'd like to hear," I snapped. "I'm supposed to arrive in Juniper and lay waste to all before me? No, it's impossible. I may have ambitions, but they don't lie in that direction. Right now, my only goal is to help our father as much as I can."

"But Freda saw—"

"I don't care! I don't believe in fortune-telling. I told Freda as much."

"Freda's *not* some carnival witch, scrabbling for pennies!" He seemed almost hurt at the suggestion. "She's been trained since childhood to see emerging patterns in Chaos. It's a great science."

"And I'm a great skeptic."

"Well, you shouldn't be. It's what got you here." He shrugged, sighed, looked away again. Clearly I had confused him.

"Go on."

"I wasn't supposed to say anything about it, but Locke already hates you." He hesitated. "Locke didn't want Dad to bring you to Juniper. If he hadn't been so vocal about it, Dad would have fetched you here many years ago."

Years ago...so *that's* why Dworkin abandoned me, I thought. New pieces to the puzzle of my life suddenly fit neatly into place. Locke, not Dworkin, had kept me stranded and alone in Ilerium all these years.

Although I didn't enjoy making quick decisions about people, I found myself disliking Locke. Hating him, even. He had given my enemy a face...a decidedly *human* face.

Could Locke have sent Ivinius the assassin-barber to my room? It seemed entirely possible. It wouldn't be the first time brother killed brother to secure a throne.

"What made Dad change his mind about bringing me here?" I asked.

"Freda did. She saw you in her cards. She told Dad we needed you here, and now, or you would die...and with you would die our hopes of winning the war."

Convenient enough, I thought. She could predict anything she wanted and who would know the difference? Perhaps she felt she needed another ally. Who better than me? A soldier to counter Locke, a strong arm to do her bidding, one forever loyal to her because she had prophesied that I would one day take over.

Still, she had gotten one thing right: if not for Dworkin's timely rescue, I *would* be dead in Ilerium right now.

"All right," I said, "I have to ask. What is this war everyone keeps mentioning? Against whom are we fighting? And how am I supposed to help?"

"I don't know, exactly. I don't think anyone knows it's been all sneak attacks so far." He swallowed. "Freda said you held the key to saving our family."

"That's it?"

"Yes."

I threw back my head and laughed. "What rot! And you fell for it?"

"No!" Aber shook his head. "It's the truth, brother. Freda saw it...and everything she sees comes true. That's what really has Locke scared."

My breath caught in my throat. Aber really believed it, I saw...believed in this prophecy of Freda's. It sounded like some soothsayer's trick to me, so vague as to be useless for anything—except manipulating me to her ends. And yet...I had seen enough magic and miracles in the last day to make me wonder if I might not be wrong.

"Well," I finally said, "I do hope it's true. But I don't have any way to know—and neither does anyone else. Is that enough to make Locke hate me? The fact that Freda thinks I can help save the whole family?"

"No." He hesitated again.

"There's something else," I said. "Spill it."

"Dad has always spoken fondly of you—perhaps too fondly—Oberon this, and Oberon that; how great a swordsman you were becoming. Locke has always been jealous. Dad never talked about *him* that way when *he* was growing up in the Courts of Chaos, as he's quick to remind us all"

I said, "And now that I'm actually here...now that Locke's greatest rival is flesh and bone instead of tall tales around the fireplace...and now that Freda has predicted that I'll save the whole family instead of him...Locke's feeling threatened. Almost desperately so."

"He *is* the first-born son, after all," Aber said, almost apologetically. "But Dad could easily name another heir...one he likes better...*you.*"

*Me!* That's what all this was about, I realized. Freda believed I stood a chance of inheriting the family titles and lands, whatever they were. Perhaps she'd read it in her cards. Perhaps Dworkin had somehow given her the impression he favored me. Or perhaps she hated Locke so much that she'd throw in with any promising rival who happened along.

It didn't matter. The impossibility of it all struck me then, and I laughed out loud.

Aber stared at me like I'd gone mad.

I said, "It's unlikely that I will inherit anything."

"Titles often pass to the strongest, not necessarily the first-born."

I shook my head. "I'm hardly the strongest. I have no friends or allies. I don't know anyone here. And I have no interest in titles."

"Maybe that's what makes you dangerous. Look at it this way. Locke's never been Dad's favorite. He knows it. But as the first-born son, he's always had advantages over you. For one, he's always been here, helping Dad. For another, he's already got a large and incredibly loyal army behind him."

I raised my eyebrows. "And I'm just supposed to walk in and take both of these advantages away from him? How?"

"Well, you *are* here." Aber shrugged almost apologetically. "Late is better than never. And you do have military experience ...more than Locke, probably, considering you've been a career soldier. Dad's told us about the battles you've fought against those you call hell-creatures. The army here demands a strong leader...an experienced soldier. And since you're the one apparently destined to win this war for our side, as everyone here already knows, well...why *not* you?"

Why not indeed, I thought. No wonder Locke hated and feared me. There is nothing quite as powerful as a leg-end...and apparently my own talents had grown with every telling.

Add to that Freda's prophecy....

I almost hated to tell Aber I was just a man with no interest or ambitions beyond reclaiming my own name and place in our family. He wouldn't like it.

But I did so. I denied everything.

"Freda made it all up," I said. "It's a joke, a hoax, designed to hurt Locke's position in the family. I don't want to rule in Juniper or anywhere else. I'm too young to settle down. And now that I've seen the way you can all travel through Shadows...well, I want to do it, too!"

"But you must!" he said. "Everyone wants to rule!"

"Not me."

"And Freda saw it—"

"No, Freda *said* she saw it."

"You're calling her a liar?"

"No." I shrugged. "All I'm saying is this: I don't believe in the power of Freda or her magical future-telling cards. Since I don't believe, I don't feel bound to live by their forecasts. I have no intention of taking lands, titles, or armies away from Locke...or anyone else."

"You really mean that, don't you?" he asked. I could hear the awe in his voice.

"Yes."

"Then you are the best of us all." He bowed slightly. "And you may be the only one of us who actually deserves to rule."

"Nonsense." I gave a dismissive wave. "Leave that to those who want to rule."

He put his hand on my shoulder. "I mean it, brother...I'm happy you're here. And I hope we can be friends."

I clasped his shoulder, too. "We already are."

"Freda was right, you know," he said, releasing me. "You are the prize of the family. I see it now. Locke has every reason to feel threatened, whether you admit it or not."

"Then let me ask you this—if Dworkin prizes me so much, why did he abandon me in Ilerium all these years? Locke's opinion be damned. If he'd wanted to, he could have gone and fetched me at any time."

"I don't know. Ask him." He glanced toward the main corridor. "He's waiting...we should go."

"Answer one more question first."

"All right—"

"Truthfully—what's all this about? The war, the killings. How did it start? Who's behind it?"

He frowned, and I could tell it troubled him.

"We have hereditary rivals in the Courts of Chaos. Enemies for generations. Somehow, one of us—Freda thinks it's Dad, but she isn't sure—did something to rekindle one of those old feuds..."

"And it can't be laid to rest? What about the King in Chaos? Couldn't he stop it?"

"Perhaps. But we have our pride. We'd never have any power again if we ran crying to King Uthor."

"I see your point." I shook my head. "Do you have any idea who might be responsible?"

"No...just that it's someone very powerful. Whoever it is began the war by trying to kill off our whole family...everyone in Shadow has been attacked in one way or another."

"To what end?"

"Destroying the bloodline, I guess. That's the ultimate revenge, isn't it?"

"That's more than a little pissed off."

A sudden, horrible realization hit. Dworkin *had* been right—the hell-creatures in Ilerium *had* been after me...and me alone. The whole invasion had happened just to find and kill *me*.

He had said the hell-creatures would leave our country alone after he had rescued me. No wonder—they had no reason to continue the fight if I wasn't there any more. By simply leaving, I had probably done what King Elnar and all his men had been unable to do in a year of fighting.

"I think Freda's right about you," Aber went on. "You won't take Locke's orders blindly, the way the others do, and that's worth a lot. If you're even half the warrior I think you are, you could end up heir."

"Even if I wanted it—which I don't—" I gave a sweep of my arm, taking in all of Juniper. "I wouldn't know what to do with it."

"Juniper?" He chuckled. "This is just a Shadow, and you could easily find another like it, if you wanted. I meant heir to the family. To *us*...to our position within the Courts of Chaos. Dad holds a title there, and of course all the rights and privileges that go with—"

He broke off when the heavy oak door before us opened suddenly. From inside, Dworkin squinted up at me. He seemed older and much more tired looking now, as if our adventure over the last twenty-four hours had taken their toll.

"I thought I heard you," he said, taking my arm and pulling me inside. His grip still felt like iron. "You certainly took your time getting here, Oberon."

He closed the door in Aber's face.

## EIGHT

I found myself in a cluttered, windowless, musty-smelling workroom. Long wooden tables lined every wall; they held a confusing jumble of papers, scrolls, wooden boxes, oddly shaped rocks, countless crystals of varying sizes, and many other less readily identified materials. Dusty racks on the walls contained neatly labeled jars; doubtless they contained ingredients for potions and spells, I decided. At one table, he had been wiring a skeleton together from sun-bleached bones. It had at least four arms...and possibly as many as eight. At another table, candles warmed strangely shaped bottles containing liquids of various hues, some of which gave off curiously spiced scents. Ahead and to the left, narrow doorways led to additional workrooms, these just as cluttered from what little I could see.

"Come on, come on," he said impatiently, turning and leading the way. "I have wasted enough time on your rescue already—we have work to do, and it is best to get on with it."

"All right," I said, falling back into the patterns of my youth. All the time an inner voice told me to stand up to him right here, right now...to demand answers to everything that had happened.

But I couldn't. Not yet. He was still Uncle Dworkin to me, still the mentor I admired and respected...and obeyed. All the years of leading men, all the years without his presence, seemed to have melted away. I could have been ten years old again, following his instructions without question.

We passed into the next room, which was filled with unshelved books and scrolls, more than I had ever seen in anyone place before. There had to be thousands of them.

He didn't stop but led me into yet another room, which held larger machines he had obviously been building. Odd bits and pieces lay half-assembled (or half-disassembled, I couldn't tell which) on the floor and the worktables. Some had pipes and wires leading from large stones to what looked like corroding copper spheres, the largest of which had to be at least four feet across, the smallest no more than a hand's width. Others looked like fairy tale castles built from spun glass, and pink and white and yellow lights flared or pulsated briefly within them. Across from us, in a giant fireplace that took up the entire wall, liquids bubbled in three large cauldrons, though no fire heated them that I could see. These potions or brews let off a curious combination of smells—something like the air after a thunderstorm had just passed, but slightly sour. I felt the hairs on the back of my neck start to bristle. Against my will, I shivered.

Dworkin—*Dad*—noticed and chuckled.

"What are you doing in here?" I asked.

"Distilling."

"Brandy?" I guessed, but knowing it couldn't be anything so simple.

"Life forces."

"Oh." I didn't quite know what to make of that. He pulled over two straight-backed wooden chairs, and we sat facing each other, though he did not look me in the eye. Could he be feeling...guilt? For never letting me know I had a father, a family? For hiding my birthright? For abandoning me these many years?

A long, awkward silence stretched between us, punctuated by faint dripping noises from one of the machines and a steady hiss from one of the cauldrons.

"Dworkin—"I finally said. "Or should I call you Dad, like Aber and the others?"

He shifted uneasily. "Either one is fine. Perhaps Dworkin is best...I have never been much of a father to you. Though 'Dad' *does* have a nice ring to it..."

"So be it—*Dad.*"

"What else have you found out since you arrived?" he asked softly.

"Not as much as I would have liked." I swallowed, my mouth dry, and for the first time in my life I suddenly found words difficult. I had a lump in my throat the size of an apple; it was hard to speak to him calmly with all I now knew. "Apparently you have enemies in the Courts of Chaos, at least one of whom is trying to destroy your bloodline. Unfortunately, I seem to be included."

He nodded. "Two attempts have been made on my own life in the last year. And seven of my children—two daughters and five sons—are now missing, I assume murdered." He shook his head. "I do not know who to blame, but I have been gathering the rest of you from all your scattered Shadows, bringing you here, protecting you while I investigate...and preparing to defend Juniper if we are attacked."

"Why didn't you tell me?" I demanded, rising and pacing the floor. I simply couldn't sit still any longer. "I had a right to know you were my father!"

"Your mother wanted it this way," Dworkin said softly, "to protect you. She knew you would never rest easily if you discovered your true nature. You would want to meet the rest of your family, pass through the Logrus and master Shadows—"

"Damn right!"

"I became a friend of the family," he said, "so that I could be near you, guide you, watch you grow."

"You made sure I learned what I needed to learn," I said, guessing the truth. "You prepared me for a life in the military. And apparently you have been secretly watching and perhaps even guiding my career all these years."

"It *is* what any dutiful father would have done."

"No." I glared at him. "A dutiful father would have told me the truth!"

"And ignored your mother's wishes?"

"She was *dead.* I wasn't. You abandoned me! Your own flesh and blood!"

*"I promised* her. I do not give my word lightly, Oberon ...I loved her too much for that."

*"Loved* her?" My voice raised to a shout. "When you sired how many more sons on other Shadows? How many wives do you have, anyway? Ten? Twenty? No wonder you never had time for me!"

He recoiled as though struck across the face. I'd hurt him more with those words than I could have with any physical blows, I realized. Perhaps I'd meant to do it—I certainly didn't feel sorry for him now.

"You don't understand the way of Shadows," he said. "And I'm older than you realize. Time moves differently on each world—"

I turned away. I didn't want him to see the tears welling up in my eyes. *Soldiers don't cry.* It was all happening too fast. I needed time to think, to sort through the strange unfolding secrets and half-truths that made up my life.

Dworkin—Dad—my father—came up behind me. He put a hand on my shoulder.

"I'm here now," he said softly. "I cannot change the past, but I can apologize for it. Perhaps I should have told you sooner. Perhaps I should never have made that promise to your mother. But what is done cannot be undone. Make the most of it. You have your heritage now. You have...a family. Embrace us all."

I faced him. "I don't know where to begin."

"You must have questions. Ask them."

I hesitated, trying to decide where to start. "Tell me about the—what did you call it? The Logrus?" I said, trying to remember his words. "Tell me about Shadows and how to move among them like you and the others do. I want to learn how."

"It's...difficult to explain." He frowned. "Think of a single world, a place at the center of the universe...a primal source of life and power and wisdom."

"The Courts of Chaos?"

"The Courts are built upon it there, yes. They are a part, but not the whole. Now, imagine time and the universe as a lake so huge you cannot see the shore when you are in the middle. The Courts of Chaos floats at the center of this lake, casting reflections into the water. And every reflection is a world unto itself, a shadow of the Courts."

"All right," I said, not sure what he was leading up to. "How many of these reflections are there?"

"Nobody knows. Millions. Billions. Perhaps more than can ever be counted. Each is separate and distinct—a world of its own, with its own languages, peoples, customs. The farther you get from the Courts, the more different these worlds become, until you cease to recognize them. We call these worlds Shadows. Anything you can imagine exists in one, somewhere. Any many things you cannot possibly imagine."

"And Juniper is just a Shadow," I said, brow furrowing. "And Ilerium...everything I've ever known?"

"Yes."

I felt stunned. With those few words, he had completely undone my view of the universe—and of my place within it. No wonder Ilerium now seemed a distant, fading memory. None of it mattered. None of it had *ever* mattered.

And yet...every fiber of my body told it *had* mattered. I *had* loved Helda. I *had* given my heart and soul to serving King Elnar and Ilerium. It had been my whole life...my whole reason for existing. It *had* been real...at least to me.

Now, suddenly, Dworkin reduced all I had ever known to a single mote of dust floating in a great ocean of a universe, a place so vastly, unimaginably huge that I could only just begin to take it in.

"But it felt so *real!*" I whispered.

"The Shadows *are* real. People live and breed in them, build cities and empires, work and love and fight and die, all the while never knowing anything of the greater universe that lies beyond."

"And the Logrus? Is that what controls it?"

"No. The Logrus is—" he hesitated, as if searching for the words to describe the indescribable. "It is a key to finding your way amongst all the Shadow worlds. It is like a maze. By traversing its length, from start to finish, someone born of Chaos may have the Logrus imprinted on his mind forever. It frees your perceptions, allows you to control your movements. You can pass freely through the Shadows and find your path among them."

Freda's words on the journey in the carriage came back to me. "That's what you did on the way here."

"Yes. We traveled through many Shadows. We took an indirect route."

"When can I go through this Logrus?"

"Soon. The Logrus is difficult and dangerous. It is not something to undertake lightly, and you must prepare for it. And, afterwards, it leaves you disoriented...sick for a time." He hesitated. "Besides the ability to travel through Shadows, it confers other powers, too."

Other powers? That caught my attention.

"Like what?" I asked cautiously.

"This." Dworkin reached into the air and suddenly plucked a sword from nothingness.

I gaped at him. "How—"

"I had it in my bedchamber. I knew where I left it, and I used the Logrus to reach for it...to bridge the distance between my hand and where it lay. A kind of mental shortcut, if you will, between here and there."

He set the sword down on the closest table. I stared at it, still hardly able to believe my eyes.

"And I can do that?" I asked skeptically.

"Not now. Not yet. You must first master the Logrus. That, at least, is your birthright...by tradition, no one, not even King Uthor himself, can deny it if you ask. Of course, there is the problem of getting you to the Courts and back safely, without our enemy finding out and killing us. And once in the Courts, you must survive the Logrus. Not all of us do, you know. My brother died on his first attempt. It destroyed him, mind and body. It is not so simple a matter after all."

"I want to try," I said firmly. "You cannot show me this gift and then tell me I can't have it!"

"In due time."

"You're playing games with me again!"

"Do I need to remind you of how many children I've already lost? It is not safe for any of us to leave here," Dworkin said firmly. "Not now, not yet. Juniper is well defended for a Shadow, but beyond the lands we control, there are creatures watching us. They are waiting for a mistake...any mistake."

"Then we'll kill them!" I felt a yearning inside to be off, to walk the Logrus and gain the powers due me...the powers my father and brothers and sisters already possessed. "That crystal you used against the hell-creatures you must have more of them."

"It is not so simple. Some of these watchers are relatives. The Courts of Chaos are...unlike anything you can imagine, with your limited experiences. Struggle and conflict are encouraged there, and only the strongest wield any real power. I have been away too long and have now lost whatever influence I once may have held."

"I don't understand," I said.

He folded his arms, looking away. "There are ancient codes of honor that are supposed to prevent death among us, among the Lords of Chaos. But out here in the deepest, farthest Shadows, those rules are often bent...or overlooked entirely. I am not important enough to try to demand observance of the rights and protections due me. But some of our enemies are very, very important, I suspect. And if *they* were to die—murdered or assassinated, whether by my hand, or yours, or our agents'—it would call the wrath of King Uthor himself upon us all. We could not survive it, not one of us."

I frowned, not liking the sound of that. "Damned if we do, dead if we don't. When we kill our enemies, it has to be in self defense."

"Or it must look like an accident." He sighed and shook his head slowly, and I realized he did not like the situation any more than I did. "After all," he continued, "there is no harm in their watching us, or so they would say."

"Spying on us."

"Well, yes."

"Then those hell-creatures in Ilerium—"

"They were soldiers drafted from another Shadow, sent to find and kill you, my boy. They are just the *hands* of our enemy...cut off the head and the body will die. It's the only way, if we are to survive."

"And this head...whose is it?"

"I wish I knew. It could be any of a dozen Lords of Chaos. My family has its share of hereditary rivals and blood-feuds. And I freely admit I have made mistakes over the years...my own list of personal enemies is larger than it should be. It could be anyone of them."

"Is that why you left the Courts?"

"One of the reasons. I thought they would forget me if I lost myself among the Shadows."

I chewed my lower lip thoughtfully. His story pretty much matched Aber's, and every word rang true. Sometimes, I'd found, just being alive was enough to make an enemy. I may have found my family...but I'd also gotten more than my share of trouble along with them.

"Before we can proceed," Dworkin went on, "I must check something. It will only take a moment...."

He crossed to a table cluttered with wires and tubes and beakers, crystals and glass spheres and copper pots—the cast-off paraphernalia of a wizard or alchemist, as far as I could tell. He rummaged among the bits and pieces, tossing first one then another aside, muttering to himself.

"How long have these feuds been going on in the Courts of Chaos?" I asked.

"Longer than anyone can remember. The Courts are *ancient.*"

"How old is that?" King Elnar's family had ruled in Ilerium for nearly a thousand years.

"Every family in the Courts can trace their lineage back through the generations," he said, "to the man who first recognized the Logrus for what it was. His name is lost to us, but it is known that he created if from his own blood and magics that came to him in a vision. He built it, and then he went through it. Once he completed the journey, when he discovered he had the power to move through Shadows, he forged an empire that still stands. Every one of his children went through the Logrus as they came of age, and they in turn gained the ability to walk among Shadows, becoming the first Lords of Chaos and begetting all the noble houses and the great families that still hold power in the Courts. Thus has it come down through the generations to us, to you and me and all the rest of our family."

"How many generations?" I asked. "How many years?"

"It could be ten thousand. It could be more. Who can say? Time has little meaning for those who travel in Shadows..."

It seemed inconceivably ancient to me. A ten-thousand-year-old blood feud...

"How many of these great families are there, anyway?" I asked. "And how many Lords of Chaos?"

"There are hundreds of houses, though many are minor, like our own. The Lords of Chaos must number in the thousands. King Uthor himself keeps the Book of Peerage, where all the bloodlines are detailed, from the greatest house to least. Should any of us survive the coming war, we should annotate it. I...did not provide anyone in the Courts with the details of my children born in Shadow."

That piqued my interest. "What of me? Did you tell them of me?"

"No."

"And yet they found me anyway. How is that possible?"

"Yes, they *did* find you." He paused, frowning. "An interesting question. You *should* have been safe in Ilerium. Nobody in the Courts knew of you."

According to Aber, Dworkin had spoken often of me to Locke and Freda and the other members of our family. That's how I'd been found. I knew without a doubt that we had a traitor in our midst—someone who had given away my name and location.

But whom? Locke? Freda? Aber? One of the others? I swallowed, picturing them one by one. I couldn't see Blaise or Pella betraying me, somehow. Davin, perhaps?

Still searching, Dworkin continued, "There is a science behind the Logrus. A reason it works. It creates a kind of mental shortcut, a way to hold its image in your mind without trying. That is the key to moving through Shadows."

"Are there other ways? I thought the Trumps—"

"Yes, there are other ways through Shadow, and there are...legends, I supposed you would call them...of at least one other device which had similar properties, though it was lost or destroyed generations ago. The Logrus is all we have. I do not yet know why, but it makes some of us better able to manipulate Shadows than others."

"And you're one of the best, I suppose."

"Me?" He chuckled. "Perhaps it seems that way to you, but in truth, compared to some of the great Lords of Chaos, I am still but a clumsy child."

I shrugged. Clearly he underestimated his own abilities. Our journey in his horseless carriage, in which he had laid a series of traps for anyone following, had impressed Freda greatly, and I didn't think that was an easy accomplishment.

"You said I'd need to get ready for the Logrus. How? Is there some training I need? A new skill?"

"You need strength and stamina and determination," Dworkin said. "When I went into the Logrus nearly two hundred years ago, it almost killed me. I lay feverish and near death for two weeks, and weird visions filled my mind. I dreamed of a new kind of Logrus, one with a different kind of pattern, and finding it has become one of the goals of all my work and research." He gestured grandly, taking in this room and the ones beyond. "In fact, the more I think about our enemies, the more I think this new pattern may be the cause."

"How? Did you actually create it?"

"No...but I spoke openly of it when I was young, and I know it brought me undue scrutiny. After all, if I had created a new Logrus...a new source of power over Shadows...who knew what abilities it might confer on me!"

"And you think someone is trying to kill you and all your children," I said, "to prevent it."

"That is one possibility," he admitted, "though a dozen others have occurred to me as well. Locke's mother is from a powerful family. They opposed our marriage...and took insult when I left her and kept our offspring."

"It was your right," I said. "Locke is your first-born and heir apparent. Of course he had to stay with you."

"Valeria did not see it that way."

"Ah." I nodded. Never underestimate the power of love. More than a few wars had been fought in Ilerium over less. And mothers are not always rational when their sons are involved.

Now we had two possible causes for the attacks, a disagreement with Locke's abandoned mother, and Dworkin's vision of a new pattern. And he had admitted there were more.

I found the idea of a new Logrus intriguing, though. If he made it, and if it worked the way the original worked, it could easily threaten the whole stability of the Courts of Chaos. Dworkin could set himself up as a king. And if his Logrus, too, cast Shadows, created whole new worlds in its image....

I shivered. Yes, I could see how anyone with a high position in the Courts of Chaos would feel threatened by it—perhaps threatened enough to want to kill even me, poor bastard son that I was, ignorant of my heritage and abandoned on a backwater Shadow with no way to escape.

"Tell me more about this new Logrus," I said.

Dworkin paused for a heartbeat, scratched his head, and crossed to the other worktable, where he began his search anew.

"I have come to believe that the reason I had so much trouble walking the Logrus is because it did not quite match the one within me. They are close as first cousins, but not the same. And this new one has begun to emerge in my children, too. Freda has it. Aber and Conner, too. But not Locke, alas, poor boy...or perhaps he is the fortunate one. Ah!"

He pulled what looked like a silver rod studded with diamonds from the jumble, then turned and motioned toward the far corner of his workroom. A small machine full of glass tubes and wires and tiny interlocking gears stood there. I had barely noted its presence before, in the midst of all the other more impressive looking devices. At its center sat a high-backed chair with armrests.

"This is what we need," he went on. "Sit there. We will start at once."

"What is it?" I asked dubiously. "Start what?"

"I must see the pattern contained within you," he said. "Sit. Make yourself comfortable. It takes but a few minutes, and it will tell me how hard or easy it will be for you to walk the Logrus."

It seemed sensible enough, and yet some instinct made me hesitate. For an instant I had a vision of an altar with a dying man spread upon it, strange patterns floating in the air above him, and then it was gone. *Alanar.* I recognized the man from Freda's Trump. What did this little flash of memory mean? Why had I glimpsed a dead man?

A coldness touched my heart. A panic. I did not want to be here right now.

*"Sit,"* Dworkin commanded.

"I don't like it," I said warily, taking a step back. "I don't think this is a good idea."

"Nonsense, my boy." He took my arm and propelled me forward. Almost by reflex, I sat in the chair. "I have done this to all your brothers and sisters...and to myself. It *is* necessary."

He stepped back, raised that rod, and pointed at me. I half flinched, expecting a brilliant flash or a burning beam of light-but nothing happened...or at least, nothing *seemed* to happen. No sounds, no lights, no growl of thun, der. The only sounds came from the bubbling cauldrons in the fireplace.

I discovered I had been unconsciously holding my breath, and I let it out with a sudden gasp. Apparently I'd been concerned over nothing. The metal wand either didn't work or didn't hurt. I relaxed.

"Just a minute more," Dworkin said.

"What is it doing?" I asked.

"Tuning itself to the forces within you," he said. "Hold still. Do not get up."

He made a few adjustments to the rod, and suddenly the machine around me came to life with a whirring and a creaking of wooden gears. I must have jumped three feet. Turning my head, I peered up into the intricate machinery. Blue sparks ghosted across its surface as wheels and cogs turned. It began to hum like a kettle about to boil.

Dworkin stepped forward and inserted the silver rod into a hole in the center of the mechanism, and at that moment I felt a strange probing in the back of my head, almost like the start of a headache, but not quite. Without warning, memories sprang forth then vanished, images from the whole of my life, the early times with my mother, later years with Dworkin, and even my service with King Elnar. I glimpsed Helda and a dozen other women I'd loved before her.

The images jumbled together in no particular order. Faster and faster they came, and the humming noise of the machine became a deafening whistle that cut through my soul.

Cities and towns—battles and grueling marches—festivals and high holidays—my seventh birthday, when Dworkin gave me my first sword-fighting the hell-creatures—childhood games in the streets—faces of people I'd long forgotten—

Slowly, in the air before me, a pattern began to form, full of elegant sweeps and curves, loops and switchbacks, a twisting geometry like something I might have seen long ago in a forgotten dream. Blue sparks drifted around me. Through everything I could just make out Dworkin's form, hands raised as he traced the pattern between us with his fingertips. Where he touched it, it took on a ruby glow.

Still the memories surged, more faces, more battles, more times long gone. Faster and faster they came, all blurred together now, and the whistle in the back of my head became an unimaginable screech of sound that tore through my skull. My eyes burned. My skin crawled. I tried to leap out of that seat, to get away from Dworkin's machine, but I couldn't move my arms or legs. When I opened my mouth to beg Dworkin to stop, the only sound was an agonized scream.

The machine was killing me.

I tried to block it from my thoughts, but it only hummed louder. Squeezing my eyes shut, I felt my thoughts shredding, the memories fleeing, all thoughts now impossible, only pain—pain—pain—

I gasped like a fish out of water, tried to breathe—

Blackness fell like a stone.

## NINE

*I dreamed.*
*Flying...floating...drifting...*
I saw snake-headed monsters and an ever-shifting tapestry of worlds...Ilerium, under the thrall of hell-creatures...

The Courts of Chaos, just like on Freda's card, the air overhead pulsating with those weird lightning-patterns, while all around me the buildings moved like living creatures and comers turned in on themselves with angles that couldn't possibly exist but somehow did...

Then worlds of vast deserts, endless oceans, and virgin forests where no man had or ever would set foot...

*Come...*
Deserts and swamps...
Cities buzzing with movement like the hives of bees...
Wind-scoured rocks with no sign of water or life...
*Come to me...*
I felt a chill, a remembered feeling of hate and loathing surging up inside. That voice—I had heard that voice before!
*Come to me, sons of Dworkin...*
Against my will, I found myself drawn forward like a moth to its flame. I soared through blackness, through vast cold and dark distances, to a world of strange colors. Patterns turned in the air, odd shapes and geometries that drifted like snowflakes, patterns within patterns within patterns. My vision began to brighten, then dim.

Slowly, I turned and discovered a tower built entirely of skulls. A grim shock of recognition swept through me. I had been here before, I thought, long ago.

*Come* to me, *sons of Dworkin...*

I could not resist the voice. Like a phantom, I passed through the tower's wall. A stairway of arm and leg bones circled the inside wall, ascending into shadows, descending into a murky, pulsating redness.

I drifted down. The redness became the flickering glow of torches. They showed an eerily familiar scene, guards in armor who surrounded an immense stone altar. And on that altar a body lay chained and bleeding...

*Taine!*

Though his face had become gaunt and gray, and he looked ten years older, I still recognized my new brother from the Trump in Freda's deck. He had a dueling scar on his left cheek just as Aber had drawn it. And he had Dworkin's face...more so now than when his portrait had been done.

Naked and blood-smeared, he lay spread-eagle on the stone slab. But he lived. As I stared at him, I saw his chest rising and falling steadily.

His arms and legs had been heavily chained, and dozens of long, shallow knife wounds—some days or weeks old, some clearly fresh—marred the smoothness of his arms and face. His captors had made an effort to keep him alive, I thought. While clearly painful, none of the wounds appeared life-threatening. The real risk would come later from infection.

Blood still seeped from the most recent wounds, but instead of falling toward the floor, drops of scarlet floated *up* around him, lazily drifting through the air. As I watched, first one then another flattened, spreading out and becoming miniature windows into other worlds.

In many of those windows, I glimpsed Juniper and the army camp that surrounded it.

*They're spying* on *us,* I realized. No *wonder someone knew to send Ivinius to kill me. They see everything that happens.*

Suddenly everything in the tower grew flat, muted, distant. The colors washed out; the world around me began pulling back like a sudden outrushing tide. The tower of skulls-this world of strange geometries—receding into darkness—

Abruptly I found myself back in my body. It was a shock, like leaping into an icy lake, and I gasped.

*"Drink..."* a voice commanded.

I sat up, sputtering, liquid fire in my mouth and throat.

"What—" I tried to say. It came out as a muffled *"Waaa."*

Opening bleary eyes, I found Dworkin crouched over me. He held a small silver cup, which he pressed to my lips. This time when he poured, I tasted brandy, old and smooth.

What had he done to me?

My whole body ached and refused to obey my commands. My hands shook. When I tried to push him away and sit up, I flailed like a fish out of water.

*"Taine..."* I gasped.

Dworkin jerked, spilling the brandy all over us both.

"What?" he demanded. "What did you say?"

I took a deep breath and summoned my strength. Raising one hand, I pushed him away. My limbs felt numb and weak, like all the blood had drained from my body and been replaced with lead. Rolling over onto my hands and knees took intense effort, but I managed it.

The room swayed dangerously. Grasping the edge of the closest table, I stood.

"Where...?" I tried to ask. It came out more or less right.

"Give yourself time to recover, my boy," he said. "You went through a difficult test."

I frowned. "Yes...I...remember."

As I sat on the edge of the table, trying to recover my sense of balance, he pressed the cup into my hands. Gingerly I took another sip.

"I know what I did was...difficult for you. But it had to be done."

"What ...had to be done?" I levered myself up on my elbows, sick and dizzy inside.

"I looked within you, within your essence. Turned you inside out, saw what needed to be seen, then put you back together."

"My head hurts." Groaning a little, I pressed my eyes shut and rubbed them. What felt like thousands of little needles piercing my skull resolved itself into the sort of headache I'd only had after a night of cheap rotgut and too many women.

"Oberon..." He hesitated.

I forced open my eyes and gazed blearily up at him.

"You said something just now. It sounded like a name."

"Taine," I said, remembering my dream.

"What about him?"

"He's hurt."

"Where?"

"It was just a nightmare." I shook my head. "I can barely recall it."

"Try," he urged. "Taine...you saw him?"

"Yes...in—in a tower made of bones, I think." I frowned, trying to recall the details. "I heard a voice...a serpent's voice. They had Taine on an altar."

"They? Who are they?"

"The guards...hell-creatures...but not like the ones in Ilerium..."

"And Taine was alive? You *are* sure of it?"

"Yes. I think...they needed his blood for something...it dripped *up!*"

"Go on." He spoke softly. "What were they doing with his blood?"

"I don't know..."

*"Think!* It is important! Try to remember!"

I half closed my eyes, trying to see the tower in my mind's eye, blood dripping into the air. "They were look, ing for us, I believe. I saw Juniper in a window made of blood...I think."

I shook my head, the dream-images slipping away, elusive as will-o'-the-wisps. In another minute they would be gone.

Dworkin sank back on his heels. "Blood drips toward the sky in the Courts of Chaos," he said numbly. "You have never been there. You could not possibly know..."

"It couldn't have been real," I said.

"I think it was. And if you saw Taine...then he *is* alive! That is good news. I had given up hope."

"Better off dead, from the look of him."

"All the children of Chaos heal fast and well. If we can find him...if we can rescue him—"

"Do you think that's possible?"

"I will see."

"And the Logrus!" I said, levering myself up with my elbows. I felt a rising sense of excitement at the prospect of traversing it. "How soon can we go there?"

He hesitated.

"What is it?" I demanded. "You said it was my birth-right. You said King Uthor couldn't deny me my chance to go through it."

"Oberon...the news is bad. You cannot use the Logrus. Not now. Not ever."

"No!" Anger and outrage surged through me. I'd spent my whole life being denied. Denied a father. Denied a family. Denied all that should have been mine. I had no intention of missing out again. I *would* master the Logrus, even if I had to borrow one of Aber's magical Trumps and go to the Courts of Chaos on my own.

"Listen to me," he said urgently. "The pattern within you is *wrong,* somehow. It is more distorted than mine...so crooked, I almost did not recognize it."

"So?" I said. His news meant nothing to me.

"You cannot enter the Logrus. It would destroy you, as it destroyed my brother, as it almost destroyed Freda and me. You would *die,* Oberon."

I looked away. My headache returned with a vengeance, little knives piercing the inside my skull.

"So that's it, then?" I said. I felt like he had kicked my legs out from under me. "There's nothing you can do? No way you can fix it, somehow? Make it work?"

"*I am* sorry, my boy." His eyes grew distant, thoughtful. "Unless..."

"Unless what?" I demanded. If he had any idea, any plan that might help me, I would have seized upon it.

But Dworkin simply sighed and shook his head. "No. It was a crazy thought, best left unspoken. You must be content with who and what you are. If nothing else, that may keep you alive. I know it gives you small comfort now, but perhaps it is a blessing in disguise. Put all thoughts of the Logrus behind you. There is nothing else we can do for now."

*For now.* That still hinted of plans for the future, I thought. Plans which, it seemed, he had no intention of sharing with me. At least, not yet.

"Very well," I said. I had a blinding pain behind both of my eyes, like twin needles pushing into my brain. I didn't feel up to fighting with him about the Logrus. There would' be time enough for that later.

Let him think I'd given up. I'd ask Aber about it later. My new-found brother seemed eager to volunteer information. If another way existed to get to the Logrus, or to have it imprinted on my mind, he might well know of it. Too many of Dworkin's lies had been exposed for me to blindly trust him now, when he said the Logrus would kill me. For all I knew, he'd made it up to keep his control over me.

I considered the evidence. First, my childhood face-changing game...no one else I knew had been able to do that. And what about my great strength? I *was* two or three times stronger than any normal man. Or the speed of my reflexes—the quickness with which I healed—? If the pattern inside me came out so distorted, why had I been able to do all these things?

No, I thought, everything added up to more than Dworkin wanted to admit. I already had a measure of power over the Logrus-small as it was compared to everyone else's. Judging from all these little signs, the Logrus within me worked just fine.

*But what if he's right?* a small voice at the back of my head asked. *What if I can't master the Logrus? What if this is as much magic as I'll ever have?*

I didn't like the thought.

"Take my arm," he Said.

With his help, I made it to the chair without falling. My head still swam, but not like before. A clarity had come over me, a sense of warmth and well-being. Probably from the brandy, I thought.

He moved to refill my cup, and I didn't stop him. I drank it in a single gulp. After a moment's hesitation, he filled the cup again, and again I drained it all.

A warm glow spread down my throat and into my belly. I pressed my eyes shut, turned away, tried to envision Taine on the altar's slab and failed. My dream or vision or whatever it had been had left me.

"You've had enough brandy," he said.

"No," I said, shaking my head. That was a mistake; waves of nausea engulfed me again. "I haven't had enough yet—not by far. I feel like I need a good three-day drunk."

"Do not feel bad about the Logrus, my boy," he said, patting my shoulder. "You grew up without it. You will not miss what you have never had."

"Won't I?" A wild fury came over me. My mind was racing, cataloging every sin he'd ever committed against me, and the words just poured out. "Do you know what it's *like,* growing up in Ilerium without a father? Yes, you were there, but it wasn't the same. It wasn't *real.* When my mother died in the Scarlet Plague and you simply disappeared—do you know how *alone* that left me? You cannot imagine it. No father or mother or brothers and sisters. No uncles or aunts, no cousins. *No one.* Now, ten years later, you magically sweep back in and expect everything to be perfect because, oh yes, you really *are* my father, and my whole life up till now had been a lie!"

"Oberon..." he whispered. He took a step back, face ashen.

"It's the truth!" I yelled. My whole body quivered with rage. "And now...after you've shown me all these wonders...told me about the Logrus and the powers that should be mine...*now* you tell me I'll never have them! And never miss what I've never known!"

"I—" he began.

I drowned him out. "I never knew my father, and I missed him. I never knew a real family, and I missed it. I never knew my brothers and sisters, and I missed them every day of my childhood.

Every time I saw other children, it reminded me of what I lacked. Don't tell me I won't miss what I've never had—I know the truth!"

"Perhaps I deserve that," he said heavily. His shoulders slumped; he seemed old...old and tired and beaten. In that moment, he looked every day of his two hundred years of age.

A pang of guilt touched me, but I pushed it away. *He* was the one who should feel guilty, I told myself. *He* was the one who had lied to me, denied me a normal childhood, and now planned to deny me everything else.

I had lived too long in Shadow. *Never again.* I would not be denied my birthright.

Whatever it took, whatever it cost, I *would* master the Logrus. I vowed it to myself.

Distantly, I heard a bell toll.

"Time for dinner," Dworkin said softly. Then with a touch of almost bitter irony, looking up into my eyes, he added, "Time for you to meet the rest of our happy little family."

## TEN

To my displeasure, I needed Dworkin's steadying touch on my arm to navigate the corridors. Luckily, by the time we reached the dining hall, much of my strength had returned. We paused outside, looking at each other, and I shrugged his hand away.

"I suppose I should thank you," I said bitterly.

Silence stretched uncomfortably between us.

"You cannot help your nature," he said simply. "You were always a rebellious child, never content."

"You make me sound ambitious. I'm not. I only want what should by rights be mine."

"I know," he said, "and I do not blame you, my boy. It is a lot for me to ask...but try to fit in, and try to be a part of this family. I know it will be difficult—none of us is perfect, me least of all. But...we are all worth the effort. I have to believe that. It keeps me going."

"Very well," I said. "I'll...try. For now."

"Thank you."

Turning, he pushed the door open and we entered the dining hall—a large oak-paneled room with a crystal chandelier over the table. Logs blazed, snapping and popping cheerfully, in the fireplace against the far wall, and they took the dampness and chill from the air.

The table had been set for fifteen, though only ten had arrived so far: Freda, Aber, Pella, Blaise, and six others, four men and two women. All twisted in their seats to stare as I came in. Aber grinned happily and waved.

I forced myself to smile and gave the whole table a polite, "Hello." No sense letting them know how I felt right now; our problems should stay private between Dworkin and me. Freda's warning echoed in my mind: *trust none of them*. If any of the others found out what had happened between us in Dworkin's workshop, they might try to use it against me. No matter how I felt about my father, I wouldn't allow that to happen.

Locke and Davin I recognized from their Trumps, and from seeing them in the courtyard earlier that day. And, of course, I'd already spoken with Freda, Pella, Blaise, and Aber. The other four were strangers. As I looked over my siblings, I noticed again that all bore a striking resemblance to Dworkin...and to me.

"This is Oberon," Dworkin said heavily. He started to put a hand on my shoulder, hesitated, let it drop to his side. I caught Freda pursing her lips—she'd noticed, and she didn't like the tension between us.

"I'm pleased to be here," I said in even tones. Be bland, be harmless, I told myself. One of them may be trying to kill me—I wouldn't let on that I knew. "I hope we'll all grow to be friends as well as family."

That got a snort of derision from Locke, which he tried to hide behind a quick cough. I gave him a cool appraisal as if to say: I *know your type. You will not get to* me.

Dworkin did a quick round of introductions, starting with my half-brothers: Locke, of course, tall and stout, with a full black beard and a brooding expression; Davin, a year or two younger than me and slender as a reed, smooth-cheeked and serious; Titus and Conner, clearly identical twins, both as short as our father and both with his eyes and wary expressions; and Fenn, who was taller than Dworkin but not as tall as me, with blue eyes and a hesitant but honestly welcoming smile. Aber came last; he gave me a quick grin.

I nodded and smiled at each in turn. Be calm and polite, reveal nothing, I reminded myself.

As for my half-sisters, I had already met Freda, Pella, and Blaise. That left Isadora and Syara, as alike as two peas in a pod: reddish hair, pale complexions, broad cheeks and eyes, and the slender figures of goddesses. Clearly both shared the same mother. Had we not been related, I would have lusted after them. As it was, I could now only admire them from afar as objects of feminine perfection.

"I want you at my right hand tonight," Dworkin said to me, starting for the head of the table. "We have a lot of catching up to do. Locke, slide down for Oberon."

Locke tried to hide his annoyance as he rose to make room *for* me. Luckily the seat next to his was vacant. As the eldest son, clearly he was used to the place of honor next to our father, and clearly he resented my taking it. So much *for* our getting off to a good start. If he truly feared my replacing him, as Aber claimed, this would only feed his paranoia.

I gave a mental sigh; surely he would realize that I couldn't control our father's whims. And, I had to admit, it seemed only natural *for* me to sit next to him tonight, on my first evening in Juniper.

"Locke, you may have my seat," Freda said, rising. She had the place to Dworkin's left.

"Are you sure?" he asked. To my surprise, he seemed hesitant. I would have expected him to leap at the chance...though perhaps he knew Freda's motives too well and expected to pay some later price for her favor.

"You and Father need to talk about military matters," she said with a dismissive wave. "I will sit next to Oberon tonight. I think it best."

"All right. If *you* want it so."

Locke still looked a bit puzzled, but he traded places with her quickly, before she could change her mind. Being one seat closer to our father seemed important to him. I reminded myself that he had grown up knowing his noble heritage...and playing politics in the Courts of Chaos. Perhaps having the right seat at dinner was important, and I simply didn't have sense enough to realize it. I definitely would have preferred a spot at the far end of the table next to Aber.

I glanced at my father. Better to sit with a friend, even in exile, than with an enemy. No, I had to correct myself, not an enemy. A tired old man, sad and out of his element. Dworkin wasn't meant for war, I realized suddenly, thinking of his workshop and all his experiments. He should never have been head of our family...he should have been tinkering and building and playing with his toys.

And I knew, then, why Locke commanded the army instead of him. Everything—our family, our plight—began to make sense in that context. Dworkin was weak, and our enemy had to believe we made easy prey. Weakness had often been the cause of war, I knew from my studies of Ilerium's history...and the history of the Fifteen Kingdoms, which had once numbered twenty-seven before conquest and consolidation had dwindled their number.

Try as they might, Locke and Davin would not be able to win this war, which clearly had already begun. And from the look of things, we were far outclassed.

I gave Freda a sad little smile as she sat to my right.

"You're looking particularly lovely this evening," I told her sincerely.

She all but preened, smoothing her dress and looking entirely pleased. "Thank you, Oberon. You cleaned up rather well yourself."

"Thanks to *you*, dear sister. You sent the barber up, didn't you?"

"Me? No—it was probably Anari."

"Probably," I said blandly. I took a glance around the table to see if my mentioning Ivinius's visit had gotten a reaction, but apparently it hadn't. Side conversations had sprung up, and only Locke and Freda and our father were paying attention to me—Locke pretending not to, of course, but I could tell he took in every word as a man too long in the desert takes in water.

I chatted amiably enough with all of them over the first course, a cold creamy soup made with some kind of yellow pumpkin, telling one and all a bit about my childhood in Ilerium. And, in turn, I learned more about them.

Dworkin certainly *had* been busy over his 200 years. Almost all of them had different mothers on different Shadows. Most had been raised with the knowledge that they were children of Chaos, and all had gone through the Logrus in the Courts of Chaos except for me. I felt a pang whenever they mentioned it.

Freda must have sensed it, for she touched my arm and murmured, "Your turn will come," she murmured. "You must have patience."

Patience...I'd had too much of that already. So I simply smiled a little sadly and made no reply: little sense in letting them know my bitter news just yet, I thought.

I did find out some interesting facts. Locke turned out to be more than eighty years old—though he looked no more than thirty. Our whole family aged quite slowly, it seemed, which explained not only Dworkin's condition despite his advanced age, but how he had managed to sire so many offspring. He had left more than a few women—or had them leave him, as with Locke's mother, a Lady of Chaos—but most had been normal humans found on Shadows such as my own. They had died of old age while he remained young and hearty.

And at least twice Freda hinted that time moved at different speeds in different places. A year in the Courts of Chaos might well be two or five or ten years on other Shadows.

It was Aber who broached the question I had hoped to avoid. "So, Dad," he said happily, and I could tell he thought he was helping me, which made it all the more painful. "How soon will Oberon go through the Logrus?"

"Never," Dworkin said flatly. No tact there, just a sharp and unpleasant truth.

I looked down, studying the tablecloth, fingering my napkin. *Never.* It had a final ring.

"What!" Aber sounded honestly shocked. "But not even King Uthor can deny Oberon his birthright. He must gain power over Shadow!"

Dworkin shook his head. "Though he *is* my son, Oberon does not carry the Logrus within him. It is so distorted, it has become nearly unrecognizable. He *cannot* try the Logrus...*ever.* It would destroy him, as it destroyed my brother Darr."

## ELEVEN

Utter silence followed. I took a quick glance down the length of the table. To a one, my every half-brother and half-sister, even Locke, had a look of stunned disbelief on his or her face. They took their magical powers for granted, I realized. That one of their own might be unable to use them—unbelievable!

And yet it was true. Despite my anger and hurt and earlier denial, I could find no reason for Dworkin to lie to me. If anything, he needed me to go through the Logrus...needed another strong son to help defend Juniper. Clearly such a task now lay beyond my meager, mortal abilities.

"How can that be?" Freda finally asked, looking troubled. "Anyone born of Chaos carries the Logrus within. It is a part of our very essence. You have said it yourself many times over, Father."

Dworkin said, "He does carry it...only it has gone wrong within him." Slowly shaking his head, he regarded me thoughtfully. "I do not know why or how, but the problems we have all had except of course you, Locke—with the Logrus are so much the worse in him."

"But to forbid him from ever trying the Logrus!" Aber protested. "That has never been done before!"

"I did not forbid him," Dworkin said sharply. "I said it would kill him."

"It is the same thing," I said.

"Perhaps the problem is simpler than you realize," Locke said, leaning back and regarding me with a half taunting, half triumphant smile. He clearly scented my blood and was moving in for the kill, the strong attacking the weak. "Perhaps his mother whored around on you. It wouldn't be the first time we had a bastard in the family."

I rose from my chair smoothly and silently. "Take that back," I said, voice cold as a grave, "while you still can." If I'd had my sword, I would have drawn it.

"Oberon! Sit!" Dworkin barked. "Locke, apologize."

My nerves stretched toward their breaking point. Nobody had ever insulted my mother and lived. If not for Dworkin, I would have leaped across the table and twisted Locke's head off with my bare hands—brother or not.

Instead of responding, my half-brother slowly tilted his chair back on the rear two legs and grinned mockingly at me. "The pup thinks he has teeth."

My voice was hard. "More than enough to rip your throat out."

He shrugged. "My apologies, *brother.*" I noticed how he emphasized the word, like he doubted its truth. "I chose my words with insufficient care. I *meant—*"

So softly I almost missed it, Freda hissed, "Shut up, Locke, or I will make you wish you had. This is dinner."

Locke glanced at her, looked away, didn't finish. Clearly he didn't fear me. But could he be afraid of Freda?

She touched my hand softly. *"Sit,* Oberon. Please."

It was not a command, but a soft, kind suggestion, and somehow it took the fight out of me. I let out my breath and did as she instructed.

Pointedly, she said, "Bickering is forbidden at dinner, as our *brother* knows." And her voice carried the same insulting inflection Locke had used.

In that instant I discovered I liked her even more than I had known.

"Thank you," Dworkin said to Freda. He cleared his throat. "Now, where was I?"

Dutifully picking up my spoon, I returned to my soup. I wasn't really hungry anymore, but I couldn't let Locke know he'd spoiled the meal for me.

"Oberon *is* my son," Dworkin said with conviction. "I have known it since the day he was born. And my tests here today proved it. The problem lies with the Logrus...it *is* a damnable mystery still, even to me. Its pattern *is* within Oberon—without any doubt, it *is* there—but some trick of fate, or our family's poor degenerate blood, has distorted its pattern in him more than in the rest of us. That is the true and only answer."

Silence stretched again. My siblings stared at the table or the walls or went back to their soups, now and then glancing furtively at each other or Dworkin—anywhere but at me.

"Well done, Locke!" Aber finally said after more than a few awkward minutes had passed. He began clapping. "That's the way to make a new-found brother feel at home and brighten up the dinner conversation."

"Shut up!" Locke growled at him.

Then Freda began clapping, then Blaise and Pella, then most of the others. Dworkin threw back his head and howled with laughter.

I stared from one to another, bewildered. This was hardly the reaction I would have expected.

Locke glared around the table, gaze settling first on Aber then me, but he must have remembered Freda's threat because he said nothing. Instead, rising, he threw down his napkin and stalked from the room.

"Send up my meal," he called to one of the servants. "I prefer to eat with civilized company—alone!"

If anything, the applause grew louder.

"First time *that's* ever happened," Aber said brightly, the moment Locke was safely out of earshot. "Can't say it will hurt the dinner conversation."

He picked up his bowl and spoon and made a big show of moving to Locke's former place. As he settled in, he gave me a quick wink.

"Hey!" he said to everyone down at the other end of the table. "The food tastes better up here!"

That got a laugh...from everyone except Davin, who sat next to him. He was Locke's righthand man, I reminded myself. Clearly he took that position seriously. He frowned, and I half expected him to rise and leave, too, in a show of solidarity...but he didn't.

Then he glanced at me, and I recognized the look in his eyes.

It wasn't hate or mistrust.

It was pity.

They now had a cripple in their midst, I realized suddenly. They could all work wonders like Dworkin. All travel through Shadow-worlds, summon weapons from great distances, contact each other with magical Trumps, and only the gods knew what else.

And now they *pitied* me, like the soldier who had lost his sword-arm in battle and would never fight again, or the scribe who had gone blind from too much reading. They pitied me because I would never share our family's one great gift...the Logrus.

As I looked across their faces, not one of them met my gaze. They all felt the same way, I saw. Only Freda and Aber seemed willing to accept me as I was.

Freda was patting my arm.

"You do not need the Logrus," she said. "It almost killed Father and me, you know. I lay unconscious for nearly a month after I completed it."

"Oh?" That interested me.

"It is supposed to be a family problem." She lowered her voice so only I could hear. "Locke had the least trouble. Poor breeding, if you ask me. Dad had him by his first wife, a Lady of Chaos—an arranged marriage, you know, well before he inherited his title. The biggest mistake he ever made was falling in love with her; he said it a hundred times if he's said it once."

I forced a chuckle.

"Thank you," I told her softly. "It helps to have a friend."

"None of us is truly your friend," she said softly, but in an almost wistful tone. "Trust no one, but love us anyway, even Locke, since we *are* family. Betrayal is our nature and we cannot change, none of us."

I regarded her curiously, thinking of Ivinius. Could this be a confession? Or just the bittersweet words of a woman who had been hurt too often by those around her?

"You're too much of a pessimist," I finally said. "I prefer to think of everyone as a friend until it's proved otherwise."

"You are naïve, dear Oberon."

"I've been disappointed in the past...but I have also been pleasantly surprised."

She smiled. "You do not truly know us. Soon...too soon, I fear, you will." She patted my arm again. "You do have a good heart. I admire that. Now finish your soup."

I took a few more spoonfuls to satisfy her, but I didn't enjoy them. Mostly I wanted to be alone now...to think things through, to reconsider the day's events. So much had happened, and so quickly, that I could barely take it in.

Locke's departure had definitely lightened the mood around the table, though. Small conversations resumed around us, and the next course came right on schedule: braised pheasant, or a game bird close enough to pheasant that it didn't matter, accompanied by spicy roasted potatoes and strange yellow vegetables the size of walnuts that tasted, somehow, like fresh salmon.

I ate slowly, eavesdropping on the chatter around me: Davin telling Titus and Conner about a new horse he had broken to saddle. Blaise telling Pella and Isadora about a kitchen scandal involving the pastry chef and a pair of scullery maids; apparently she's just heard it from one of the seamstresses, who had gotten it straight from the herb gardener. Aber and Freda talked about new Trumps that Aber planned to paint. And Dworkin...Dad...looked down across us all and smiled like the benevolent ruler he so desperately wanted to be.

Almost pointedly, nobody discussed me...or so much as looked in my direction. Being ignored hurt almost as much as being insulted.

*Oberon the weak.*

*Oberon the cripple.*

*Oberon the* doomed-to-be-powerless.

There *must* be an answer, I thought. Maybe Dworkin—*Dad,* I corrected myself—had made a mistake. Maybe a true version of the Logrus *did* exist somewhere within me, only he hadn't seen it. Maybe...

No. I couldn't give in to wishful thinking. I forced all thoughts of the Logrus from my mind. After all, I told myself, I'd spent my whole life with no knowledge of it or the powers it bestowed. For years I'd relied on my wits and the strength of my arm. I didn't need Dworkin's tricks, nor magic cards nor spells, just a good sword and a sturdy horse.

As servants cleared our plates in preparation for the next course, Dad leaned back in his seat and focused his gaze on Davin.

"How are the new recruits working out?" he asked.

At last something I knew, I thought, leaning forward and regarding Davin with interest. Hopefully Locke managed troops better than he managed relations within our family.

"As well as can be expected," Davin said. He gave a short report, mentioning company names like "Eagles" and "Bears" and "Wolves," none of which meant anything to me. A company could have been anything from a hundred to a thousand men, depending on how it had been set up.

The report seemed to satisfy Dad, though. I also liked what I heard. Locke and Davin seemed to have a solid grasp of military matters. From the sound of things, their newest recruits had begun to pull together into an able combat force and would be ready to join the rest of the troops in just a few weeks.

"How many men are under your command?" I asked Davin, hoping to win a few points with him by showing an interest. Perhaps he could use whatever influence he had with Locke to put us on better terms.

"Nearly two hundred thousand," he said off-handedly. "Give us another year and we will have half a million...the finest force ever assembled, if I do say so myself."

"We may not have a year," Dworkin said.

"Did you say—two hundred *thousand?*" The number shocked me.

"Well, a few thousand more, actually," Davin said with a little shrug. "I haven't seen the latest figures yet. More keep arriving all the time."

"Where are they coming from?" I wasn't sure all of Ilerium had that many able-bodied fighting men.

"Oh, far and wide." He met my gaze. "We recruit from a dozen Shadows, including some where we are worshipped as gods. They are eager to join."

"I would have guessed fifteen or twenty thousand men in total," I said, thinking back to the size of the camp around the castle. Their numbers made King Elnar's fight against the hell-creatures look like an alley brawl in comparison. "Where do you keep them all quartered?"

"There are additional companies stationed to the north and east of Juniper. We only have so much space around the castle, after all."

"With a tenth that many," I mused aloud, "it would be a simple matter to drive the hell-creatures from Ilerium once and for all..."

Davin brayed with laughter. I flushed, realizing how ridiculous that must have sounded to him. Ilerium was but one world amidst all the Shadows cast by the Courts of Chaos, meaningless to anyone except me...and well beyond the concern of anyone else at this table. Never mind that I had spent the last twenty years there, and that I had dedicated my life to serving my king and my country.

And never mind that those vows still weighed on me.

"With you gone," Dworkin reminded me in gentle tones, "the enemy no longer has any reason to attack Ilerium. They will leave it alone to concentrate on other battles."

"Like here," I said, realizing the truth. "That's why you've brought all these soldiers to Juniper, isn't it. You're getting ready for an attack."

"Very good!" Davin said in lightly mocking tones, a pale imitation of Locke now. "Give the man a prize."

I gave a shrug and did not bother to reply. Sometimes it's better to say nothing. Locke had taken an instant dislike to me, and Davin had obviously taken his cue and done the same. Even so, I hoped they both might eventually be won over as allies—perhaps even as friends—with some effort on my part.

I said, "Two hundred thousand men...all fully trained? Armed and armored? Ready for battle?"

Davin smiled. "That's right. We've been preparing them for a year now."

I frowned. "The logistics of keeping such a force—the food supply alone, not to mention the costs! How is it possible? Juniper looks well off, but surely it can't support a standing army of such size for long!"

"All we need is taken from Shadow," Davin said with a grand wave of his arm. "We're worshipped as gods on countless thousands of worlds. People are happy to tithe us all we need—food, weapons, gold, jewels. Everything."

"But why so many? Do we really *need* two hundred thousand men? Or half a million? How many hell-creatures do you expect will attack?"

Freda said, "If we command this many, so too may other Lords of Chaos. They have had longer to prepare...they might well command more. Perhaps millions more."

I found the numbers incredible. That my family could sustain a force of two hundred thousand, let alone train and manage it, spoke greatly of their general competence in such matters.

Dworkin said, "An attack is coming, and soon. Freda has seen it."

"In her cards?"

I glanced at her, and she gave a little nod.

"Soon," she said.

"Oberon *has* given me some good news, though," Dworkin said happily. "Taine is alive."

There were exclamations all around the table.

"How? Where?" Freda demanded.

I took a minute to tell them of my dream or vision or whatever it had been—the few details I could still recall, anyway. Dworkin had to remind me of several key points as I stumbled through the narrative.

"Are you certain it was real?" Davin asked me, sounding more than a little skeptical.

"No, I'm not," I said. I had more than a few doubts myself. "I have no experience in such things."

Dworkin said, "Remember, Oberon has never been to the Courts of Chaos. He had never even heard of it before today. In his dream, however, the blood flowed *up*. That is a detail he could not have guessed or imagined. I believe his vision is true. Somewhere, somehow, Taine is still alive."

"Indeed," Freda said.

Davin looked thoughtful suddenly and regarded me with what I thought was a new-found respect.

"The question now," he said, "is what do we do? How can we rescue Taine?"

"Perhaps his Trump..." Aber said.

Freda shook her head. "I have tried that too many times now. He cannot be reached."

"When was the last time?" I asked.

She thought carefully before replying. "Perhaps two weeks ago."

"It never hurts to try again," Dworkin said. "Perhaps, knowing he is alive, you will have a better chance of reaching him."

"I will try," she said, "as soon as dinner is over. We should all try."

There were murmurs of agreement from all present. It seemed they all had Trumps depicting Taine and could use them.

I felt a measure of pride. Perhaps I *was* more than a cripple after all. Maybe I had my own form of magic to fall back upon...visions that showed more than Freda's Trumps.

Servants began bringing in platters bearing the next course—cubes of beef, nicely pink and steaming, artfully arranged with waxy looking yellow-and-red striped beans. Unfortunately, as delicious as it looked, I found my appetite completely gone. A restlessness came over me, a need to get up and do something active rather than sit and wait for the meal to end.

Pointedly, I stifled a yawn.

"If you don't mind," I said to Dworkin, "I'd like to retire. Everything I've been through today is starting to catch up with me. I'm going to fall asleep in this chair if I don't get some rest."

"Off you go, then." He made shooing motions with his fork. "Pleasant dreams, my boy. I will send for you again tomorrow. There are still a few matters we must discuss."

"Yes, Dad," I said, rising.

Freda, Aber, and all the rest—even Davin—bade me good night. They all had interesting expressions on their faces: not so much pity, now, as a kind of awe or wonder. I might not be able to walk the Logrus as they had done, but it seemed I shared at least some of their powers. Dworkin had been right to show it off before them. This way they wouldn't dismiss me outright, the way Locke had done.

I strode out into the corridor, pausing only long enough to get my bearings. Although exhaustion really did threaten to overwhelm me, I knew I had work to do: Ivinius's body remained hidden behind that tapestry. I had to dispose of it without being seen.

Instead of going back to my rooms, however, I decided to explore the castle a bit more. There might be a safe, easy passage out—I just had to find it.

Unfortunately, every way I turned, I found more servants moving on errand or scrubbing the floors or changing candles or filling reserves in oil lamps. The castle's staff had to number in the hundreds.

I passed one of the guard rooms Aber had pointed out earlier that afternoon. Through the open door, it looked like any of a hundred guard rooms I'd seen over the years—a rack of swords against the far wall, armor and shields on wooden pegs, a table and plenty of sturdy chairs.

At the moment, three guards sat at the table throwing dice. Unfortunately, the one facing the door recognized me—the moment he saw my face, he leaped to his feet.

"Lord!" he cried. He saluted, and the other two shoved back their chairs and did the same.

"Please, continue with your game." I gave a polite wave, then strolled on. No need to involve them; they were probably off duty and unwinding from a long day's work.

Kitchens...servants' quarters...the still-guarded corridor by Dad's workshop...the main hall...everywhere I went, I found people. *Lots* of people. And all seemed to recognize me. Clearly, I thought with some frustration, getting Ivinius out of Juniper would not be as easy as I'd hoped.

Then I remembered Aber's gift—my own set of Trumps. I could make them work on my own—after all, I had been able to contact my brother earlier from Dworkin's horseless carriage. Perhaps I could use one now to get rid of Ivinius's body. Frowning, I tried to recall all their pictures. I had barely glanced at them—but hadn't one showed a forest glade with Juniper in the distance? That would be perfect, I thought.

Excited now, I hurried back up to my rooms. The hinges squeaked when I entered. Servants had lit an oil lamp on the writing table, but everything else looked just as I had left it: my sword across the back of one of the chairs, the stand and washbasin beside the now-dark windows, the desk shoved up against the wall, its paper, ink, and blotters all in slight disarray.

The carved wooden box containing my set of Trumps sat atop the stack of unused towels on the tray atop the wash-stand.

Feeling a growing sense of elation, I opened the little box and pulled out my stack of Trumps. They felt cool and hard as ivory in my hands. Slowly, one by one, I leafed through them. Portraits came first: Aber...Locke...Pella...Blaise...Freda...

Yes—there was the one I needed! With a trembling hand, I drew forth the card I had half remembered. It showed a dark forest glade, lush grass underfoot, trees all around, with Juniper's towers just visible in the distance. This seemed an ideal place to dump a body...far enough from Juniper to be safe from any immediate discovery. Let Ivinius's masters try to figure out what had happened to him!

Card in hand, I started for the sitting room. Then I stopped myself. How would I get back after I'd disposed of the body? I gave a chuckle. I was catching on to this game of Trumps—I would need one to bring me safely home.

I returned to my set of cards, selected the one that I had confiscated from Aber, which showed my bedroom, and only then headed for the sitting room. This would be a fast and simple job using magic, I thought. I would go to the glade, dump the body, and come straight home.

Hurrying now, I swept back the tapestry.

My elation died. I had come back too late.

The body had disappeared.

## TWELVE

A quick search of my suite revealed no sign of Ivinius anywhere. No blood had been spilled, so no tell-tale stains remained. Only the tray with the razors and towels told me he had actually been here...and the ink stain beneath the small carpet, but that could have been spilled any time. It spoke of a clumsy scribe more than of an assassin.

I had no proof now that I'd been attacked, or that he'd been a hell-creature impersonating a servant. Without his body, I'd lost my one clue...and my one slight advantage. Since no alarm had been raised, I assumed either another hell-creature or a traitor in Juniper had come searching for him, discovered his body, and spirited it off.

I frowned. I hadn't seen a single empty hallway or corridor all the way back to my rooms from dinner. Someone could have snuck into my rooms by normal means—it only took a moment of turned backs to slip through my unlocked door. But anyone smuggling out a body would have encountered witnesses. Clearly the body had been removed by other, perhaps even magical means. A Trump? It seemed likely.

And a Trump meant one of us ...one of my half-brothers or half-sisters...

But which one?

Puzzled, annoyed, and more than slightly frightened by the implications, I carefully bolted my doors, checked the windows (there didn't seem to be any way short of flying to get to my balcony from the balconies to either side), and I moved my sword to within easy reach of the bed.

Only then did I undress and crawl between the sheets.

Exhaustion surged like an ocean tide. I was asleep almost before my head hit the pillow.

Polite knocking has never been the way to rouse me in the morning, nor softly called invitations to breakfast. As with all soldiers, I liked to sleep the same way as I ate, fought, and bedded my women—heartily, fully, deeply. Trumpets sounding a call to arms, or the clash of swords, are the only things that stir my blood in the early hours. Otherwise, as my men had found out over the years, it's best to let me be.

It should have surprised no one, then, that I scarcely heard the knocking, or the politely incessant "Lord? Lord Oberon?" that followed from the hallway when I refused to be awakened.

When someone threw back the curtains and bright sunlight flooded the room, I half opened one eye, saw it was only Aber, rolled over, and continued to snore.

"Oberon!" he called. "Wakee wakee!"

I opened my eyes to slits and glared at him. Hands on his hips, my half-brother gazed down at me with a bemused expression. Behind him, in the doorway to my bedchamber, stood a clump of anxious servants in castle livery.

"I thought I bolted the door!" I said.

"Dad wants to see you. The servants have been trying to rouse you for half an hour. Finally they came and got me."

"Why didn't they say something?"

Growling a little, I threw back the covers and sat up, naked. A couple of the women hurried from the doorway, blushing. Anari hurried forward with a robe which turned out to be several sizes too large—but it would do. I shrugged it on.

Then I noticed a Trump in Aber's hand...and plucked it from his grasp before he could object.

"Aha!" I said. A miniature portrait of my antechamber, done just like the one I had confiscated yesterday. "I knew I locked the door last night!"

He laughed. "Well, how else do you think I'd get in?"

"You told me you didn't have any more Trumps of my rooms!"

"No," he said with a grin, "I didn't. I told you I didn't have any more of your *bedroom*. This one isn't of your bedroom, is it?"

"A fine distinction," I grumbled. He looked entirely too pleased with himself. Served me right for not being specific enough, though I didn't appreciate the service. Clearly I needed to do a better job of watching out for my own interests. "I'll hang onto this one, too. Do you have any other Trumps of my rooms? *Any* of them?"

"Hundreds!" He tapped his head. "I keep them up here." I snorted. "Make sure they stay there. I don't like people sneaking up on me!"

"Oh, all right." He sighed. "You're no fun."

Yawning, I stretched the kinks from my muscles. "Now what were you saying? Dad wants to see me?"

"Yes." Aber folded his arms. "You'll find things run much more smoothly when you stick to his schedule. Rise early in the morning, stay up late at night, and try to catch a nap in the afternoon if time allows."

"Lord," said Anari, "I have found you a valet and taken the liberty of preparing your schedule for today."

Schedule? I didn't like the sound of that.

"Go on," I said.

Anari motioned toward the doorway, and a young man of perhaps thirteen or so dashed forward and bowed to me. "This is my great-grandson, Horace," Anari said. "He will serve you well."

"I'm sure," I said. I gave Horace a brief nod. He had Anari's features, but black hair to the old man's white. "Pleased to have you, Horace."

"Thank you, Lord!" He looked relieved.

"Call me Oberon," I told him.

"Yes, Lord Oberon!"

"No, just Oberon. Or Lord."

"Yes...Oberon...Lord." He seemed hesitant at such familiarity. Well, he would get used to it soon enough. I needed a valet, not a toady.

Anari said, "The castle tailors will be here after breakfast. They will prepare clothing to your tastes. After that, lunch. You will be fitted for armor in the afternoon...and Lord Davin wishes to accompany you to the stables. He says you need a horse."

"A peace offering?" I asked Aber.

"Who understands them?" he said with a shrug. "I don't."

I didn't care; I did need a horse. "It sounds fine," I said to Anari. "But all must wait until after I see my father."

"Of course."

Horace was already making himself useful, laying out clothes for me—a beautiful white shirt with a stylized lion's head stitched on the chest in gold thread and dark wine-colored pants that shimmered slightly in the bright morning light. They looked about my size, too...certainly closer than the robe.

"These were Mattus's," Aber said. "I don't think he'd mind if you took them."

"They're beautiful." I ran my hand over the fabric, wondering at the incredible softness and the silky texture, unlike anything I'd ever seen in Ilerium. No one there, not even King Elnar himself, had garments such as these.

"They were made in the Courts of Chaos," Aber said.

"What's the secret? Magic"

"Spider-silk, I believe."

"Incredible!"

Horace had continued his work while we talked, setting out a wide belt, cape, and gloves in colors to match the pants, plus clean socks and undergarments.

"You know where to find me," Aber said, starting for the door. "I'll walk down with you when you're ready. Don't dawdle...Dad's still waiting!"

"And growing more annoyed by the moment, I'm sure," I added with a smile. "I remember."

Shaking his head, he left, and the few servants still outside the door followed. Anari started after them, then paused in the doorway to look back.

"Don't worry," I told him. "Horace will be fine. I can tell he's a hard worker. And I'll watch out for him, you have my word."

He seemed relieved. "Thank you, Lord Oberon."

Ten minutes later, I collected Aber from his rooms across the hall and started down for Dad's workshop. I have always had a fairly good sense of direction, and I unerringly retraced our journey from the previous evening.

As we walked, I asked Aber what had happened at dinner after I left.

"Not much," he said. "Everyone was too shocked."

I chuckled. "Shocked? By Taine's being alive or my being a cripple?"

"A little of both, actually." He swallowed and wouldn't meet my gaze. "After dinner—"

"Everyone tried to contact Taine with his Trump," I guessed. "But it didn't work."

"That's right."

"So he's either dead, unconscious, drugged, or protected somehow from your Trumps."

"That's how it looks to me."

We reached Dworkin's workshop. Two new guards—one of whom I recognized from the dice game in the guardroom—snapped to attention as we passed.

"Is there anything else you can do?" I asked. "Is there any way to just reach through his Trump, grab him whether he's awake or not, and just drag him through?"

"I wish we could. But Trumps don't work that way."

I raised my hand to knock on the workshop door, but it swung open for me. The room blazed with light. I couldn't see Dworkin for a moment—but then I spotted him on the other side of the room. He hadn't opened the door, but there didn't seem to be anyone else present. Ghosts? No—probably just the Logrus again, I realized with a gulp. If he could snatch swords from the other end of the castle, why not open doors from ten feet away?

"Ah, there you are!" Dworkin said. "Come in."

Disconcerted, I stepped inside.

"Good luck!" Aber said to me, and then the door slammed in his face.

Dworkin sat at a table in a tall-backed wooden chair. The table held a box, and in the box sat what looked like an immense ruby. I must admit I stared at it; I had never seen a jewel of its size before. Surely it belonged to some king...which is what Dworkin probably was in this Shadow.

He chuckled. "Impressive, is it not?"

"Beautiful," I said. I raised it, studying the carefully faceted sides, which gleamed seductively in the bright light.

"This crystal is special. It holds a replica of the pattern within you."

"Where did you get it?"

"I...acquired it some time ago. It has unusual properties, one of which may prove useful in your situation. Your Pattern, I now believe, is *not* a mere distortion of the Logrus after all."

"Then...you were wrong last night?" I felt a mounting excitement. This might be the answer to my hopes and prayers. "I can walk the Logrus after all?"

"No—that would kill you!"

"But you said—"

"*I said* your pattern is not a distortion of the Logrus. It is something else...something new. A *different* pattern."

I frowned, confused. "How can that be? Isn't the Logrus responsible for everything...for the Courts of Chaos and all the Shadow worlds?

"In some ways, perhaps."

"I don't understand." I stared at him blankly.

"Few are the things that cannot be replaced."

"You mean I really *am* a cripple. I cannot draw on the Logrus like you do."

"No!" He threw back his head and laughed. "Exactly the opposite, my boy—you do not *need* to draw on the Logrus. You have something else to draw upon...your own pattern."

"My own..." I stared at him dumbly.

"I hold the design of your pattern fixed clearly in my mind now, and it burns with a primal power. You are like that first nameless Lord of Chaos. You hold a pattern—this new pattern—inside you. It is unlike the Logrus! It is a pattern from which whole worlds may spring, once it is traced properly!"

*Not the Logrus....*

I felt a sudden joy, a boundless euphoria, as I realized what that meant. Perhaps I *could* master Shadows the way the rest of my family had. I *might yet* travel between the Shadow worlds and work the wonders I had seen. Suddenly it all lay within my grasp.

And I wanted it more than I had ever wanted anything in my life. More than a father, more than a family, I wanted my heritage...my destiny.

*Only*—

"Traced properly?" I asked slowly. "What does that mean?"

He hesitated, and I could tell he was trying to find the words to explain it to me.

"I believe the Logrus exists not just inside, but outside the universe as we know it," he finally said. "The first Lord of Chaos partly traced its shape using his own blood...putting a form to the formless, making it *real* in a way that it had not been before. It is my belief that when someone of our bloodline passes through it, the Logrus's pattern is imprinted forever in his mind, enabling him to use it—to draw on its power and move between worlds."

"I understand," I said. I'd heard the whole history-of-our-powers speech already. "You said the Logrus wouldn't work on me...it would destroy me."

"That is correct. What we must do for you is something similar to what the first Lord of Chaos did...find a way to trace the unique pattern within you, so that your pattern is imprinted on your mind, much the way the Logrus is imprinted on *my* mind."

"All right," I said. It sounded reasonable enough. And yet...something still bothered me.

Dad hesitated.

"You're leaving something out," I said accusingly.

"No..."

"Tell me!"

He swallowed. "I have never tried this before. It may work. It *should* work, if my theories about the Logrus and its nature are correct. But then again...what if I am wrong? What if I have made a mistake?"

"It might kill me," I said, recognizing what he had been unwilling to say.

"That, or worse. It might destroy your mind, leaving your body little more than an empty shell. Or...it might do nothing at all."

I didn't know which would be worse. My hopes had been raised; it *had* to work. It *would* work. I had run out of options.

"What are my chances of living?" I asked.

"I cannot guarantee anything, except that I have done my best."

"Would you do it?" I asked. "Would you risk your own life on tracing this pattern?"

"Yes," he said simply. No arguments, no explanations, just a single word.

I took a deep breath. This was the moment of truth. I could risk everything and try to gain power unimaginable. Or I could be safe, forever trapped in the world of mortal men.

Could I live with the Lockes of the world sneering at me, pitying me? Could I live with myself if I passed up my one last chance for power?

Only cowards choose the safe path.

I had known what my answer must be even before Dworkin told me of the risk. I wanted power. I *wanted* magic of my own. After seeing what Dworkin and the rest of my family could do, how could I step back now?

I swallowed hard. "I want to try it."

Dworkin let out his breath. "I will not fail you, my boy," he said softly.

He held up the ruby. I gasped as it caught the light, sending flashes of color dancing and slashing around the room.

Holding the jewel higher, at my eye level, I found it glowed with an inner light. I leaned forward, wanting to fall into its center like a moth is called by an open flame.

"Look deep inside," Dworkin continued. His voice sounded as if he were standing far away. "Fastened within, it is a design...an exact tracing of the pattern within you. Gaze upon it, my boy—gaze and let your spirit go!"

A shimmer of red surrounded me. The world receded, and light and shadow began to pulsate rhythmically, shapes and forms seeming to appear, then vanish.

As though from a great distance away, I heard Dworkin's voice: "Follow the pattern, my boy...let it show you the way..."

I stepped forward.

It was like opening a door and entering a room I never knew existed. The world unfolded around me. Space and time ceased to have meaning. I felt neither breath in my lungs nor the beating of my heart; I simply *was*. I did not need to breathe, or see, or taste, or touch. When I reached for my wrist, I felt no pulse...I felt nothing at all.

Lights glimmered, moved. Shadows flowed like water.

*This isn't real....*

And yet it was. Before me, behind me, to the sides and all around me, I saw the lines of a great pattern. It blazed with a liquid red light, curves and sweeps and switchbacks, like the twisted body of some immense serpent or dragon. It held me transfixed within it, just as I held it within me, and together we balanced perfectly. I felt a calm, a harmony of belonging.

*"This way..."*

I felt a hand on my shoulder, pushing me on. I took a step.

"Dad?"

*"Yes. I am here. I have projected myself inside the jewel, too. Come, Move forward, onto the pattern. Walk its length. I will be with you..."*

I stepped forward, heading for the pattern. This was no mere distortion of the Logrus. It was separate, different, and yet...two parts of some greater whole.

Distantly, as though in a dream, I heard Dad's voice talking to me. I could not make out the words, but the tone nagged and insisted. I had to do something...go somewhere...

So *hard to concentrate*. And yet I knew there was something I had to remember...something I had to do....

*"Forward,"* said the voice. "Do *not stop.*"

Yes. Forward.

I moved on, into the pattern, following the glowing red light. At first I found it easy, but it grew steadily harder as I progressed, like wading through mud. The light pushed at me, trying to drive me back, but I refused to give up. I thought. I would not stop no matter what happened.

And abruptly the resistance ceased. I moved easily down the trail. The light, clear and brilliant, lit the path. Around the turn, forward—-another turn—

The whole of my life flashed before me, but strangely vivid—all the places I'd been, all the people I'd ever met.

*My mother—*
*Swearing to serve King Elnar—*
*Sword lessons* on *the town green—*
*Our house in Piermont—*
*Fighting the* hell-creatures—
*Dworkin as a younger man—*

The path curved and again grew difficult, and I found myself straining for every inch, forcing myself forward. I would not stop. I could not stop. The lights ahead beckoned. Images of my life flashed and danced through my mind.

*The beach at Janisport—*
*King Elnar's crowning—*
*Fishing* on *the banks of the Blue River—*
*The women* I *had known before Helda—*
*The battle of Highland Ridge—*
*In bed with Helda—*
*Mustering troops for battle—*

For some reason, I seized upon the image of the battlefield. Here King Elnar had fought the hell-creatures to a standstill. Here we had known our first real victory in the war against the hell-creatures.

In my mind's eye, I still saw our troops again rallying valiantly to the king, swords and pikes raised, screaming their war-cries—

And, reaching the center of the pattern, where it had wound in upon itself—

—I staggered across mud and matted grass, then drew up short, half gagging on the stench of death and decay. Bodies of men and horses lay all around me, rotting and covered with flies. A low buzz of wings came from the corpses.

I looked up. It was late afternoon on a dark, overcast day. A chill wind blew from the east, heavy with the promise of rain. It could not remove the stench of death, however.

Slowly I turned in a circle. The battlefield stretched as far as I could see in every direction. There had been a massacre here, and I saw uncountable hundreds, perhaps thousands of bodies, all human, all dressed in King Elnar's colors.

From warmth to cold, from dry to damp, from the safety of a castle to the horrors of a battlefield in an instant. What had happened? How had I gotten here?

*Dworkin's ruby...*I remembered it now. I had seen the fields outside of Kingstown while gazing into the jewel. Somehow, it had sent me here.

But why? To see the destruction?

I covered my mouth and nose with my shirt tail, but it did little to hide the stench. Slowly, I turned full circle, taking in the horrors around me.

These men had died at least four or five days ago, I estimated. Broken weapons, a burnt out war-wagon toppled on its side, and fallen banners caked with mud and gore spoke to the magnitude of the loss. King Elnar's army had been destroyed, and from the number of bodies, probably to the last man.

A cold drizzle began to soak my hair and clothes. The stench of carrion grew worse. Carefully I began to pick my way among the bodies, looking for the king, for anyone I knew.

I shivered, suddenly, soaked to the skin. Then I forced myself to look at the battlefield, at all that remained around me. Birds and dogs and other, less savory carrion, eaters had worked on the corpses for several days, but I didn't need to see faces to recognize them.

All had been human.

I climbed onto the burnt-out wagon's sides, my fingers growing black and greasy from the char, and when I stood above the battlefield I saw the true scope of the disaster.

The battlefield stretched as far as I could see. Proud banners lay in the mud. Swords, knives, pikes, and axes by the score lay rusting on the ground. And everywhere, piled or singly as they had fallen, lay more bodies.

No one, not wife nor child nor priest, had come to sing the funeral songs and bury the dead. I did not have to look to know that Kingstown too had fallen, or that the hell,-creatures had slaughtered all whom they met along the way.

So much for Dad's prediction that the hell-creatures would leave Ilerium once I went to Juniper. As I picked my way through the battlefield, a numb sort of shock settled upon me. Severed limbs, empty eye sockets that seemed yet to stare, expressions of terror and pain etched on every face—I could scarcely take it all in.

Then I came to a place where the bodies and debris had been cleared away. A line of seven chest-high wooden poles, each stuck into the mud perhaps two feet apart, held ghastly trophies: the severed heads of King Elnar and six of his lieutenants.

Staring at what little remained of my king, I felt my stomach knot with pain. I stumbled forward to stand before him. His eyes were closed; his mouth hung open. Though his grayish skin had begun to crack from exposure to the sun, he had a peaceful look, almost as though he slept.

It was a struggle to keep from throwing myself to the ground and sobbing helplessly. How could this have happened? Dad had said the hell-creatures would leave once I fled Ilerium. I had believed him.

"I'm sorry," I told him.

Suddenly, impossibly, King Elnar's eyelids flickered open.

I felt a jolt of terror.

His eyes turned slowly to regard me. Recognition shone in them.

"You!" he croaked, barely able to form the words. A black tongue darted out, licking cracked and broken lips. "You brought this punishment upon us!"

"No..." I whispered.

The other heads on the other poles began to open their eyes, too. Ilrich, Lanar, Harellen—one by one they began to call my name: *"Obere...Obere...Obere ..."*

Voice growing stronger, King Elnar said, "You fled your oath of allegiance. You abandoned us in our hour of need. Know, then, our doom, for you shall share it!"

"I thought the hell-creatures would leave," I told him. "They were looking for *me,* not you."

"Traitor!" he said. "You betrayed us all!"

And the other heads began to shout, *"Traitor! Traitor! Traitor! Traitor!"*

"No!" I said. "Listen to me! It's not true!"

"Hell-creatures!" King Elnar began to scream. "He's here! He's here! Come and get him! Come and get the traitor!"

"Quiet!" I said, voice sharp. "Don't call them—"

"Help!" one of the other heads shouted. "Hell-creatures! Come help us! Lieutenant Obere is here!"

I cried, "Shut up!"

Another called, "This is the one you want, not us! Help! Help!"

"Come and get him!" shouted the rest of the heads. "Come and get him!"

I tried everything to quiet them—explanations, reasoning, orders. Nothing worked. They just wouldn't stop shouting for the hell-creatures to come and get me.

They were no longer men, but bewitched *things,* I finally told myself. The people I had known would never have betrayed me this way...not the king I had sworn to serve till my dying breath, not my brothers-in-arms...not one of them.

Raising my boot, I knocked over King Elnar's pole. His head did not roll free. I bent to pry it off, but then I discovered it was not stuck on top of the pole, but had somehow become a part of it...flesh and wood grown together in a horrible mingling of the two.

"Liege-killer!" the heads shouted.

"Traitor!"

"Murderer!"

"Assassin!"

"Hell-*creatures—help us!*"

I pulled the pole free from the ground. A little more than four feet from end to end, it only weighed twenty pounds or so. I raised it easily over my head and smashed the head-part on the nearest stone with all my strength.

King Elnar's face shattered, but instead of bone and brains, a pulpy green mass and what looked like sap sprayed out. It smelled like fresh-cut lumber.

Half sobbing, I smashed it again and again until the head was completely gone. Then I used the pole to smash the other heads, too. All the time they screeched their insults and called on the hell-creatures for help.

They couldn't help it, I told myself. They were no longer the people I had known.

Finally it was done. Alone again, I stood there, listening to the wind moan softly through the battlefield, the smell of fresh wood mingling with the carrion stench. Rain pattered down harder. Darkness began to fall. Lightning flickered overhead.

Turning, still dragging the pole, I looked toward Kingstown. Perhaps I could find answers there...or a way back to Juniper. I needed time to rest and think and gather my wits.

Then I heard the one sound I feared most: distant hoofbeats. A lot of them. Hell-creatures? Answering the heads' frantic calls?

I didn't doubt it. The hell-creatures must have left the heads to watch for my return. And they had betrayed me as soon as I arrived.

Desperately, I looked around. There was no one left alive to help me here, and no place to make a stand. I might hide among the fallen bodies for a time, but a search would find me soon enough, and I didn't look forward to a night spent lying motionless in cold mud.

I snatched up a fallen sword, only to discover it was chipped and bent in the middle. The second one I grabbed was broken. Damn Dworkin and his no-swords-in-the workshop rule! If I'd had my own blade, I might have stood a chance.

With darkness falling rapidly now and rain drumming incessantly, I didn't have time to hunt for a weapon I could use. With the hell-creatures approaching, I had to find cover, and fast. In my current condition, I didn't think I'd last two minutes against any determined attack.

I ran toward Kingstown. Perhaps it still stood. Perhaps the remains of King Elnar's army had rallied there and still held it. Though I knew the chances were slim, it seemed my only remaining option.

At the very least, I might find a place to hide until morning.

## THIRTEEN

Kingstown was a burnt-out ruin.

When I topped the small hill over-looking the town, tongues of lightning showed nothing but blackened rubble. Not a single building remained. Here and there stone chimneys still stood, marking the passing of this place like gravestones. I would find no help here.

*Oberon...*

A distant voice seemed to be calling my name. I gazed around me in surprise.

"Who's there?"

*Aber. Think of me. Reach out with your thoughts.*

I tried to picture him in my mind. As I concentrated, an image of him grew before me, wavered, and became real.

"It *is* you!" I gasped. Perhaps my situation wasn't as desperate as I'd thought.

*"Yes. Dad said he...lost you, somehow. I thought I'd try your Trump. Where are you now? What happened?"*

"I'm cold, wet, and tired. Can you get me back home?"

He hesitated only a second. *"Sure."*

"Thanks."

He reached out his hand toward me, and I did the same toward him. Our fingers touched somewhere in the middle. He gripped my wrist firmly and pulled me forward. I took a step—

—and found myself standing in a room lined with tapestries of dancers, jugglers, and scenes of merriment. An oil lamp hung from the ceiling, spreading a warm yellow light. A rack of swords, a cluttered writing table, a high canopied bed, and two plain wooden chairs completed the furnishings.

I glanced behind me, but another wall stood there now, this one lined with shelves full of books, scrolls, shells, rocks, and other odds and ends such as anyone might accumulate over the years. Ilerium, Kingstown, and the hell-creatures had vanished.

"Is this—?" I began.

"My bedroom."

Only then did I relax. *Safe. Back in Juniper.* I found myself trembling from sheer nervous exhaustion. I had never felt so helpless before.

But I had escaped.

"You look like a drowned rat!" he said, laughing a bit.

I glanced down. Rain had plastered my clothes to my body. Mud and sap and wood-pulp had splattered my pants and boots. Water dripped from my hair, trickled down my forehead and cheeks, and dripped from my chin.

"I *feel* like a drowned rat," I told him. "Sorry about the mess." Gingerly I lifted first one then the other foot. My boots left a muddy brown smear. Water began to pool all around me.

"That's okay."

"But your carpets—" They had to be worth a small fortune!

He shrugged. "Oh, I don't care. They can be cleaned or replaced. Having you back safe is what matters. Now, sit down—you look like you're about to collapse!"

"Thanks." I took two steps and sank heavily onto one of his spare wooden chairs. My clothes squished. Water ran in my eyes. I just wanted to find a warm dry place and curl up there for the next month. "I think this has probably been the worst night of my life."

"What have you got?" Aber asked.

"Huh?" I looked down and realized I still held the pole...the one upon which King Elnar's head had been stuck. I let it drop to the floor. Somehow, I never wanted to see it again. It was cursed or bewitched or both.

"I was going to defend myself with it," I said half apologetically. "Hell-creatures were hunting me."

His eyes widened. "Hell-creatures! Where were you?"

"Back home...the Shadow I came from...Ilerium."

"How did you get there?"

"Dad did something. He was trying some experiment some idea he had to get around my using the Logrus." Taking a deep breath, I pulled off first one boot, then the other. Half an inch of water sat inside each. After a moment's hesitation, I put them down next to the chair.

"Well?" he demanded. "Did it work?"

"I don't think so. It gave me a headache, then somehow he dumped me back in Ilerium—that's the place I grew up. King Elnar—his whole army—had been butchered. The hell-creatures had burned the town, too. I don't think anyone survived. And they were still there, waiting for me. If not for you..."

"I'm sorry," he said sympathetically.

"It can't be helped," I said heavily. It seemed I'd escaped my destiny. Dad really *had* saved me. "If I'd stayed behind to fight the hell-creatures, I'd be dead, now, too."

"You look half frozen as well as half drowned," he observed. "How about a brandy?"

"Please!" I pushed wet hair back out of my eyes.

An open bottle and a glass sat on the writing table. He poured me a large drink, which I downed in a single gulp, then a second one, which I sipped.

Rising, I went over to the fireplace. It had been banked for the evening, and its embers burned low, but it still radiated warmth. It felt good to just stand before it, basking like a cat in a sunny window.

Aber threw on a couple more split logs, then shifted the coals with a poker. Flames appeared. The logs began to burn. The room grew warmer, and I toasted myself quite happily front and back.

"How did you bring me here?" I asked him. "The Logrus?"

"Yes." He went back to the writing table, picked up a Trump, and brought it back to show me. It had my picture on it. In typical fashion, he had drawn me holding a candlestick and peering into darkness.

I had to chuckle. "That's exactly how I feel right now," I told him. "Lost in the dark. Or perhaps found but still in the dark."

I reached out to take the card, but he said, "Sorry, it's not quite dry yet," and carried it back on the writing table.

Taking another sip of brandy, I felt its warm glow spreading through my belly. Maybe there were some advantages to belonging to this crazy family after all. A last-second rescue by a brother I'd only met the day before...it was the sort of thing a bard could easily spin into a heroic song.

Frowning, I thought back to King Elnar and my fellow lieutenants, all dead now, their ensorceled heads smashed to pulp. If only the story had a happy ending...

Aber had taken a blanket from the bed and now handed it to me.

"Get out of those wet things and dry yourself off," he said. "I'll bring you another set of Mattus's clothes. As soon as you're up to it, you must see Dad. He's worried sick about you."

"Thanks," I said gratefully.

*     *     *

Aber returned in short order with shirt, pants, and undergarments, plus my valet. Horace looked half asleep and I guessed Aber had dragged him from bed to help me.

It didn't take them long to get me changed and cleaned up. I found myself moving slowly; after all I'd been through, the lateness of the hour, and the effects of the brandy, my arms and legs felt like lead weights, and my head began to pound. I wanted nothing more than to crawl into bed and pass out for the next day or two.

Aber had a spare pair of boots"but they proved several sizes too small. Horace went out and soon returned with a larger pair—I didn't ask where he'd found them, but I suspected he swiped them from another of my brothers. Not that I cared at this point.

"You'll do," Aber said finally, looking me up and down. "Just try not to collapse."

"I feel better," I lied.

"That's just the brandy. You look terrible."

"Could be." I took a deep breath and turned toward the door, swaying slightly. Time to visit our father, I thought. I couldn't put it off any longer. I said as much.

"Do you want me to go with you?" Aber asked suddenly, steadying my arm.

"No need," I said. "He'll want to see me alone. We have a lot to discuss."

"You're right, he never wants to see me. But still..." He hesitated.

"I know the way," I said with more confidence than I felt.

"Are you sure?"

"Yes."

"I'll just wish you luck, then." He glanced at Horace. "*Go* with him," he said, "just in case."

"Yes, Lord," Horace said. He stepped forward, and I leaned a bit on his shoulder.

"Thanks," I said to Aber for  everything."

"You don't know how lucky you are!"

"Sure I do." I grinned at him.

"Go on, get out of here. Dad's waiting."

Horace helped me into the corridor, where I took a deep breath and forced myself to stand on my own two feet. I thought I could make it successfully downstairs on my own. I didn't want the other servants to see me limping and leaning on Horace—rumors of some personal catastrophe would be all over Juniper before daybreak.

With Horace trailing, I made my way unerringly downstairs and through the maze of corridors, past two sleepy looking guards, and straight to Dworkin's workshop.

I didn't bother knocking, but pushed the door open and went in. Dworkin had been seated at one of his tables tinkering with a four-armed skeleton.

"What happened? Where have you been?" he demanded, leaping forward. "You just—vanished!"

I swayed a little, and Horace leaped forward to steady me. I leaned on his shoulder as he helped me to a chair.

"That will be all," I told him.

"Yes, Lord," he said, and he bowed and hurried out.

Slowly I told my father everything that had happened to me: my sudden unexpected appearance at the battlefield north of Kingstown, the heads of King Elnar and his lieutenants and how they had betrayed me, my flight from the hell-creatures, and how I discovered the town had been burned.

"Aber saved me," I said. "He made a trump to check on me, then used it to bring me back here."

"Then it worked," he said, awed. "The jewel really does carry a true image of your pattern. You are now attuned to it, and it to you."

"I don't understand."

He smiled kindly. "You traveled to Ilerium on your own, drawing on the pattern within you. You can master Shadows now."

I felt stunned. "It worked? Really?"

"Yes!"

"Like the Logrus?"

*"Yes!"*

I sighed with relief. "Good...."

"The very nature of Chaos lies in the Logrus," he said. "It is a primal force, alive and vibrant. It is incorporated into the very essence of the Lords of Chaos, from King Uthor on down to the smallest child who shares his blood."

"Including you," I said. "And everyone of *your* blood...except me."

"That's right."

"But why *not* in me?"

"Oh, I know the answer to that now," he said with a laugh, "but we must save it for another day. Come, I have a bed in one of the back rooms for when I work too long here. Lie down, sleep. You will be the better for it tomorrow."

I still had a thousand questions—how had I transported myself to Ilerium without a Trump? Did I need the ruby to work magic? Would it take me to any Shadow world I could envision, even ones I've never been to before?—but I didn't have the strength to argue. Rising, I followed him through several different rooms than the ones I'd seen before, all equally cluttered with magical and scientific devices, until we came to one with a small bed pushed up against the wall A pair of mummified lions sat on top of the covers, but he tossed them into the corner and pulled back the blankets for me.

"In you go, my boy."

Without bothering to undress, I threw myself down.

Dreams came quickly, full of weird images of burning patterns encased in ruby light, talking heads, and Dworkin cackling as he loomed over me, pulling strings like a mad puppeteer.

## FOURTEEN

I don't know how long I slept, but when I finally awoke the next day, I felt groggy and out of sorts with the world. Dworkin had vanished. Slowly I sat up, stretched, rubbed my eyes, and climbed unsteadily to my feet. My muscles ached and my head pounded.

I wandered out of the workshop, past two new guards on duty in the corridor, and into the banquet hall. Perhaps food would help, I thought.

Blaise and a couple of women I'd never seen before were eating what looked like a cold lunch at one end of the table. I nodded politely to them, but took my own meal at the other end. They barely seemed to notice me, going on about various people I'd never heard of.

"How may I serve you, Lord?" a servant asked, appearing at my side.

"A bloody steak, half a dozen fried eggs, and beer."

"Yes, Lord."

He returned five minutes later with plates filled with the food I'd ordered, plus a basket of fresh bread, a cake of butter, a salt cellar, and a large bowl piled high with fruit. I recognized apples and pears, but most of the others strange knobbed balls of green and yellow, mottled red-dish-orange blades, and puffy white globes the size of my fist—I had never before seen.

I ate in silence, thinking back to events of the previous day. It all seemed distant and unreal, as though someone else had voyaged to Ilerium. And yet I could still hear King Elnar and his lieutenants' voices—

*Traitor!*
*Murderer!*
*Assassin!*

It sent a cold knife through my heart.

After eating, I felt much like my old self. I had slept well past noon, I realized. I couldn't spend the whole day lounging around the castle, so I went in search of Anari. He had set up a whole day of appointments for me with tailors and the like, but unfortunately, between Dad and everything else, I hadn't kept a single one. Perhaps, I thought, he could reschedule them for later.

I finally found him in a small room off the audience chamber, looking over reports and making staff assignments. He greeted me warmly when I walked in.

"I trust you are satisfied with young Horace, Lord?" he said.

"Quite satisfied," I said. "He seems able and enthusiastic. I have no complaints."

"I am happy to hear it." He smiled, and I thought the news genuinely pleased him.

"Do you know where my father is?"

"Prince Dworkin has gone to inspect troops with Lord Locke and Lord Davin. They should return before dinner."

"Ah." I couldn't expect Dworkin to neglect his duties and wait for me, I supposed. Still, I'd hoped he would still be here.

"What of the tailors?" I said. "I'm afraid I missed all the appointments."

He consulted a set of papers on the desk before him. "I believe...yes, they are with Lady Blaise now," he said. "She is selecting fabrics for new officers' uniforms. That should take most of the afternoon. Will tomorrow morning be soon enough for you to see them?"

"Yes." I could always borrow more of Mattus's wardrobe, as needed.

"Very good, my Lord." He dipped a quill pen in ink and made a note of it. His handwriting, I noticed, was thin and ornate.

I continued, "Is there a workout yard in the castle?"

"Of course, Lord Oberon. Master Berushk will be at your service." He motioned to a page of perhaps nine or ten years, who wore castle livery and stood attentively by the door. "Show Lord Oberon to the workout yard," he said.

"Yes, sir," the page said.

\*     \*     \*

The boy led me outside to the front courtyard, with its broad flagstones, and then we passed through a small rose garden. The gate on the far side opened onto an enclosed courtyard perhaps fifty feet square. This had to be the place, I thought, looking at the practice dummies, racks of swords and other weapons. It even had a pivoting drill machine with wooden arms and swords.

Two men, stripped to the waist, now fought there with swords and knives, pivoting and thrusting, parrying and riposting. A third man, older and much scarred on his hands and face, looked on critically.

"This is it, Lord," the page said to me.

"Thanks. You may go."

"Yes, Lord." Bowing, he ran back the way we had come.

I turned my attention to the fighters, whom I now recognized as my half brothers Titus and Conner. They were workmanlike at best in their swordsmanship, I decided.

"Hold!" the third man said. Titus and Conner drew up short, panting and sweating.

"You're letting your guards down again," he said to both of them. I silently agreed with his assessment. "You cannot count on your opponent being as tired as you are. In a real battle, such mistakes would cost you your lives."

I pushed open the gate and went in. They all paused to look at me.

"Who is this?" Berushk asked.

"Oberon, our brother," Titus—or was it Conner?—said to him.

"Another soft and useless child?" said the weapons-master with a sneer, giving me a dismissive look from head to heel. "Well, young Oberon, I haven't seen you here before. Are you lost on your stroll through the roses? Off with you, and leave swordplay to real men."

I had to laugh. King Elnar's weapons-master had used almost exactly the same insults the first time we'd met. My temper had been hotter in those days, and as a fresh young officer, I'd had a lot to prove. Of course, I'd taken offense, drawn my blade, and demanded a fight on the spot. He'd obliged...and I'd very nearly killed him, the first student ever to do so. I *would* have killed him, had several others not dragged me away from the fight.

Only later had I found out that weapons-masters often goaded new pupils into fights to get a fair assessment of their abilities.

I just grinned at Berushk and said, "I'm happy to show you how it's done, old man. Do you have a spare sword?"

"Wood or steel?" he asked, grinning back.

"I'll borrow Conner's," I said. "With his permission."

"Of course." The twin on the right stepped forward, offering me the hilt of his sword. As he grew close, he turned his back to Berushk and whispered, "Watch yourself, he changes hands in the middle of a fight, and he likes to give dueling scars."

I gave him a wink.

"Now, let's see if I remember how this works," I said aloud. "I believe I hold it *so,* and the object is to poke you with the pointy end?"

Berushk smiled. "Enough games, boy." He made little circles with the tip of Titus's blade. "Show me your best."

I gave his a quick salute with the blade, then assumed a classical attack stance, right foot forward, left hand on my hip, blade up and ready.

He attacked fast and high, and I parried with little apparent grace or skill, making it seem—once—twice—again!—as though luck more than skill protected me. As sword rang on sword, I yielded ground steadily before him.

When he deliberately left an opening, I didn't take it. Instead, I hesitated, trying to appear indecisive. Let him think he had me confused and on the run, I thought. I was the master of this fight, not him. I would determine when and how it ended.

Sighing a bit, wanting to get our fight over and done so he could get on with lessons, he attacked with renewed vigor, this time using a quick double-feint designed to get around my guard.

My parry came a beat too slow. He twisted, lunged, backslashed with what should have struck a stinging blow to my right thigh.

Only his blow didn't land.

This was the chance I'd been waiting for. With the speed of a striking panther, I closed instead of retreating, moving inside his reach. His eyes grew wide. He realized too late!—what had just happened when his blade whistled through empty air.

I flipped my sword over to my left hand, grabbed his wrist with my right hand, and gave twist and a jerk. He staggered, off balance and over-extended. Without hesitation, I pivoted and kicked his left leg out from under him, and he sprawled onto his back with a whoosh of expelled air.

Stepping close, I pointed my sword at his throat.

"Yield?" I asked quietly.

He chuckled. "Well done, Oberon. Worthy of a Lord of Chaos. I yield."

Conner and Titus were staring at me like I'd just grown a second head.

"You *won?*" Titus said. "You actually *won?*"

I offered Berushk my hand, and he pulled himself up and dusted *off* his clothes somewhat ruefully.

*"That,"* he said to Conner and Titus, "is the way to fight a battle. Never reveal your strengths. Let your opponent misjudge and make the first mistake." He turned to me. "Who trained you, Lord Oberon?" I have never seen the *clave-à-main* used in such an *energetic* manner before!"

"My father," I said evenly. I tossed Conner his sword.

"That would explain it," Berushk said, smiling. "I have never seen him fight, though tales of his wild youth are still legend in the Courts of Chaos. He must have been quite accomplished."

"He still is," I said, thinking back to our battle with the hell-creatures in Kingstown. His swordsmanship had been nothing short of amazing. I went on, "I take it I've passed your test?"

"Lord Oberon," he said, "I fear there is little you can learn from me."

"I just came for a workout."

"That," he said, "we can do." He looked at Conner and Titus and winked at them a little too happily. "Can't we, boys?"

Berushk proved true to his word. I spent the next two hours in one of the most grueling exercise sessions of my life, fighting the three of them singly, paired, or all three at once.

I didn't lose a single contest, not even when Berushk tied back my left arm and put weights on my feet. It left me soaked in sweat and shaking, but I managed to tag them all with a wooden sword before my strength gave out.

"That's it for me today!" I said, panting.

"Well fought, Lord," Berushk said. He bowed to me.

I noticed our audience had grown to include a good dozen army officers and castle guardsmen. They began to clap and cheer, so I gave them a quick salute with my sword before returning it to the practice weapons rack. I had a feeling they'd be talking about my workout for some time.

Then I toweled off, thanked Berushk for his time and trouble, and headed inside. The watchers parted silently as I passed through their ranks.

Conner and Titus hurried to join me.

"I think you're as good as Locke," Conner told me.

"Maybe better," said Titus. "Berushk still beats him now and again."

I laughed. "That's just because they work out together. They know each other's tricks."

"Even so..."

And we spent the walk up to our rooms chatting like old friends. I had found them dour and distant at dinner, but once they relaxed, I found I actually enjoyed their company.

We reached our floor and went our separate ways. That's when I noticed the door to my rooms stood open. So much for my plans for a quiet rest before dinner.

I peeked around the door frame, expecting the worst.

Instead of lurking assassins, however, I found Freda and Aber waiting inside for me. Freda, at the writing table, had her set of cards out and was turning them over one by one, studying the emerging pattern. She did not look happy.

"Problems?" I asked Aber quietly as I entered. "Doesn't she like what she sees?"

"The problem is, she's not seeing *anything.*"

I raised my eyebrows. "Is that bad?"

"I don't know." He folded his arms and frowned. "She won't tell me."

That made me smile. "You should join me in the workout yard tomorrow," I said, heading for my bedroom and the washbasin. I'd need to get cleaned up for dinner. "It's a good way to get your exercise and bond with your brothers."

"The problem with that," he said, "is that I don't *like* my brothers all that much. Present company excepted, of course."

"Of course," I said.

"And as for bonding with them?" He gave a mock shudder. "No thank you! Who did you work out with?"

"Conner and Titus. And an interesting weapons-master named Berushk."

"I met him once. All he did was insult me!"

"What did you do?"

"I told him to grow up and went back inside."

I had to laugh. "Everyone says a battle is coming. Don't you want to be ready?"

"Oh, don't worry about me. I have a plan. If we're attacked, I'm going to stand well out of the way while you and Locke and Dad kill everyone."

I snorted. "That's not much of a plan."

"It will do for now."

"Have you seen Horace?"

"Who?"

"My valet."

"Oh, him. No. Want me to send someone to find him?"

"No...just show me the way to Mattus's closet, will you? I need some clean clothes."

"Sure. Come on." He started for the door, and I trailed him.

Before we made it out, though, Freda said, "Oberon, please come here first. I want you to shuffle these Trumps."

"All right," I said. "If you think it will help."

As I reached for them, a loud bell began to toll close by, its peals loud and incessant, coming every few seconds. I paused, listening, counting. Five then eight then ten strikes, and then it stopped.

Freda had an anxious expression on her face. Rising, she began to pack up her cards.

"What does that bell mean?" I demanded.

"An emergency!" Aber said. "We have five minutes to report to the main hall!"

## FIFTEEN

Let me get my sword first," I said. I wasn't making the mistake again of getting sent off gods-knew-where without being properly armed.

Running back into my bedroom, I grabbed my swordbelt and buckled it on. Then I rejoined Freda and Aber, and together we hurried downstairs. Titus and Conner followed almost on our heels.

We met Locke and Davin on the ground floor. Both looked grim.

"Anyone know what the problem is?" Locke asked us.

"Sorry, no," I said. "You?"

"No." He turned and headed for the audience hall at a jog, Davin at his heels. Aber and I followed them.

"How often has the alarm been rung?" I asked Aber.

"First time that I know of," he said. "It's only supposed to be rung in the direst of emergencies."

"Like an attack?"

He gulped. "Yes!"

We reached the audience chamber, and there Anari directed us to a small antechamber off to the left. Inside, Dworkin sat at a table covered with maps of the lands around Juniper. A soldier with that extra joint in his arms stood stiffly at attention before him. I noticed he had minor wounds on his hands and arms, and what appeared to be burns on the left side of his face.

I nudged Aber. "He's been fighting hell-creatures," I whispered.

Aber looked suddenly terrified. "Here?" he whispered back. "Then it's begun?"

"What is it?" Locke demanded of our father and the soldier. "What's happened?"

"Tell them, Captain," Dworkin said.

"Yes, Prince." Slowly, in strangely accented tones, the officer began his report. "We were on the dawn patrol—"

"That's ten men on foot walking the forest line," I overheard Davin whisper to Blaise.

"—and there was a wind blowing from the forest. I smelled fresh horse manure and knew it could not have come from our camp. No horse patrols go there. I ordered everyone to spread out, and we entered the trees to investigate.

"Almost immediately we came upon a small campsite, well hidden. Three devils were waiting for us with their fire-breathing mounts. They attacked and killed four of my men. We killed one, and when that happened, the other two fled. We could not catch them on foot. They seemed to vanish into the trees. Men are searching for them now, but…" He shrugged. "I do not have much hope for the finding."

"Hell-creatures come and go like that," I said, half to myself. "You never see their raiders—or their spies—until it's too late, and you never find them when they run."

Davin shot me a curious glance. "You know them?" he demanded. "How?"

"They tried to kill Dad and me the day before yesterday. I've been fighting them for the last year in Ilerium."

"How can we be sure it's them?" Aber said.

I shrugged. "How many other armies have fire-breathing horses?"

Locke said to the captain, "How long had they been there?"

"No more than two or three days, General."

Locke turned to our father. "I must see that campsite. They fled quickly. Perhaps they left something behind."

"A good idea," Dworkin said, nodding. "Take Davin with you…and Oberon."

"Oberon?" Locke asked. I heard doubt in his voice. "Are you sure—?"

I stepped forward. "As I just said, I've been fighting hell-creatures for more than a year now. I think I know them better than anyone else here." *Or almost anyone else,* I thought, looking around the circle of faces. We still had a traitor in our midst.

"Very well," he said with a shrug of acceptance, no taunting or baiting now, when it really mattered.

I had half expected a childish display of temper, and my opinion of him as a soldier went up a notch. A very small notch.

"Get your wounds looked after, Captain," Locke said. "Meet us at the stables in twenty minutes. We'll have a fresh horse ready for you."

"Yes, General," he said. He gave Locke a raised-palm salute, then hurried from the hall.

"The time is here," Dworkin said softly, brow creased. "They will move against us shortly, if they are sending watchers. We must be prepared." He looked up at us, at Locke, Davin, and me. "Be on your guard. They will kill you if they have a chance. Do not give them one!"

I trailed Locke and Davin to the stables. Now that we had a task to do, Locke moved with the deftness and speed of an experienced commander, calling for horses and a mounted squad. Grooms hurried to obey, and guards went running to the camp outside to summon the men he wanted to accompany us.

"Better add more guards to Juniper's walls," I suggested in a quiet voice as we waited for our horses. "Put more guards at the gates, too. Have everyone searched coming in...and going out. The hell-creatures are shape-shifters. No telling what they might try to smuggle in...or out."

"Shape-shifters! You're certain!"

"Yes," I said, thinking of Ivinius, so well disguised as a human barber that he had gotten close enough to slit my throat.

"Very well. I'll take your word on it."

With a frown, he waved over the Captain of the Guard and gave him instructions, The man took off running a moment later.

"Extra guards," Locke told me, "at the gate. Extra patrols on the walls. Anything else you'd suggest?"

"Just...after this, trust no one."

He raised his eyebrows at that, but made no reply.

"Aren't you going to ask...?" I said.

"No. I recognize Freda's words."

Instead of denying it, I chuckled. "Yes. But she's right, at least in this particular instance. A hell-creature almost killed me once by impersonating a barber. I'd hate to have the same thing happen to you."

Locke gave me another odd look. "You aren't what I expected," he admitted. "You surprise me, brother."

"This is the second time I've been told that since I got here."

"Freda—?" He hesitated.

"No. If you must know, it was Aber. He expected me to be just like you, from Dad's tales, and apparently you two don't always see eye to eye."

Locke shrugged. "Such is life," he said philosophically. "There are only sheep and wolves. I have never much wanted to be a sheep."

"As for me...I simply don't care about our family's politics," I told him. "You're all strangers...except, of course, our father." I'd almost said Dworkin. "My only concern is keeping alive—and the best way for me to do that is to keep the rest of you alive, too. We all want the same thing, so we might as well work together."

"Well spoken." He hesitated. "Later, tonight perhaps, we must have a talk...just you and me, alone."

"I'd welcome it."

He gave a curt nod and looked away.

A private talk...I took his invitation as something akin to an apology—or at least as an admission that I wasn't as horrible as he'd thought. Slow progress, but progress nonetheless.

Our horses had been saddled and were now being led into the courtyard. He stepped over to a handsome black stallion, about sixteen hands high, who nuzzled his palms looking for sugar. I felt a pang of envy—the stallion was a magnificent animal, and Locke patted his neck affectionately.

They had brought me a dappled gray mare, who seemed good tempered and fit. She would do, I decided, looking her over. Davin had a chestnut gelding with white socks on both front feet, full of nervous energy. The extra-jointed captain who would be leading us had another dappled gray mare like enough to mine that I couldn't have told them apart.

"Mount up!" Locke called.

I swung into the mare's saddle and followed Locke and the others out through Juniper's gate. Twenty more horsemen waited outside for us, and they fell in behind, two side-by-side columns, as we turned left and cut through the army camp. Ahead, perhaps five or six miles away, I could see the dark line of trees that marked the edge of a dense forest. The land had been cleared for farming all the way to its edge, but no crops had been planted and the military camp didn't extend all the way to its edge. It seemed an ideal place from which to spy on us.

When I glanced over my shoulder, I spotted extra guards just now coming out onto the castle battlements, and the two men normally stationed at the gates had grown to eight.

I caught up with the captain who'd found the hell-creatures. His wounds had been cleaned and dressed, and the minor burns on his face gleamed with ointment.

"I'm Oberon," I told him. "I am called d'Darjan, Lord." He inclined his head. "If it pleases you."

"These spies you found...had you ever seen their like before?"

He hesitated. "No, Lord."

I had the impression he knew more than that, but didn't want to speak too openly to me. After all, he had never seen me before today and didn't know my loyalties. And who knew what rumors were circulating among the guards about me...one overheard insulting remark between Davin and Locke might well fuel a dozen stories among the guards and soldiers of my treachery, cowardice, or worse.

I let my mare fall back, and he spurred his to catch up with Locke. They talked in low voices, with Captain d'Darjan pointing ahead. Then Locke glanced back at me and nodded, and I guessed d'Darjan had asked what he could safely tell me. Nothing to do but wait, I thought with growing impatience.

A thirty-minute ride brought us to the edge of an ancient forest. A thick hedge of gorse bushes and blackberry brambles, threaded with trails, grew along its edge.

I studied the tall oaks and maples, many with trunks as wide around as my arms could reach, that towered a hundred feet over us. They would provide ample vantage points for spying, I thought.

I rode forward to join d'Darjan and my brothers. The rest of the soldiers reined in behind us.

"This is it, General," Captain d'Darjan said, indicating what looked like a deer track that wound between the gorse bushes and circled out of sight. It would be a prickly, uncomfortable ride, but I thought a horse could make it through. "There is another path on the other side, but it is no larger."

"Fan out into the forest and keep watch," Locke called to the soldiers behind us. He dismounted. Davin and I did the same. "Be on your guard. Shout if you see anything unusual. If you spot the enemy, fall back at once."

His men wheeled their horses and began moving slowly into the forest down various trails, sharp-eyed and ready for battle. I didn't think anything or anyone would be able to sneak up on us.

"Let's take a look at their camp," Locke said. He tethered his horse, drew his sword, took a deep breath, and marched into the thicket.

Davin followed him, and I followed Davin. Captain d'Darjan brought up the rear.

I had to admit the hell-creatures had chosen their hiding spot well. From the outside, you would never have guessed their camp lay hidden within the thicket. The trail, little bigger than a deer track, widened after a few paces and a turn, and only there did I spot the impressions of horse hooves in the soft earth.

We circled in toward the center of the thicket. There, an area perhaps twenty feet across, with a tall oak at its center, had been cleared with small axes.

The hell-creatures had clearly left in haste, abandoning three bedrolls, a small coil of rope, and a wickedly barbed knife. They had even dug a small fire pit and rimmed it with large rocks to hide the flames.

I found a stick and stirred the ashes, uncovering the well-gnawed bones of what looked to be rats or squirrels. A few embers still gleamed faintly orange-red.

Rising, I looked at the tree. A broken branch at eye level still oozed sap, I found. From the evidence, they probably hadn't been here more than a day or two, as captain d'Darjan had said.

"Here's where they tethered their horses," Davin said, squatting and examining the markings. "Three of them, all right."

I turned slowly, looking for anything else out of the ordinary. The oak tree at the center of the thicket had several more broken branches about twenty feet off the ground.

"They climbed up to spy on us," I said, pointing.

"Take a look," Locke said.

I grabbed a sturdy looking limb and pulled myself up. It was an easy climb, and sure enough, when I reached the broken limbs I discovered I could see both the military camp and the castle with an unobstructed view.

"Well?" Locke called up.

"I can see everything," I said, squinting. "Troops, horse pens, even Juniper." "So they know how many we are," Davin said, "and where we're placed."

I began to climb down, then dropped the last five feet. "And they know the lay of the land now," I added. "They were scouting for an attack."

"They may come back," Locke said. He hesitated, looking up the tree, then down the trail. "We're going to have to clear out all the brush at the edge of the forest and post sentries. This can't happen again."

"Burn it off?" Davin asked.

I left them and went to the abandoned bedrolls. When I picked the first one up, something small fluttered down from its folds...a Trump, I realized from its blue back, complete with gold lion. I glanced at Locke and Davin, but they hadn't noticed.

"No," Locke was saying. He had turned to face the other way, toward the heart of the forest. "We can't risk a fire spreading out of control and reaching the camp. It will have to be done by hand."

Carefully, trying to avoid attracting my brothers' attention, I turned my back to them, picked up the card, and flipped it over.

It had Locke's picture on it.

The hair on the back of my neck prickled with alarm. I glanced over my shoulder, but he and Davin were busy talking and weren't paying the slightest attention to me. They hadn't seen my discovery.

And I couldn't let them see it. I saw the need for great care; in this family, it seemed I could never trust anyone if there was an alternative.

"I'll get a detachment out as soon as we get back," Davin said. "It's going to be a two-day job, possibly three."

I tucked the card into my sleeve, then rejoined them with a sigh of mock disgust.

"Nothing else here," I announced.

Locke gave a nod, then turned and led the way back toward our horses. The cool touch of the Trump against my arm was a constant reminder of my discovery.

*Locke...*

Why would the hell-creatures have *his* Trump...unless they needed to contact him?

And why would they contact him...unless he was the traitor?

## SIXTEEN

On the trip back to Juniper, I ranged ahead of the others, leaving Locke and Davin with their men. I rode neither hard nor fast enough to attract undue attention, but managed to get back a good ten minutes ahead of them.

All the way, winding through the tent city of their soldiers, crossing the drawbridge, and into the castle's courtyard, I kept turning the implications of my discovery over and over in my mind.

We had a traitor in our midst. Ivinius's presence—and the disappearance of his body—proved it. And the traitor had to be someone capable of using Trumps...which meant a family member.

But *Locke?*

Well, why *not* Locke?

He had been nothing short of hostile until this morning. And since Dworkin—I still found it hard to call him Dad—trusted him with the defenses of Juniper, his betrayal would be truly disastrous.

Or was I allowing personal dislike to cloud my judgment?

Safely ahead of the others, I pulled out the Trump I'd found, turned it over, and studied it without concentrating too hard on the picture. Locke...drawn exactly the same way as Freda's Trump had been.

In fact, I realized with some dismay, this could be Freda's Trump. But they couldn't *both* be in league with hell-creatures...could they?

I knew one fact that might help: Aber had created this card. I'd ask him who it belonged to as soon as we got back to Juniper. If he could identify it...

I left my horse with the grooms and went looking for Aber. I found Freda standing in the audience hall with Pella, Blaise, and a couple of women I didn't recognize. The warning bell must have brought everyone out looking for news or rumors.

I joined them.

"Did you find anything?" Freda asked me, once suitable introductions had been made. As I had suspected, the women I didn't recognize were the wives of two of Dworkin's chancellors.

"I'm afraid not," I said. I didn't mention the Trump I'd found. "It was just a camp site. They had been spying on us for a couple of days."

"Too bad. Are you all back now? Safe?"

"I'm a little ahead of the others," I said, glancing toward the door. "Locke wants to clear the brush at the edge of the forest, and I'm sure he's going to stop and detail those duties before reporting back. He and Davin shouldn't be too long."

She nodded thoughtfully, then took my arm and drew me aside. "And how did you find Locke today?" she asked more softly.

"Less..." I searched for the right word. "Less upset by my presence. I think he's begun to accept me. Who knows, we might even end up friends."

"Davin gave him a complete report about what Father said about you last night."

I smiled lightly. "Yes, I got the feeling he knew about it. He has nothing to fear from me now. I cannot take his place without the Logrus."

"Do not place too much trust in him yet. He may not view you as an enemy, but you are still a rival."

"I won't," I promised. What would she think if she knew he wanted a private chat with me tonight? "Trust must be earned. He certainly hasn't earned any yet."

*And he won't earn it as long as there's a chance he's our traitor,* I added silently.

"Good." She smiled, the small lines at the corners of her eyes and mouth crinkling. "I hope you both make an effort at it. You can be of great help with the army, I know."

"I hope so," I said. Deliberately changing the subject, I asked, "Have you seen Aber?"

"Aber Not since you left. You might look in his rooms. That's where he spends most afternoons."

"Thank you," I said. I gave her and the chancellors' wives a polite nod, then headed for the stairs. "Until dinner."

Today I felt more comfortable navigating the castle's seemingly endless stairs and corridors, and found my way safely to my rooms. I found Horace in my bedroom. My bed was covered with heaps of clothing.

"What's all this?" I asked, staring.

"Mattus's clothing, Lord," Horace said, folding a shirt deftly and placing it in the wardrobe. "Lord Aber said I should bring it in for you."

"Thoughtful of him."

"Yes, Lord."

I realized I hadn't had a chance to change yet from my workout, and now I stank not just of sweat, but of horse.

"Pick out new clothes for me," I said, heading for the washbasin. "Then get the rest of them put away." I'd clean up before going to see Aber, I decided.

Five minutes later, I went to Aber's room and knocked sharply.

He called, "Enter at your own risk!" in cheerful tones.

I went in and found him sitting at a drafting table by the windows. Small bottles of colored pigments sat all around him, and he held a tiny horsehair brush in one hand.

He paused in his work. "What news from the woods, brother?" he asked.

"Nothing more than we already heard," I said with a shrug. "The hell-creatures were long gone."

"A pity," he said.

I came closer, looking at the half-dozen Trumps sitting out on the table. "What are you doing?"

"Making a Trump."

He picked it up and turned it so I could see...and though only half finished, it clearly showed a man standing with feet spread and sword raised, ready for battle. He was dressed all in deep blues with black trim, and his cloak ruffled faintly as though from a steady breeze. In the white spaces of the unfinished background, ever so faintly, I noticed a lacework pattern of thin black lines...curves and angles that seemed to reach deep into the card, somehow, like a three-dimensional puzzle. A representation of the Logrus? I suspected so.

Aber had just begun coloring the face when I walked in. With some surprise, I realized it was a miniature portrait of me.

"What do you think of this one?" he asked. "I'm making it for Freda. She told me she wanted it last night, after dinner."

"No more candles?"

He chuckled. "Actually, that one was supposed to be Mattus. I finished it up this morning with your face." He shrugged apologetically. "I was in a hurry."

"And a good thing you were. You probably saved my life."

"Ah, how ironic! The artist saves the warrior."

I laughed. "It was still a good likeness, even if it started out as a picture of Mattus. And I'm even more flattered by this one."

"Really?" He seemed honestly delighted. "You know, I think you're the first person who's ever said that to me!"

I regarded his new card carefully. "Blue is not really my color, though," I said. "How about red next time?"

"The colors don't matter, it's the person and how the image is drawn." He set it back in the last of the dying sunlight. "Have to let it dry now, anyway," he said. "So, what brings you here?"

I hesitated. *Trust* no *one,* Freda had said. But this was something I couldn't do alone. I needed an ally...and of all my family, I liked Aber most of all. If I had to trust someone, it had to be him...for no other reason than he was the one most likely to recognize the Trump I'd found. It wasn't an easy decision, but once made, I knew it was the right one.

"I want you to look at something." I pulled out the Locke's Trump and handed it to him. "I found it. Is it yours?"

"Well, I made it." He turned it over and pointed to the rampant lion painted in gold on the back. "I put a lion on all of mine. Dad never bothered with such niceties when he made Trumps."

"Do you know who you made it for?"

He shrugged. "Why not ask at dinner? I'm sure whoever's lost it wants it back." "I...do have a reason."

"But you're not going to say."

"No. Not right now."

"Hmm." He studied me thoughtfully, then raised the Trump for a second, studying it more carefully. "Honestly, I'm not sure who I made it for," he admitted. "I've done at least twenty of Locke over the years, and I always copy my original. They all look pretty much the same."

He opened a drawer in the table and pulled out a small teak box similar to the one he'd given me, but with polished brass corners. He swung back the lid and pulled out a set of perhaps fifty or sixty cards, fanned them open, and pulled one out.

When he set it beside the Trump I had found, they appeared identical. I wouldn't have been able to tell them apart. No wonder it had looked like Freda's—he really *had* been copying his original card over and over. And with twenty of them out there...this Trump could belong to anyone.

"Sorry," he said. "Like I told you, ask at dinner. That's your best bet."

I shook my head. "I can't do that. Do you think it might be Locke's?"

"No."

"Why not?"

"I never give anyone their own Trump. It's a waste of my time. Why would you want to contact yourself?"

It made sense. And yet, when I thought back to my carriage ride, envisioning the Trumps I'd seen on the table, I was pretty sure Freda had one of herself.

"What about Freda?" I asked. "Doesn't she..."

"Oh, that's different." He laughed. "She reads patterns from them, so she needs one of everyone in the family, including herself. That's what you get for growing up in the Courts. People are...different there. They think and teach and learn things that the rest of us, who grew up in Shadows, can only long for."

I nodded. It all fit. "So Locke wouldn't need it. He couldn't use it. But Davin..."

"Yes, it might be his." Aber's eyes narrowed a bit with sudden suspicion. "Why are you asking all these questions? Something's wrong. Where did you *really* get it...in the enemy's camp?"

I hesitated. If I could trust one family member, somehow I thought it would be Aber. Should I tell him? I needed an ally someone in whom I could confide and seek advice...someone who knew Juniper. And if anything happened to me, if another hell-creature managed to assassinate me, I wanted the truth known. He had just guessed where the card had come from, after all. What could it hurt to tell him the truth...or as much of it as he needed to know?

"That's it, isn't it?" He took my silence for confirmation. "So...they have our Trumps."

I took a deep breath. Against my instincts for secrecy, I told him how I had found the Trump, hidden it from Locke and Davin, and brought it back with me.

Then I told him my suspicions about a traitor in Juniper.

"And you thought these spies had been talking to Locke," he said, folding his hands together under his chin thoughtfully. "You thought Locke might betray us."

"That was the general idea," I admitted. "He's been the most, ah, *hostile*, after all."

"You're wrong," Aber said bluntly. He looked me straight in the eye. "Locke doesn't have the imagination or the ambition to betray anyone. He and Davin spent the last year training the army for Dad. They will both fight to the death, if necessary, to protect us."

"Maybe he thinks we're going to lose and wants to be on the winning side."

"They are trying to wipe out our bloodline. Why would they let *him* live?"

"Deals have been made before."

"Not with Locke."

"Then how do you explain this?" I tapped the Trump with my finger. "Maybe they agreed to let him live out his years in exile. It's a small price it he can deliver Juniper...all of *us.*"

"I don't know." His brow furrowed again. "There are at least four sets of Trumps missing...Mattus, Alanar, Taine, and Clay all carried them. This card could easily be one of theirs."

"Then why *Locke?*" I demanded. "Why would hell-creatures carry *his* card and no others?"

"And why would they forget it when they left?" Aber countered. "It's not the sort of thing you'd *accidentally* leave behind when you clear out camp. And, for that matter, it's not the sort of thing a routine scout would carry."

"I see your point," I admitted.

"What if they *wanted* us to find it," he went on. "What if they *planned* the whole thing, right down to hiding that card in the bedroll?"

The idea hadn't occurred to me. It was devious...exactly the sort of trick a hell-creature might try.

Aber went on, "If Dad stripped Locke of his command, it would do us real damage. The men love him and will follow him to the seven hells and back, if he asks. Davin isn't half the leader Locke is. And the men don't know you well enough to follow you. Losing Locke would be a terrible blow."

"You have a good point," I admitted

"So, what are you going to do?" he asked. "Tell Dad or keep it to yourself?"

"I'm not sure yet," I said. "If only you recognized the Trump!"

I began to pace, thinking. Everything had seemed much clearer before I'd talked to Aber, when Locke looked guilty. Now, according to Aber, finding the Trump meant the traitor could be anyone *except* Locke.

*Who?*

I sighed. "Plots and schemes have never come easily to me," I told him.

"Nor to me," he said. "It takes a lot more patience than I have. You'd be better off talking to Blaise, if you want that sort of advice."

"Blaise?" His suggestion left me faintly baffled. "Why her? I would've thought you'd send me to Freda."

"Freda is no amateur, but Blaise is the *true* master when it comes to intrigue. Nothing happens in Juniper without her hearing about it."

*"Blaise?"* I said again. "Our *sister* Blaise?"

He gave a chuckle at my bewildered expression.

"Don't let her fool you," he said. "She's got a regular network of spies. Half the staff is in her pay."

"And the other half?"

"Sleeping with her."

I snorted. "Well, it saves money, I suppose," I said.

*Blaise...*It was something to think about. I hadn't even considered her. From our first meeting, I'd gotten the impression she knew little beyond what jewelry to wear with which clothes to such-and-such a court function—an important skill in its way, I'm sure, but not one I'd ever found particularly useful. Perhaps I had been too quick to dismiss her.

And then, just when Aber had me half believing I'd been fooled into believing we had a spy among us by the planted Trump, I remembered Ivinius the barber, who had tried to kill me in my rooms. He'd been smuggled into the castle for the sole purpose of killing me, and by someone who knew who I was and what I needed to hear to put me off my guard.

So who had sent Ivinius to kill me? And how had he or she gotten the body out of my rooms without being seen?

"But I do know—without any doubt—that we have a traitor in Juniper," I continued.

He blinked in surprise. "What! Who?"

"I don't know—yet."

Then I told him how Ivinius had tried to slit my throat in my room. It felt good to share this secret, too.

"So *that's* why you jumped at me when I Trumped in," he said. "You thought I'd come to check on your murder!"

"Or to finish the job."I sighed and shook my head. "If it had only been Locke instead of you...things would certainly be a lot simpler right now."

"You were lucky," he said slowly. "If it had been Locke, you'd be dead. He's the best swordsman among us."

"You've never seen me fight."

He shrugged. "I concede the point. But Locke's the best swordsman *I've* ever seen. He was schooled by a dozen weapons-masters in the Courts of Chaos. He grew up with blades in both hands. His mother, after all—"

"Freda mentioned her," I said. "Some sort of hell-creature?"

"The Lady Ryassa de Lyor ab Sytalla is hardly a hell-creature."

"Then you've met her?"

"Not formally, no...but I've seen her half a dozen times."

I shrugged. "You're probably right. Father never would have married her otherwise."

"True."

"And," I said, "if you say Locke's a great swordsman, I'll accept that, even though I've never seen him fight."

"Good."

"It's just that I made the mistake of letting down my guard, thinking I was safe here. It won't happen again. Not with anyone."

He pursed his lips again. "A traitor...that's something none of us has ever talked about before. Yet it makes a lot of sense. This Shadow is very, very far from the Courts. About as far as you can get and still use the Logrus. We should have been safe here...and yet they found us fairly quickly."

I spread my hands in a half shrug. "So...what now?"

"Blaise ..." he hesitated.

"The same qualities that make her a likely ally also make her a likely suspect. She could have gotten Ivinius into the castle and sent him to my room."

"True. She saw what you looked like when we had drinks, so she knew you needed a shave and a haircut. But you could say the same for Pella, Freda, and me, too. Or Dad, for that matter. Or anyone you passed in the corridor."

"Or anyone who saw me get out of the carriage when we got here," I said, remembering the crowd that had surrounded Dad. Locke and Davin had been among them...plus several dozen others, anyone of whom could have said the wrong word to the wrong person and set me up.

I sighed. Clearly we weren't getting anywhere.

"What do we do now?" I asked.

"Tell Blaise about the Trump you found," he said, "and your suspicions. The more I think about it, the more I believe she'll be able to help you. I'll tell Freda. Perhaps one of them will have an answer."

"Don't tell them about the hell-creature barber yet," I said. "I don't want to tip my hand."

"No...you're right, of course. Save that. It may be important later."


I found Blaise's rooms on the floor above, and her serving girl showed me into a sitting room done in bright colors, with fresh cut flowers in intricate arrangements all around. My sister reclined on a small sofa, a glass of red wine in one hand and a pretty young man in the other. He kissed her fingers, rose with a sideways glance at me, and slipped out the side door. I watched him go without comment, thinking of Aber's jibe that she slept with half the serving staff. An exaggeration, of course...at least, I hoped so.

"Oberon," she said, rising.

I kissed the cheek she offered.

"Blaise," I said. "You're looking lovely."

"Thank you." She wore that wide, predatory smile again, and all my mistrust came flooding back. "I'm glad you've come to see me," she said. "May I offer you some wine?"

"No, thank you." "It's time we had a talk. But I certainly hadn't expected to see you so soon."

Glancing pointedly at her serving girl, I said, "This isn't really a social call."

"No?"

"Aber thought I should seek your advice."

"Interesting." She smiled. "Go on."

"Alone, if you don't mind."

She made a little motion with one hand, and her serving girl curtsied and withdrew, shutting the door. Only then did I turn back to my half sister.

"I'm listening," she said, more businesslike than before. She set down her glass, folded her hands in her lap, and looked up at me curiously.

I took a deep breath. What did I have to lose at this point? I didn't know who to trust and who to suspect, so I might as well put all the evidence out in the open. Perhaps she would have more insight than Aber and I did.

Quickly, before I could change my mind, I told her everything, starting with Ivinius trying to slit my throat and ending with the Trump I'd found in the hell-creature's camp. A little to my surprise, she neither interrupted nor showed the slightest concern. She merely looked thoughtful.

"What do you think?" I asked.

"That you are a damned fool," she said sharply. "You should not have hidden an assassination attempt. This isn't a game, Oberon. If we are in danger in Juniper, we all have a right to know!"

I bristled at that, but did not reply. Unfortunately, I thought she might be right. I *had* handled it wrong. I should have gone straight to Dad as soon as I'd killed Ivinius.

"What's done is done," I finally said, "and cannot be changed. I thought I made the right decision at the time."

"And now you've come to me?"

"Aber seems to think you might have a certain...*insight* into whatever plots are going on around us."

"Hmm." She leaned back on the couch, drumming her fingers on its arm, eyes distant. "I'm not sure whether to be flattered or insulted. There has never been much love between Aber and me, you know."

"We don't need love. We need cooperation."

She looked me in the eye. "You are quite right, Oberon. This is not a petty squabble among siblings. We are all involved, and we are all in mortal danger. If we are not careful, we will all end up dead."

"Do you know anything about Ivinius?" I asked.

"He performed his job well and faithfully for many years. He was married. I believe his wife died about a week ago."

"Murdered?" I asked.

She shrugged. "When a woman of seventy-odd years dies in her sleep, who questions it? Not I."

"I suppose not." I sat on the chair opposite her. "*Of* course, Ivinius's wife would have known *immediately* if someone began impersonating him. I bet they killed her to keep her quiet."

"A hell-creature impersonating Ivinius would need help. A stranger could never sneak into Juniper, replace a skilled tradesman, and impersonate him perfectly without some assistance. It had to be someone with a knowledge of the castle's routine, who brought him here and coached him on what to say and what to do."

I reminded her that the body had been removed from my rooms.

"That narrows down our list of suspects."

"Not really," I said. "The door wasn't locked. Anyone could have walked in, found Ivinius's body, and escaped with it."

"Anybody might have slipped in," she said, "but no one saw a body being carried out. I would have heard. You cannot hide a death here...which means whoever took the body used a Trump."

"A family member?"

"Yes."

"That's what I concluded," I said. "Someone who knew I arrived in need of a shave and a haircut. You, Freda, Aber, Pella, Davin, and Locke all saw me. I don't know whether any of the others did."

"And then you found Locke's Trump in the hell-creatures' camp," she said, frowning.

"Yes. But Aber doesn't think he's the traitor."

"Locke is guilty of many things, but he wouldn't plot with our enemies. They planted that card for us to find."

"That's what Aber said, too. But if not Locke, then who?"

"I think I know."

"Tell me!"

Blaise shook her head as she rose. "Not yet," she said firmly. "I have no proof. We must see Father first. This can, not wait."

She hurried me out and down a series of back staircases and plainly furnished corridors through which a constant stream of servants moved until I had quite lost all sense of direction. Juniper was *big*. But when we pushed out into a main hallway, I realized we'd taken a shortcut and reached Dad's workshop in about half the time it normally would have taken from my suite.

Now that she had a purpose, she moved with a speed and determination that surprised me. Who did she suspect? As Aber had said, there was more to her than I'd thought.

She swept past the two guards, with me still trailing, and knocked on our father's workshop door.

Dworkin opened it after a heartbeat, peered up at the two of us, then stood back for us to enter.

"This is an odd pairing, I would say. What brings you here together?"

"Tell him," Blaise said, looking at me.

So, for the third time that afternoon, I repeated my story, leaving nothing out. Then I told him our conclusions, down to our having a traitor in the family.

"I know I should have come to you sooner," I said, "and I'm sorry for that. I didn't know who I should trust...so I trusted no one."

"You thought you were doing the right thing," Dworkin said. "We will get to the bottom of this matter."

"Blaise thinks she knows who the traitor is," I added.

"Oh?" He looked at her, surprised and pleased.

"That's right, Father. It can only be Freda."

## SEVENTEEN

"Freda!" he and I said as one. I couldn't believe it.

"That's right."

*"But—why?"* I said.

"Who else could it possibly be?" Blaise said. "She has more Trumps than any of us except Aber. She's said several times that we cannot win the coming battle. And she refuses to name those who have set themselves against us."

"I am not sure *refuses* is the correct word," Dworkin said. "She cannot see who they are."

"She has named the guilty often enough before," Blaise said, folding her arms stubbornly. "Why not this time...unless she is helping them?"

"No," Dworkin said. "I cannot believe it. Wild accusations prove nothing."

"Then how about proof." She leaned forward. "Freda went into Oberon's rooms yesterday morning...after he went downstairs to see you. She went in alone, and she didn't come out."

"How do you know this?" Dworkin demanded.

"One of the scrubwomen told me."

"A spy?" I said.

She smiled at me. "Not at all. I simply asked some of the servants to keep an eye on you, in case you needed help. She noticed Freda going in after you had left, and when Freda didn't come out, it struck her as odd. She mentioned it to me this morning."

Dworkin turned away, and when he spoke again, his voice shook. "Summon Locke," he said. "And Freda."

We had quite a little gathering in Dad's workshop: Locke arrived with Davin in tow, and Freda came with Aber. No reason had been given, just that our father wanted them.

I had to repeat my story a fourth time for Locke's benefit, and I went through the details quickly and surely. When I mentioned finding his Trump hidden in the bedroll, he leaped to his feet.

"I had nothing to do with them!" he said.

"Sit down," our father said. "We know that. They clearly planted the card there, hoping to discredit you." He looked at me. "Continue, Oberon."

I finished up with the discussion Aber and I had, where we agreed that the hell-creatures were trying to get Locke removed.

"See?" Davin said to him in a whisper. "They fear you."

Then Blaise told how Freda had been seen entering my rooms...and how she hadn't come out.

I stepped forward. "Unfortunately, eyewitnesses don't prove anything," I said. "Remember, the hell-creatures are shape-shifters. One of them could easily have disguised himself as Freda."

"How could they—" Blaise began.

I said, "Look!"

Closing my eyes, I envisioned Freda's face in my mind, her long hair, the thin lines around her eyes, the shape of her jaws and cheeks. I held that image, made it my own, and then I opened my eyes.

"See?" I said with Freda's voice. From the shocked faces of everyone around me, I knew my old childhood trick still worked. My face now looked exactly like Freda's. "Anyone can do it."

"How—" Blaise breathed.

Dworkin chuckled. "A simple enough trick. You have never tried to change your face, have you, my girl?"

Blaise looked from Freda to me and back again. Then, when she opened her mouth, no words came out.

"I have something to say," Freda said, standing. She glared at Blaise. "First, my comings and goings are of no concern to anyone but myself. I don't need your *spies* peeking at me from behind every wash-bucket in the castle. Second, I *did* go to Oberon's rooms yesterday. He wasn't there, so I left. And I used a Trump—we all do."

"Where did you go?" Blaise countered. "Off to hide the body?"

"If you must know, I returned to my room," Freda said coolly.

"What did you want with me?" I asked her.

"I wanted to read your cards. Just like this afternoon...only I didn't get a chance then, either."

"See?" Dworkin said. "A simple explanation."

"Then who removed the body?" Locke said.

Nobody had an answer.

Then, for the second time that day, a distant bell began to sound an alarm.

Locke led the way out to the audience hall, where a man dressed as a lieutenant stood waiting with two other men. They were panting and soaked in sweat.

"General!" he gasped, saluting Locke, "they're doing something to the sky!"

"What?" Locke demanded.

"I don't know!"

As one, we ran to the windows and peered up at the sky.

Directly over Juniper, immense black clouds now boiled and seethed. A strange bluish lightning flickered. The cloud grew larger as we watched, and slowly it began to move, swirling, spiraling inward.

"What is it, Dad?" I asked Dworkin.

"I have never seen its like before," he admitted. "Freda?"

"No. But I do not like it."

"Nor I," said Locke.

"Where is Anari?" Dworkin said.

"Here, Prince." He had been standing to the back of our little crowd, also staring up at the sky.

"I want everyone out of the top floors," Dworkin said firmly. "Bring the beds downstairs to the ballroom, dining hall, and audience chambers. No one is to go above ground level."

"I'm going to pull some of our troops away from Juniper," Locke said, starting for the door. "I don't know how, but that cloud means ill for us." To Dworkin he said, "You and Freda need to find something to stop it. If you need to swallow your pride and ask for help at the Courts of Chaos, do it!"

Turning, he ran for the door, with Davin and the lieutenant close behind.

"Oberon, come with me," Dworkin said, turning and heading back toward his workshop.

I hesitated. Part of me wanted to join Locke in the field, getting the army camp moved farther from Juniper. There was something about those clouds that made me more than a little bit afraid. But a good soldier—and a dutiful son—obeys orders, and I followed him back to his workshop.

Inside, he bolted the door, then turned and went to a large wooden chest pushed up against the wall. He opened the top and drew out a blue velvet bag with its drawstring pulled closed.

He opened it slowly, carefully, and pulled out a set of Trumps similar to Aber's. Looking at them over his shoulder, I saw portraits of men and women in strange costumes. I didn't recognize any of them as part of our family.

He flipped past these people quickly, then drew out an image I did recognize...a gloomy castle almost lost in night and storm, with strange patterns of lightning around the silver-limned towers and battlements: The Grand Plaza of the Courts of Chaos, drawn almost exactly as it had been on Freda's card.

"You're going to the Courts of Chaos?" I asked slowly. Just looking at the Trump sent my skin crawling.

"Yes. Locke is right—I have avoided it too long. This fight has gotten out of hand. I must petition King Uthor to intercede. It is a disgrace...but it must be done. You will accompany me."

I swallowed. "All right."

He raised the card and stared at it. I took a deep breath, held it, expecting to be whisked off to the world on the card at any second.

But nothing happened.

I let out my breath. Still Dworkin stared. And still we stayed in his workshop, unmoving.

"Uh, Dad…" I began.

He lowered the card and looked at me. I saw tears glistening in his eyes.

"I can't do it," he said.

"Want me to try?"

Silently, he handed me the card. I raised it, saw the courtyard, concentrated on the image…and nothing happened. I stared harder. Still nothing.

Rubbing my eyes, I turned the card over and looked at the back—plain white—then at the front again. I remembered how other Trumps had seemed to come to life as I stared at them, and I tried once more, *willing* it to work.

*Nothing.*

Was I doing something wrong?

Dworkin took the card out of my hand.

"I thought so," he said softly, returning it to the bag and tightening the drawstring. "Now we know what the clouds are for. Somehow, they are interfering with the Logrus. We are cut off."

"Perhaps it's just the cloud," I said. "If we ride out from under it…"

"No," he said, eyes distant. "They are here, now, and they are close. Now that we cannot retreat, cannot run, they will march on us…and they will kill us all."

## EIGHTEEN

I swallowed. "It can't be as bad as all that."

"Why not?"

I had no answer.

"I'll tell Freda," I said, starting for the door. "Perhaps she'll know what to do."

He gave a curt nod.

I left him there, seated at one of his work tables, just staring into space. I had never seen him like this before, and it tore me up inside. How could he have let it come to this? How could he have become so helpless so suddenly?

It didn't take me long to find Freda; she still stood at one of the windows in the audience hall, staring up at the sky. Aber and most of the others were still there as well.

The black cloud, I saw, had doubled in size, and it swirled faster than before. Blue flashes and the constant flicker of lightning gave it a sinister appearance.

I touched Freda's arm and motioned for her to follow me. She gave one last look at the sky, then we went off to the side, where we could talk without being heard.

"What happened?" she asked. "Is he gone?"

"No." Quickly I told her what we had discovered. "I thought you might be able to do something."

She shook her head. "I have not been able to use my Trumps since this morning. I started to tell you when we were in your room. I wanted you to shuffle them...I thought I had done something to cause the problem."

"It had begun even then?" I said. "Before the cloud?"

"Apparently. Why?"

"Then maybe the cloud isn't the cause. Maybe it's something else."

"Like what?"

I shrugged. "You and Dad are the experts. Is there a device that could cause it? If so, could it be hidden here, inside the castle?"

"Not that I know of," she said.

I sighed. "So much for that idea. I thought Ivinius or our unknown traitor might have smuggled something into Juniper."

"Still...it *is* possible, I suppose. I will organize a search, just to make sure."

"Why don't you ask Blaise to do it?"

She looked at me in surprise. "Why?"

"She's already in charge of the servants. She can put them to work."

"You ask her, then. I cannot, after what she accused me of."

I looked into her eyes. "Trust none of them, but love them all?"

She sighed and looked away. "Advice is easier when given than taken," she said. "Very well, I will talk to her."

Turning, she headed back to the window. I saw her pull Blaise aside, and they began to talk in low voices. Since no blows were exchanged, I assumed the best. In a life-or-death situation, even bitter enemies would work together to save themselves.

I went outside, into the main courtyard. The cloud had grown large enough to blot out the sun and most of its light, and a hazy sort of twilight settled over everything. Guards hurried across the courtyard, lighting torches. I knew without doubt that something huge and terrible was about to break over us. I think we all did.

Well, let it come. I gave a silent toast to inevitability. The sooner it came, the sooner we could act against it.

Without warning, a tremendous flash lit the courtyard, followed by a deafening *crack* of thunder. Tiny bits of rock rained down on me, followed by a choking cloud of dust. Then a block of stone as big as my head hit the paving stones ten feet from where I stood, shattering. I reeled back, coughing and choking, eyes stinging and tearing.

Screams sounded from inside the castle. It took me a second to realize what had happened—lightning had struck the top floor.

I ran for the steps to the battlements, knowing I'd be safer there than out in the open. The real danger lay in falling stones, not being struck by lightning. Somehow, I had a feeling this one had been the first of many to come.

Gaining the top of the battlements, I looked out across the army camp. Men by the thousands worked frantically, packing gear, pulling up wooden stakes and folding tents, herding animals. I spotted Locke on horseback, directing their movements. He seemed to be directing everyone within two hundred yards of the castle away to the empty fields by the forest where the hell-creatures had been spying on us.

Another blast of lightning came, then a third. Each struck the castle's highest tower, cracking stone blocks and roof tiles. Debris rained down. Luckily no one was injured or killed.

"Close the gates!" I called down to the guards on duty. "Don't let anyone in except Locke or Davin! It's too dangerous!"

"Yes, Lord!" one of them called up, and two of them began to swing the heavy gates shut.

I went back down to the courtyard, waited for the next bolts of lightning to strike and the debris to fall, then sprinted across the courtyard and into the audience hall.

It was deserted. Two of the windows had broken, and I saw blood on the floor—someone had been cut by flying glass, I thought.

I spotted servants moving in the hallway, and I hurried to see what they were doing. Anari, it turned out, had taken Dworkin's orders to heart and had begun moving all the castle's beds and bedding to the ground floor. Servants would sleep in the grand ballroom. My sisters would share the dining hall. My brothers and I would have one of the lesser halls—one with no windows. Hopefully the lightning would stop or the castle would withstand its blasts through the morning.

I caught sight of Aber, who was supervising two servants as they carried an immense wooden chest down the stairs, and I strode over to join him.

"Who got hurt in the audience hall?" I asked.

"Conner," he said. "A section of the glass fell in on him. His face and hands are cut up, but he'll live."

"That's good news," I said. "What's in the trunk?"

"My set of Trumps. And a few other precious items I don't want to lose. I thought I'd store them down here until we leave. We *are* leaving, aren't we?"

I smiled bleakly. "What happened to your faith in Dad, Locke, and me? I thought you planned to sit tight until we killed everyone."

His voice dropped to a whisper. "No offense, brother, but have you noticed what we're up against? We won't be alive to fight if we don't get out of here, and soon. They're bringing the castle down on our heads!"

A particularly loud *crack!* sounded outside as if to underscore his words. The castle shook, and I heard the low rumble of falling stones.

He might have a point, I thought. But the castle walls grew stronger the closer you got to the foundations. It wouldn't be easy to destroy Juniper.

"In case you missed it," I told him, "our Trumps aren't working anymore. We *can't* go anywhere. It's time to stand and fight."

"What?" He paled. "You're wrong! The Trumps always work!"

"Try one," I said, "and you'll see. Neither Freda, Dad, nor I could get them to work."

The servants carrying the trunk had reached the bottom of the stairs, and he motioned for them to set it down. They did so, and he flipped open its lid. I peered over his shoulder and saw stacks of cards...there had to be hundreds of them.

He picked up the top one, which showed *me*...it was the same card he'd been painting in his room earlier.

"Do you mind?" he asked me.

"Go ahead."

He stared at it intently, frowning, but I felt no sense of contact. From his frustrated expression, I knew it wasn't working for him, either.

With a low moan, he dropped his arm and looked at me. His face had gone ashen; his hand trembled.

"I'm sorry," I said. I felt a little guilty for having him try the Trump when I'd known it wouldn't work. Making Trumps seemed to be his one great talent, and it had been rendered useless right now.

"I can't believe it," he said.

"We'll think of something else," I said with more confidence than I felt. "Dad has whole rooms full of magical stuff. He must have something that can help us."

Aber tossed the card back into the trunk, then slammed down the lid. Motioning for the two men to pick it up again, he told them to put it with the rest of his belongings. They started off down the hall.

"Well," he told me philosophically, "I'll just have to fall back on my other plan, I suppose."

"What's that!" I asked.

"Hide until the danger's past!"

I laughed, and he gave me a weak smile. At least he still had his sense of humor.

The lightning stopped half an hour later, with the coming of night, but I suspected it was a temporary reprieve. Perhaps whoever had sent the cloud needed daylight to direct his attack. I had little doubt but that the blasts would resume at dawn.

Our father remained locked in his workshop, leaving the rest of us to care for the castle. It was late by the time we had everyone bedded down for the night, from family to servants. The guards bravely walking the battlements were the only ones outside.

Freda, Blaise, and I retired to the audience hall, waiting for Locke and Davin to return. We didn't have much to say to each other, but the company was better than being alone.

The silence outside seemed ominous.

Finally, toward midnight, I heard horses in the courtyard and rose to check.

"It's Locke and Davin," I told my sisters.

"About time," Blaise murmured.

Locke left the horses with Davin and hurried inside. He looked grim when he saw us.

"What news?" I asked.

"The men are now a safe distance from the castle," he said. "I don't think the lightning will reach them. What have I missed? Where's Dad?"

"Locked in his rooms," I said unhappily. "He's not answering to knocks."

Freda added, "We moved everyone to ground level, and they are settled for the night."

"I saw the lightning strikes," he said. "Perhaps we should move everyone out to the fields as soon as possible."

"I think that would be a mistake," I said. "They're trying to drive us into the open. Despite the lightning, we're better off in here. Although the top towers will fall, the closer the walls get to the ground, the stronger they become. We'll be all right for a while yet."

"Good enough."

"If you're going back out tomorrow morning," I said, "you might want to do it before daybreak. I think darkness stopped the lightning."

"I will." He glanced around. "Where are we camped out tonight?" I rose. "I'll show you."


My sleep was deep and restful, for once. Even though I shared the chamber with a dozen others, most of whom snored, exhaustion took me. No bad dreams plagued me, no visions of evil serpents or dying men on stone altars, no skies of ever-shifting patterns nor towers made of human bones.

I woke a little before dawn, listening to the first stirrings of life, thinking back to events of the previous night. It seemed unreal, somehow, almost like a bad dream. Clouds didn't swirl in the sky, loosing thunderbolts upon helpless people. It seemed impossible, and yet I knew it had happened.

A silent figure crept into the room. I tensed, hand reaching for my sword. It was one of the castle guards. Another assassin?

Silently, like a ghost, he padded to Locke's side. I prepared to shout a warning and launch myself at him, but he only stretched out his hand and shook his general's shoulder.

Locke came awake with a start.

"You asked me to fetch you before dawn, General," the man said. "It's time."

"Very well," he said softly. "Wake Davin." Rising, he began to dress.

I too sat up, stretching. My muscles ached a bit from my workout the previous afternoon, but I felt much refreshed...ready to fight, if need be, to protect Juniper. The hell-creatures would not take the castle easily, I vowed. I began to dress, too.

Locke picked up his boots, noticed me, and gave a quick jerk of his head toward the door. Rising, I grabbed my own boots and followed him out. We headed toward our father's workshop.

"What are your plans for today?" I asked when he paused to pull on his boots. I took a moment to do the same.

"Prepare the men for battle," he said grimly.

"I don't think it will come today."

"Why not?"

"Why rush? Let the lightning work on our morale."

He nodded. "You're right. That's what I would do, too."

We headed for our father's rooms again, but the guards there lowered their pikes, blocking our way.

"Apologies, my Lords," said the guard on duty with an audible gulp. "Prince Dworkin said not to let anyone disturb him. Not even you, General."

Locked sighed. "I know you are only doing your duty," he said. "But I must do mine as well."

He hit the man twice, fast and hard, with the flat of his hand; the poor fellow slumped to the floor. It happened before the other guard could so much as move.

Locke glared across at him. "Remove your friend," he said, "or I will remove you both."

"It means my life, Lord," the man pleaded, eyes wide and desperate. He barred the way with his pike and raised his chin, then pressed his eyes shut. "If you please."

Locke nodded. Then he hit him twice, too, and when he slid to the floor, Locke and I stepped over the bodies. We had gone well beyond the point of fooling around.

Dworkin had left the door unbarred, so we didn't have to kick it in. Locke glanced over at me, then pushed it open and entered.

Our father sat with his head down on the table nearest us, snoring. Three large bottles sat before him. Two had been completely emptied, plus half of the third.

I picked up the half bottle, sniffed once, set it down.

"Brandy," I said.

"Dad! Wake up!" Locke shook his shoulder.

Dworkin lolled to the side and would have fallen to the floor if I hadn't reached out to steady him. We didn't get to much as a whimper. He was dead to the world.

"Typical," Locke said.

"He's done this before?"

"Once that I know of, when he got kicked out of the Courts of Chaos."

"Kicked out? Why?"

"Well, that's not exactly how he tells it. He usually says he left because he grew tired of life in the Courts. But I know the truth. He forgets that I was there, too."

I leaned forward. "What really happened? Every time someone tells me, I get a different story."

"The truth?" He gave a sad smile. "He seduced King Uthor's youngest and favorite daughter. Got her with child, in fact. Once that happened, it was hard to hide their involvement."

"Couldn't he have married her?"

"Unfortunately, she was already betrothed. Had been, in fact, since birth. Dworkin knew that, too, and he didn't care."

"Then...all this could be King Uthor's doing?"

"Could be?" He chuckled. "Oh, Uthor may not be leading the attack, but I see his hand in it. I had hoped we could outrun or outlast him. He *is* old. And all this happened forty years ago, as time goes in the Courts."

Forty years...long before my birth. I stared down at our father's unconscious form. If Locke told the truth—and I believed him; why should he lie?—then Dad had brought ruin upon himself. And upon the rest of us.

I pushed him back onto the table. He could sleep off his drunk there. Foolish, foolish man.

"Leave him," I said. "If you don't mind, I'll accompany you today. I don't want to spend the day in the castle, listening to falling rock. And if I get a chance to swing my blade a few more times in the right direction—"

"All right." He chuckled humorlessly. "I'm sure we can find something for you to do."

The grooms had emptied the stables during the night. Our horses were penned with the cavalry's mounts outside in the main camp. Davin joined us in the courtyard, now littered with fallen stone, and together the three of us walked out toward the military camp.

The sky grew lighter. I saw that the clouds still swirled endlessly overhead.

Halfway to the army camp, the lightning started again behind us. I glanced over my shoulder at the castle, as bolt after bolt of blue lanced from the sky, striking the tallest towers. More stones fell, raising clouds of dust. I didn't envy those still inside. I knew it wouldn't be a pleasant day for them.

Ahead, horns began to sound.

"That's an attack!" Locke cried, recognizing the call to arms and sprinting for the pens of horses.

Davin and I followed on his heels.

## NINETEEN

By the time we reached the horses, the grooms had already saddled Locke's black stallion. Locke mounted without hesitation and took off at a gallop.

Davin and I waited impatiently for our own horses to be readied.

"Does anyone know what's happening?" I called, but none of the grooms or the soldiers at nearby tents spoke up. The soldiers were grimly putting on armor and buckling on their weapons.

Finally our horses were ready, and we took off after Locke. It didn't take us long to find the command tent, and when we ducked through the flaps, we found our brother barking orders.

"They're marching on our men to the north," he said to Davin.

"The recruits?" Davin paled. "They're not ready!"

"They've just become our front lines. Muster the Wolves, Bears, and Panthers. We need archers at the fore. Put them...put them at Beck's Ridge."

"Got it." Davin turned and ran.

Locke looked to me. "You said you fought them for a year. What advice can you give me?"

"Are they on foot or mounted?" I asked.

"Tell him," Locke said to one of the captains standing before him.

The man turned to me. "Both," he said. "They have two lines of creatures with pikes marching at the fore. Horsemen with swords ride behind. No archers that I could see."

"That sounds right," I said. I swallowed at the sudden lump in my throat. It was just like Ilerium all over again, only larger. There, we had lost battles steadily for a year, and we had been able to fall back as necessary. Here we had a castle to defend. A siege seemed inevitable. And yet, with the lightning blasting the castle to ruin, we would find no safety within its walls.

To Locke, I said, "Their mounted troops are the biggest danger right now. Their horses breathe fire, remember, and they kill men as readily as the riders do."

"Then I'll have our archers take out as many horses and riders as they can," Locke said.

"Fight the horsemen with two weapons," I continued. "Keep a knife pointed at the horse and it won't come too close. The riders are strong and like to beat down their opponents, so keep moving and keep them off-balance. Fight two or three on one."

"What weapons are best?" the captain asked.

"Spears, pikes, and arrows." I glanced at Locke. "How many archers do you have, anyway?"

"Five thousand, more or less."

I whistled. "That many!" For the first time, I felt a surge of hope. "It may be enough."

"Best guess at their numbers?" Locke asked the captain.

"Maybe ten thousand, from what I saw. We outnumber them."

Locke frowned. "That's too few," he said. "There should be more. They've scouted us. They know how many we have."

Horns began to sound again outside. A runner came through the flaps.

Gasping for breath, half bent over with his hands on his knees, he managed to say: "More of them marching against us, General! From the east and the south! Thousands!"

Nodding like he'd expected it, Locke rose. "Sound the ready call. We march in five minutes. Split the forces evenly in thirds. Archers to the front, pikes and spears behind. I'll lead the west, Davin the east. Oberon, will you take the south?"

"Yes," I said.

He nodded. "We'll pick off as many as we can with the archers. Keep falling back around the castle. If necessary, we'll regroup there and make our stand."

"All right," I, said.

"Parketh," he said to one of his aides, "find Lord Oberon some armor. Move!"

*     *     *

The number of men assigned to my command—nearly twenty-five thousand infantry, with spears and pikes, plus two thousand archers and a thousand cavalry—seemed impossibly huge, and yet as I rode down the assembled ranks, I couldn't help but feel it wouldn't be enough. This attack had been well orchestrated...the hell-creatures knew our numbers, and still they came. Somehow, I thought we had missed some important detail.

Then I glanced up at the sky, at the swirling black mass of clouds over Juniper, and I wondered if they counted on the lightning to help destroy us. If we fell back around the castle, we would certainly be within its range...

No sense worrying about retreat now, I thought with a sigh. If we carried the day, we wouldn't have to worry about getting too close to the castle.

I reached the end of my troops, raised my sword, and cried, "On to victory!"

The men gave a cheer, then began to march forward, heading south across the fields.

As we neared the woods, troops began to pour from the forest silently, waves of hell-creatures armed with pikes. I saw no sign of their horsemen yet, but I knew they wouldn't be far behind. We couldn't wait for them—our archers would have to take out their first wave of attackers.

"Archers ready!" I called, and the bugler sounded my commands so all could hear.

Our front lines dropped to one knee, giving the archers room to aim.

"Fire!" I screamed.

They began to let loose their arrows, huge volleys of them. The front line of hell-creatures fell, but more swarmed from the trees in a seemingly endless black wave.

My archers continued to shoot, but there were too many of the hell-creatures. For every one that fell, five more took his place, advancing on us at a run. And then, behind them, I saw lines of hell-creatures on horseback making their way steadily toward us.

"Sound the call for the pikemen!" I said to the bugler, as their first men neared our lines.

He blew the call, and our archers dropped back. The line of pikemen rushed forward, screaming fierce battle cries. The archers raised their bows and fired over the pikemen's heads, killing more of the hell-creatures to the rear.

"Hold some arrows back for their horses!" I shouted. "Aim for their mounts whenever you have a clear shot!"

Both sides met in the middle of the field, a huge writhing mass of bodies. From my vantage point on my horse's back, I saw still more hell-creatures pouring from the forest, although there had to be tens of thousands already fighting.

Our archers kept firing as they found targets, but I held our horsemen back. Their mounts shifted impatiently, eager to charge.

"Steady...steady..." I murmured.

The battle slowly turned in the hell-creatures' favor. Half my troops had fallen, and the remaining half seemed badly outnumbered. The archers had begun to fall back; they couldn't pick out targets easily. I knew the time had come to send in my horsemen.

"Sound the charge," I said, raising my sword.

To the wailing call of the horn, I spurred my own mount, and together with my two thousand cavalrymen, I rode into the battle.

It became a blur of slashing, hacking, and chopping. Around me, I saw horses and riders from both sides pulled down and then hacked to bits. Still I fought on, my sword a blur as I killed hell-creatures by the dozen. Soldiers began to rally around me, and together we cut a wide swathe through the enemy's lines. I screamed my war-cry and rode, smeared in blood and gore, fighting as I had never fought before, taking a wild joy in the feel of metal slicing through armor and flesh, of killing those who had destroyed my life and my love and my home.

Suddenly, it was over. I heard the wail of enemy horns, and the hell-creatures turned and began their retreat. Archers fired at their backs, taking down dozens, then hundreds more. The men around me began to cheer.

I sagged in my saddle, grinning madly, exhausted beyond words. As I turned, taking in the battlefield, I saw bodies everywhere, human and hell-creature alike, piled three and four deep in places.

My arms trembled. My head ached. I had never felt so tired before in my entire life.

And yet I felt a wild elation—it had been a victory of epic proportion. Although two-thirds of my men had fallen, dead or wounded, we had still won the battle. And we had killed twice as many of them as they had killed of us.

"O-ber-on! O-ber-on! O-ber-on!" The men began to chant my name.

I raised my sword and sat up straight in my saddle. "Back to camp!" I cried. "Carry the wounded and our dead!"

Still cheering, they fanned out across the battlefield, looking for human survivors, killing whatever hell-creatures still lived.

There would be no prisoners in this war, I thought.

By the time we started back toward camp, scouts had ridden out to get a report and tell me what had happened. Their news wasn't good. Although Locke's men had ultimately carried the day, Locke had been badly wounded, dragged from his saddle, and left for dead by the hell-creatures. His men had carried him back to his tent, where physicians now tended him.

That was the good news.

Davin's men had lost their battle. Davin hadn't made it back. He lay lost somewhere on the battlefield, amid the corpses of eighteen thousand other men.

I left my horse and hurried to see Locke. I pushed past the physicians, ignoring their pleas to let the general rest, and knelt at the side of his cot.

Although they had bandaged his head, blood had already soaked through the bandages.

"Locke," I said, "it's me."

His eyes flickered and opened. Slowly he turned his head toward me, though I could tell it pained him greatly to do so.

"What news?" he croaked.

"We won," I said. "At least for today."

He smiled a bit, and then he died.

Taking a deep breath, I reached out, shut his eyes, and stood. Priests hurried forward and began to say their prayers, getting his body ready for burial. I'd have to ask Freda what we did with our family's dead, I thought distantly.

"Send runners if the enemy moves on us again," I told Locke's aides. "I must tell our father."

"Yes, General," they said to me.

Slowly I turned and walked out into the open. Officers called to me for news of Locke, but I ignored them.

With a heavy heart, ignoring the lightning that once again struck the castle walls, I began the long walk back. It would be dark soon, I thought. The attack would cease. I would go in and let them know what had happened.

It wasn't a duty I looked forward to.

## TWENTY

The two guards at Dworkin's door had been replaced, I noticed as I approached. They snapped to attention, but made no move to stop me.

I went past them and entered my father's workshop without knocking. He took one look at my face, then sagged into a chair.

"The news is bad," he said flatly, "isn't it."

"Davin and Locke are dead," I told him. "But we won the day."

"And tomorrow?"

"Tomorrow," I said, "I will lead the men. We will fight and hope for the best."

"Will you tell Freda?" he asked.

"Yes," I said, and without another word I turned and left.

I ran into Aber first and paused to tell him the news, but he didn't seem surprised.

"I told you Locke wasn't a traitor," he said.

"No," I agreed, "he wasn't. He may well have been the best of us all. I have to tell Freda. I promised Dad."

"She's taken over the little room off the audience hall. She won't come out. I've tried all day."

"What's she doing?"

"I don't know."

I sighed, rose. "I'll go talk to her," I said. One more unpleasant task on top of an unpleasant day, I thought.

I went to the audience hall, but when I tried the door to the little room, it had been locked from the inside.

"Freda," I called, knocking. "Let me in."

She didn't answer.

"Freda?" I called. "It's me, Oberon. Open up, will you? It's important. Freda!"

I heard bolts sliding, and then the door opened a foot—enough for me to slip inside. She closed it and locked it behind me.

"You should not have come," she said.

She looked terrible, face pinched and drawn, cheeks gray, hair a disheveled mess.

"Aber is worried about you."

"Worried about me?" She gave a laugh. "I am the least of anyone's worries. The end has come. We are trapped. We will die here."

"You've seen this in your cards?" I nodded toward the deck of Trumps scattered across the table, on top of Dworkin's maps.

"No. I cannot see anything."

I glanced at the two small windows set high in the wall. She had drawn the curtains, hiding the clouds and the incessant flicker of that odd blue lightning.

"There is an old saying," I said. "Where there's life, there's hope."

"It is not true." She gestured at the table in the center of the room. Several candles, burnt down almost to nubs, showed her Trumps laid down in rows. "The patterns are random, without meaning. We will all die. We cannot survive without the Logrus."

"I did," I said. "I have lived my whole life without the Logrus."

"And look where it has gotten you," she said bitterly. "You would be dead now if Father had not saved you."

"*No,*" I said. "I survived a year of fighting against the hell-creatures without the Logrus, or Dad, or *you*. I survived my whole life without once drawing on its power. I *still* cannot use the Logrus, and I am the one who survived today's battle."

"And...Locke and Davin?"

I swallowed, looked away. "I'm sorry."

She began to cry. I put my arm around her.

"I'm not about to give up," I said softly. "I'm not about to lie down and die here, trapped like an animal. Out of every life a little blood must spill. It makes us stronger. We *will* survive."

"You do not know any better," she said after a minute, and with some effort she regained control of herself and dried her tears. "The war is already over...we have lost."

"Our enemy wants us to believe that. I don't."

She looked at me, puzzled. "I do not understand."

"You're thinking like a woman of Chaos. Your first impulse is to reach for the Logrus...and when it isn't there, you think you're crippled."

"*I am* crippled! We all are!"

"No, you're not!" I fumbled for the right words. "Look, I've never drawn on the Logrus. Not once in my whole life. You don't need it to use a sword. You don't need it to walk or run or laugh or dance. And you don't need to see the future to live. People get by just fine without the Logrus. They always have and they always will"

"Not real people," she said. "Just Shadowlings..."

"Am I a Shadowling?"

She hesitated. "No...but—"

"But nothing! Forget the Logrus! Forget it exists! Think of what you can do without it...find ways to fight, ways to escape, ways to confuse and deceive our enemies. Dad says you're the smartest of us all. Prove it."

Her brow furrowed, but she did not argue any more.

I crossed to her table, gathered all her Trumps into a single stack, and put them back in their little wooden box. Had a fire burned in the fireplace, I would have cast them into it.

"Don't look at your Trumps again," I said in a firm voice. "Promise me!"

"I promise," she said slowly.

"Keep your word," I told her. Then I kissed her on the forehead. "I will send someone with food. Eat, then go to sleep. Something will occur to us sooner or later. Some way to win the fight...the war."

"Yes, Oberon," she said softly. "And...thank you."
I forced a smile I didn't feel. "Don't mention it."

As I left her room, I found my mind suddenly racing. She had given me an idea, with her stubborn clinging to the power of the Logrus. I knew the Logrus had become useless. Something had cut off Juniper from its power, isolated us, left Dworkin and all the rest of my family powerless. Without the Logrus, they felt like cripples.

Our enemies depended on that.

Talking to her had given me an idea...an idea so crazy, I just thought it just might work.

I sent servants running to the kitchens to prepare a hot meal for Freda, then went back to our Dworkin's workshop. Again the guards let me pass without question.

I strode straight to the door, found it standing open, and an impromptu war conference going on inside. Conner, his head and shoulder wrapped in blood-stained bandages, stood inside with Titus and our father. The jumble of experiments had all been dumped onto the floor or shoved into the corners, and maps now covered every single table.

"—not going to work," Conner was saying heatedly.

They all grew silent as I entered.

"I know I'm interrupting," I said, "but get out, both of you. *Now.* I have to speak to our father alone. It's important."

"You get out," Conner said, bristling. "We're working."

"Go," Dworkin said to them both. "We are not accomplishing anything. Get some sleep; we will talk again later."

Conner looked like he wanted to argue, but finally gave a nod. Titus helped him stand, and together they limped out.

I shut the door after them, then barred it. I didn't want to be disturbed again.

"They are trying to help," Dworkin said. "You cannot lead the whole army yourself. You are going to need them."

"Forget the army," I told him. "Aber showed me something of what goes into making a Trump. You incorporate the Logrus into it, making it part of the image. Right?"

"In a way. Yes."

"You're supposed to be good at it. He said so."

"Yes. I made thousands of them in my youth."

"I want you to make me a Trump, right now. But instead of the Logrus, I want you to use the pattern within me."

He raised his bushy gray eyebrows. "What?"

"You've seen it," I said. "You said it's in that ruby. You know what it looks like. If it's so different from the Logrus, perhaps we can use it to get away from Juniper. It took me to Ilerium, remember."

"Yes." He stared, eyes distant, envisioning something...perhaps the pattern within me, the pattern he had seen deep within that jewel. "What an interesting thought."

"Will it work?" I demanded.

"I don't know."

"I want you to try."

"It *may* be possible," Dworkin mused aloud. "If ..."

He didn't finish his sentence, but rose and fetched paper, ink, and a cup full of brushes. After clearing a space on one of the tables, he sat and began to sketch with a quick, sure hand.

I recognized the picture immediately: the street outside Helda's house. He drew burnt-out ruins where her home had been, with only the stone chimney still standing.

"No..." I said. "—I don't want to go there. Anywhere else, please!"

"You know this street well," he said, "and that will help you concentrate. It is the only place we have both been recently."

"Ilerium isn't safe!"

"It should be by now. Time moves a lot differently between these two Shadows...a single day here is almost two weeks there."

"What about my pattern?" I asked. He hadn't drawn the image the way Aber had, starting with the Logrus in the background, but went straight to drawing the street. "Don't you need to work it into the picture?"

He gave a low chuckle. "You begin to see the difference between Aber and me," he said. "Aber does not understand *why* the Trumps work. He doesn't *want* to understand. Instead, he slavishly copies my own early efforts, when I painted a flat representation of the Logrus as part of each card, behind the image. It helped me concentrate. The Logrus does not actually need to be part of the card...but it does need to be foremost in the artist's mind as he creates. It shapes the picture as much as the human hand. They are, after all, one and the same."

"I don't understand."

"You do not need to. That is my point!"

He dipped his pen in the inkwell and finished quickly. The image was sketchy, little better than a simple line drawing, with the faintest hints of shape to the background. But despite the lack of detail, it had an unmistakable power that I could feel as I gazed upon it. A power which the Logrus Trumps no longer held.

I concentrated on the scene, and it swiftly grew more real...colors entered...a deep blue sky...black for the burnt-out foundations to either side...blue-gray cobblestones littered with broken red roof tiles...and suddenly I looked out onto the street in late afternoon. Not a single building still stood, just fire-blackened chimneys by the dozens. Neither man nor beast stirred anywhere that I could see.

Had I stepped forward, I would have passed through to safety. Kingstown and Ilerium lay within my reach.

Dworkin's hand abruptly covered the picture. Blinking, I stood before him again.

"It worked!" he said, and I heard the awe in his voice. "We can leave!"

"Make more Trumps," I told him, "for five distant Shadows, places where everyone will be safe. We'll send everyone through, scatter the family to places our enemies will never find them."

"Why separate?" he asked. "Surely together..."

"We still have a traitor among us," I reminded him. "I don't know who it is. But if only you and I know where everyone has gone, they will be safe. I think that's how they found us here."

"Yes," he said, smiling now, his confidence returning. "A good plan. Freda and Pella can go together. Conner and Titus. Blaise and Isadora. Syara and Leona. Fenn and Aber. No one will be able to track them if they stay away from the Logrus..."

"Exactly."

"You and I will go last," he went on, eyes distant, envisioning some special Shadow. "We must work on mastering the pattern within you...for that is where our future hopes must rest."

"Whatever you say, Dad." I rose and clasped his shoulder. "Be strong for now. We'll win. I'll make sure of it."

"I never had any doubts." He smiled up at me.

Then I went to find the rest of our family. We had a castle to abandon.

## TWENTY-ONE

With everyone living on the ground floor, I didn't think it would take long to find all my brothers and sisters. I found Aber waiting impatiently outside Dworkin's rooms.

"Well?" he demanded.

"Well what?"

"From the way you went racing in there, I thought something had happened. Did it?"

I shook my head. "Actually, we *have* come up with a plan. I think it's going to work, too."

"Great! Tell me about it. What can I do to help?"

"We have to find everyone first."

"I just saw Freda and Pella in the kitchens," he said.

"Fetch them. I'll see who else I can find."

We split up. I headed for the dining hall, and there I found Blaise, Titus, and Conner seated at the long table—now pushing up against the far wall. A cold supper of roast chicken, grilled vegetables, and what looked like meat pudding sat before them.

They grew silent the second I walked in, and from their guilty expressions, I knew they had been talking about me.

Well, let them. I had nothing to hide. And it looked very much like I'd be their savior.

"What news?" Conner asked after a few awkward seconds.

I said, "Our father has come up with a plan. He wants to see everyone in his workshop. Right now."

"It's about time," Blaise said, throwing down her napkin and standing. "What is he up to?"

"Later," I said, "when everyone gets there. Do you know where anyone else is?"

Blaise hesitated.

"Tell me!" I said.

"It's Fenn and Isadora," Conner said suddenly. "They aren't here."

"What!" I stared at the three of them. "Don't tell me they're trying to slip past the hell-creatures—"

"No," Blaise said. "They left three days ago by Trump. Just before the problems started. They went for help. We weren't supposed to tell anyone...they swore us to secrecy."

I cursed. They might be dead or captured. Then a worse thought struck. Had we just found our traitor—or should I say, traitors?

"Do you know where they went?" I asked.

"It's Locke's fault," Titus exclaimed. "He put them up to something."

"They didn't say," Blaise said. "We were just supposed to cover for them."

"Fenn called it a secret mission," Conner added.

"And none of you has the slightest idea what it was?"

"That's right," Blaise said.

I sighed. Well, perhaps it made things simpler. Two less bodies to save. Two less possible complications to our escape.

"All right," I said. "Go join our father. I still have to find Leona and Syara."

"I think they're still in the audience hall," Blaise said.

"Thanks." I nodded. "I'll check there first."

I watched them go, then hurried to the audience hall. Sure enough, I found Leona and Syara helping tend to wounded soldiers. Some of the more grievously injured had been brought here from the battlefields.

"Father wants to see us all," I said, drawing them aside. "Leave them to the physicians."

They hesitated a second, looking at the injured and dying. Clearly they didn't want to leave their charges.

"It's very important." I linked my arms through theirs and gently steered them toward the door. "I'm not allowed to take 'No' for an answer."

"Very well," Syara said with a sigh. "But there are men dying here."

"Dad has a plan," I said. "He needs us all there."

At that, they gave in and let me lead them back to our father's workshop.

The door stood open. I brought them inside, counting heads. Yes, everyone had come. They clustered around Dworkin, chattering happily, asking questions which he answered with knowing smiles.

"Ah," he said. "Here is Oberon. Ready, my boy?"

"Yes." I shut and barred the door.

"What's this plan?" Conner asked me.

Everyone echoed his sentiments.

"Are you done with the Trumps?" I asked Dworkin.

"Yes."

"We're leaving," I told my brothers and sisters. "We're going to split up—head to different Shadows. I want you all to stay there at least a year or two. Do nothing involving the Logrus. Let's see if we can't outlast our enemies."

"But the Trumps—" Freda began.

"We now have a few that work," I told her. "That's all you need to know for the moment."

She still looked upset, so I added, "It's for everyone's safety. We're going to pair up. None of you will know where the other groups have gone. Hopefully, you'll all be safe."

"Who is first?" Dworkin asked.

"Leona and Syara," I said. They stood closest to me. "Give me the first Trump," I said to our father.

He passed me a card. I held it up, staring at it, feeling the power of the image as it sprang to life.

A placid lake, swans swimming, sailboats racing across the water. Beyond the water rose a golden-hued city, its bridges and towers like spun glass. My sisters would be happy here, I thought.

I pushed them through, saw them on the other side staring back at me with startled expressions—and then they were gone.

I held a crumpled card in my hand. Silently, I passed it to Dworkin, who thrust it into a candle's flame. It caught fire like well-seasoned tinder, burning brightly and rapidly. He dropped it to the stone floor, where it slowly turned to ash.

"Next," I said. "Conner and Titus."

They stepped forward, and as before, our father passed me one of his new Trumps. I held it up, concentrating on the image.

This scene showed a busy street in a bustling city. Men on horseback, tall buildings, shops selling arms and armor—the perfect place for two young men to lose themselves in adventures.

As the sights and smells and textures of this city leaped to life, I pushed my brothers through. As before, I crumpled the Trump in my hand, and they were gone.

Dworkin burned it, too.

"Freda and Pella," I said.

"Pick us a nice world, Father," Freda said in a soft tone.

He smiled at her lovingly, then passed me another Trump. I gazed at it.

A winter palace, with snow falling. White horses decked in bells and ribbons. Twin statues of Freda and Pella being worshipped as goddesses.

I smiled. Yes, they would be happy here, I thought. I pushed them through as the world came to life before me, and just before I crumpled the page, I heard wild cheering as they appeared. The goddesses had arrived. They would be well cared for.

That only left Aber and Blaise. I would never have paired them, but with Fenn and Isadora gone, there didn't seem much choice.

"Ready?" I asked.

"I suppose," Aber said, stepping forward bravely. "Coming, Sis?"

She glared at him. "Don't call me that!"

Oh yes, I thought, rolling my eyes, they were going to have a lot of fun together. If they didn't rip each other's throats out first.

Without comment, Dworkin passed me another Trump. I gazed down at an elegant whitewashed villa. As it came to reality before me, I smelled the ocean's brine and heard the soft calls of gulls as they wheeled in a cloudless azure sky. It seemed almost idyllic.

I helped Blaise through, then reached for Aber. But as he stepped close, he snatched the Trump from my hand, ripped it in half, and the doorway into Shadow vanished. My last glimpse of Blaise showed her with hands on her hips and a furious expression on her face.

"Are you crazy!" I demanded. "What's the idea?"

Grinning, Aber thrust the ruined Trump into a candle's flame. It burned fast and bright.

"You have to ask?" he said. "I'm not living with *her* for a year or two! I'd rather face a legion of hell-creatures naked and unarmed!"

I took a deep breath, then let it out with a laugh. "All right," I said, looking at our father. He looked distinctly nonplussed. "I guess we don't have any choice now. Like it or not, you're coming with us."

"Where?" he asked eagerly.

Dworkin held up the last Trump.

"Where they least expect us," he said, smiling like a shark about to devour its prey.

I looked down, a horrible cold feeling reaching up inside my chest. He had drawn the Courts of Chaos.


HERE ENDS BOOK ONE
OF THE *DAWN* OF AMBER

JOHN GREGORY BETANCOURT is an editor, publisher, and bestselling author of science fiction and fantasy novels and short stories. He has had 36 books published, including the bestselling Star Trek novel, *Infection,* and three other Star Trek novels; a trilogy of mythic novels starring Hercules; the critically acclaimed *Born of Elven Blood; Rememory; Johnny Zed; The Blind Archer;* and many others. He is personally responsible for the revival of *Weird Tales,* the classic magazine of the fantastic, and has authored two critical works in conjunction with the Sci-Fi Channel: *The* Sci-Fi *Channel Trivia Book* and *The* Sci-Fi *Channel Encyclopedia of* TV *Science Fiction.*

ROGER ZELAZNY authored many science fiction and fantasy classics, and won three Nebula Awards and six Hugo Awards over the course of his long and distinguished career. While he is best known for his ten-volume *Chronicles of Amber* series of novels (beginning with 1970's *Nine Princes in Amber),* Zelazny also wrote many other novels, short stories, and novellas, including *Psychoshop* (with Alfred Bester), *Damnation Alley,* the award-winning *The Doors of His Face, The Lamps of His Mouth* and *Lord of Light,* and the stories "24 Views of Mount Fuji, by Hokusai," "Permafrost," and "Home is the Hangman." Zelazny died in Santa Fe, New Mexico, in June 1995.

For sales, editorial information, subsidiary rights
information or a catalog, please write or phone or e-mail

iBooks
1230 Park Avenue, 9a
New York, NY 10128, US
Sales: 1-800-68-BRICK
Tel: 212-427-7139
www.BrickTowerPress.com
email: bricktower@aol.com.


www.Ingram.com

CPSIA information can be obtained
at www.ICGtesting.com
Printed in the USA
LVOW12s0312190817

545577LV00003B/355/P